DANCE OF DEATH

It was like a dance, turn, swing, fire, the only dance he had ever done. Turn, wheel, extend the arm. Boom! Blam! Turn again, gracefully duck, turn, fire, fire again, then go forward. . . .

Gill turned and saw the faintest glimmer of grayness penetrating the profound gloom of the hive. He let go of the depleted plasma rifle and pulled a chemical slugthrower out of a side pouch. Four quick shots blasted a close-packed group of aliens with high explosive. Then Gill turned and ran, with Stan on his shoulder, toward the light.

His feet slid on the hard clay of the tunnel's floor, and then suddenly he was out of the hive and into the sepulchral gray light of planet AR-32. . . .

D1013519

Don't miss any of these exciting *Aliens, Aliens vs. Predator* and *Predator* adventures from Bantam Books!

Aliens #1: Earth Hive by Steve Perry
Aliens #2: Nightmare Asylum by Steve Perry
Aliens #3: The Female War by Steve Perry and Stephani Perry
Aliens vs. Predator: Prey by Steve Perry and Stephani Perry
Aliens vs. Predator: Hunter's Planet by David Bischoff
Predator: Concrete Jungle by Nathan Archer

Be sure to look for all of Bantam's classic Star Trek *novels:*
The Price of the Phoenix by Sondra Marshak and Myrna Culbreath
World Without End by Joe Haldeman
Spock, Messiah! by Theodore R. Cogswell and Charles A. Spano, Jr.
The Starless World by Gordon Eklund
Fate of the Phoenix by Sondra Marshak and Myrna Culbreath
Mudd's Enterprise by J. A. Lawrence
Planet of Judgment by Joe Haldeman
Death's Angel by Kathleen Sky

Complete your Bantam Star Wars *library:*
The Truce at Bakura by Kathy Tyers
The Courtship of Princess Leia by Dave Wolverton
Heir to the Empire by Timothy Zahn
Dark Force Rising by Timothy Zahn
The Last Command by Timothy Zahn
The Jedi Academy Trilogy by Kevin J. Anderson
    Jedi Search
    Dark Apprentice
    Champions of the Force
Children of the Jedi by Barbara Hambly
The Crystal Star by Vonda N. McIntyre
Ambush at Corellia by Roger MacBride Allen
Assault at Selonia by Roger MacBride Allen
Tales from the Mos Eisley Cantina edited by Kevin J. Anderson

ALIENS™

ALIEN HARVEST

Robert Sheckley

*Based on the Twentieth Century Fox motion
pictures, the designs of H. R. Giger,
and the Dark Horse graphic novel ALIENS: HIVE
by Jerry Prosser*

SPECTRA™

BANTAM BOOKS
New York • Toronto • London • Sydney • Auckland

ALIEN HARVEST
A Bantam Spectra Book / September 1995

*SPECTRA and the portrayal of a boxed "s" are trademarks of
Bantam Books, a division of Bantam Doubleday Dell Publishing
Group, Inc.*

All rights reserved.
Copyright © 1994 by Twentieth Century Fox Film Corporation
*Aliens™, Predator™ and Aliens vs. Predator™ © 1994 Twentieth
Century Fox Film Corporation.*
Cover art copyright © 1995 by John Bolton.
*No part of this book may be reproduced or transmitted in any
form or by any means, electronic or mechanical, including
photocopying, recording, or by any information storage and
retrieval system, without permission in writing from the
publisher.*
For information address: Bantam Books.

*If you purchased this book without a cover you should be aware
that this book is stolen property. It was reported as "unsold and destroyed" to the publisher and neither the author nor the publisher
has received any payment for this "stripped book."*

ISBN 0-553-56441-2

Published simultaneously in the United States and Canada

Bantam Books are published by Bantam Books, a division of Bantam Doubleday
Dell Publishing Group, Inc. Its trademark, consisting of the words "Bantam Books"
and the portrayal of a rooster, is Registered in U.S. Patent and Trademark Office
and in other countries. Marca Registrada. Bantam Books, 1540 Broadway, New
York, New York 10036.

PRINTED IN THE UNITED STATES OF AMERICA
RAD   0 9 8 7 6 5 4 3 2 1

To my wife, Gail, with all my love.

Captain Hoban's Prologue

I was in the middle of the whole thing with Stan and Julie. I guess almost everybody on Earth knows how it ended. But they don't know how it began. I've been putting together everything I know about it. I figure it started the morning Stan got the summons.

1

That morning Stan had to go downtown to the Colonial Mercantile Building on Vesey Street. The day before there had been a ring at his doorbell. Stan hadn't been doing much when it came. He had several experiments going in his cellar laboratory. The lab took up most of the space in the old frame house on Gramercy Park that he had inherited from his father. Stan hadn't been feeling well lately, and although he tried to tell himself it wasn't anything, some little voice within him kept on intruding, telling him, "This could be very serious. . . ."

He had been avoiding his doctor for a while, but now he called up and made an appointment with Dr. Johnston at the Fifty-ninth Street clinic for the next day. That was when the doorbell rang.

The man standing outside was tall and thin, and dressed in a badly pressed gray business suit.

"Are you Professor Myakovsky?"

"I am," Stan replied.

"Are you the Stanley Myakovsky who wrote the book about Ari the ant?"

"Yes, I am," Stan repeated. He was starting to feel a little better. This guy seemed to be someone who had read his book, was probably a fan, maybe even wanted an autograph. "What can I do for you?"

"I got a summons for you," the man said, taking a folded paper out of his pocket and slapping it briskly into Stan's hand. "You are served. Have a nice day, Doctor." He turned and left.

Stan went back inside and looked over the summons. He had no idea what it was about and the document itself didn't enlighten him. It simply said he was to appear in Courtroom B at 311 Vesey Street the following day, or face the consequences.

Have a nice day.

What a laugh.

It had been so long since Stan had had a nice day, he couldn't remember what one looked like.

The next day he left early for Vesey Street. The Broadway trolley was running again, rumbling past the newly restored buildings of midtown. It was a bright day outside, and despite his depression, Stan started to feel just the slightest lift to his spirits.

That lasted until he got to Vesey Street.

Vesey Street was filled with city and federal buildings, some of them quite old, dating from before the time of the aliens, miraculously unburned during the anarchic days when the aliens ruled. Some of the buildings in this area were brand-spanking-new. There had been a lot of rebuilding since those days. Stan would have liked to have been part of the first days after humans reoccupied their own planet. It must have been exhilarating, reoccupying your own country, having a future again on your own planet. Now, of course, it was business as usual. . . . More or less.

Times were pretty good. America was experiencing

a boom. Business was strong. A lot of people were making a lot of money. Some people, of course, were losing a lot of money. It had to come from somewhere. So it came from people like Stan.

He mounted the stone steps of the Criminal Courts Building. Within, he found a clerk who checked his summons and directed him up a flight of stairs to the correct courtroom.

He walked in. It was a small room with a half-dozen chairs facing a raised desk. The sign on the door had said JUDGE JACOB LESSNER, PRESIDING. Behind the desk sat a small man in black robes. He said, "Dr. Stanley Myakovsky?"

"Yes," Stan replied.

"Come in. I suppose you know what this is about?"

"No, I don't."

Judge Lessner frowned. "Your lawyer really should keep you better informed."

Stan nodded, although he knew very well he hadn't been answering his lawyer's calls over the last few days.

"Well, this is a pretty simple matter." The judge searched among the papers on his desk until he found what he was looking for. "This is a government order seizing your spaceship."

"The *Dolomite*?" Stan asked.

The judge searched his paper until he found it. "Yes, of course, that's the name of your ship. You may no longer go aboard."

"But why?"

"You were sent a notice a month ago advising you of the government's decision to take action against your unpaid bills."

Stan thought the paper must be somewhere among the unopened mail on his desk. He had been too depressed of late to open any of it. Most of the letters had something bad to say: how this investment or that was sliding to hell on him, or how his patents weren't earning as expected. And even more papers about all his back taxes.

He felt a wave of hopelessness engulf him. He tried to struggle out of it. "They are not allowed to do that. My spaceship is one of the few ways I have of conducting business. If they take that, how am I supposed to pay them what they say I owe?"

"That is not my concern," the judge stated flatly. "You should have taken that into consideration when you fell so deeply into arrears. In any event, I am hereby notifying you of the government's decision to take your ship. If you have any difficulty with this, you or your lawyer can file a complaint with the clerk down the hall."

"Thanks a lot," Stan said bitterly, and left the courtroom. A few blocks away he found a park bench to sit on. He needed to collect himself. His heart was beating wildly and he was sweating, though it was a mild day. At least, he thought, maybe my bad news for the day is over. I've had my share.

That was before his doctor's appointment, of course.

Dr. Johnston of the Fifty-ninth Street clinic came to the dressing room just as Stan finished knotting his tie.

"How did my tests work out?" Stan asked.

The doctor looked uncomfortable. "Not so good, I'm afraid."

"But I was here a year ago; you said I was fine!"

"A lot can happen in a year," the doctor said.

Stan wanted to say, *Sure, tell me about it*, but he held back.

"Exactly what is the matter?" he asked.

Dr. Johnston answered, "I might as well give it to you straight, Dr. Myakovsky. You were correct in your surmise about those black marks on your chest and back. They are indeed cancers."

Stan sat down. He needed a moment to think about this. He couldn't believe what he had heard. And yet he had suspected it for months.

Finally he asked, "Is my condition terminal?"

"Yes." The doctor nodded gravely. "In fact, you don't have much time left. A matter of months. I'm sorry, but it's best to give you the news straight. The condition, as I'm sure you know, is incurable. But its progress can be slowed, and we can ease some of the symptoms. I've already made out a prescription for the medicine we prescribe for such cases." He handed Stan a folded slip of paper. "And there is also this."

The doctor held out a small plastic box. Within it, packed in foam rubber, were a dozen ampoules of a bluish liquid.

"This is Xeno-Zip. Have you heard of it?"

Stan nodded. "If memory serves, it is produced from the royal jelly of alien females."

"That is correct," Dr. Johnston said. "I must tell you it's no cure for what you have. But it should relieve the symptoms. The stuff's illegal and I shouldn't be giving you this ... but it could be just what you're looking for."

"Does it have much in the way of side effects?" Stan asked.

The doctor smiled grimly. "It has indeed. That's why it hasn't received government approval yet, though many people still use it. Indeed, it has become the most-sought-after consciousness-altering substance in existence. Although the effect is not invariable, it does give most people an intense feeling of well-being and competence. Others experience levels of their own being not normally perceived. Still others have an orgasm that seems to go on forever."

"At least I'm going to die happy." Stan wasn't smiling as he spoke.

2

It was cold that night. Wind demons seemed to chase up and down the streets of New York, wailing at the high-flying moon like all of the banshees of Howard Phillips Lovecraft.

The block that Stan's house stood upon had once been genteel, a part of Gramercy Park. Now, armed citizens patrolled the streets night and day. Insurrection and disorder were rife all over the city, brought on by the breakdown of law and order since the troubles with the aliens. Some people could remember the coming of the aliens, and the many deaths that had resulted from their macabre practices. Their effect on New York had been to make it seem a much older city than it in fact was, one of those ancient cities like Baghdad or Babylon. Now, after the aliens, the city felt like it had seen unimaginable evil, and was resting, a little exhausted, waiting for the good life to start up again.

After making himself a light dinner from an Insta-Pac protein ration, Stan went to the living room and started a fire in the fireplace. He sat down in a rocking chair and stared morosely into the flames, listening to the wind whistling outside the window and thinking of how little time he had left.

It was strange how, upon hearing that your life had an imminent termination date, you began to think of suicide. Stan had never before understood Schopenhauer's saying that he got through many a long night with thoughts of suicide, but now it made sense. To kill himself might even be a triumph; it would rob the cancer of its victory. No longer would he dance to death's tune. No longer could the pain curl him up and make him beg for relief. He could get out of it, laugh at it all, and, as Hamlet had said, "Make his quietus with a bare bodkin."

From the plate of apples near his chair he picked up a short, keenly edged knife and looked at it like he'd never seen one before. Where in his body should he put it in? Should it be done hara-kiri style? Or was there another manner more appropriate for a Westerner?

And yet, tempting as the thoughts of suicide were, they were mainly interesting when considered in the abstract. He didn't really want to kill himself. He wanted to do something. But he didn't know what it was.

These were long, sad winter thoughts he was thinking, and he was startled out of his reverie when he heard the front door chimes.

Stan looked up in surprise. He wasn't expecting anyone. He was a lonely man as he had been a lonely boy. He had gotten used to his solitary condition early in life, and had learned there was no sense struggling against it. He felt that it was written somewhere that he should be alone. This was his fate. He had no girlfriends—in fact, no real friends at all. No one came to take him to the movies or a concert, or for an evening's drinking. Since his parents' death four years ago in a traffic accident, he had become even less sociable. Sometimes he talked with colleagues at the laboratory, but even among people who should have been his own kind, his macabre and ironic sense of humor kept him apart. Stan lived alone in the house. He had set up a laboratory in the basement, and as far as possible, he did his experiments, wrote his papers, and lived his life at home, in solitude, among familiar things.

It was here that he had written *Cyberantics*, his children's book about a cybernetic ant named Ari, based on an ant he had actually constructed himself. In fact, Ari was in the room with him now, perched on a small box on the mantel. The ant could see Stan as he hesitated a moment at the door.

The chimes rang again. He arose and went to answer the summons. The front door creaked in his hand, almost as if it were reluctant to open. Stan peered out, his nearsighted eyes blinking behind his thick glasses.

A young woman stood under the porch light and the first thing Stan noticed was the sheen of copper on her dark chestnut-red hair. She was tall and slender, and had masses of hair pushed back and tied behind her neck with a white ribbon. She wore a dark belted trench coat, severely cut, but not severe enough to hide the fact that she had a very good figure. Her face was oval and attractive, lightly made up. An old scar, now almost completely faded but visible even in the darkness of the porch, ran from the outside corner of her left eye to the corner of her full lips. It looked like an old dueling scar, such as they had once sported in places like Heidelberg some centuries earlier. Could it really be a dueling scar? Did people still fight duels? Some accident, perhaps. But then why hadn't she had it surgically removed? One thing was certain; the scar seemed to enhance her beauty, just as ancient people believed that scarification increased a woman's charm.

"Dr. Myakovsky?" the woman said. "I am Julie Lish.

I have a matter of considerable importance to discuss with you. May I come in?"

Stan had been staring at her hard, as if she were a lab specimen. Now he came back to himself with a start.

"Oh certainly; please. Come in."

He escorted Julie Lish inside and led her through the gloomy hallway to the well-lighted room where he had been staring into the flames of a dying fire. He picked up a poker now and stirred the fire up, then indicated a pair of matching armchairs just a comfortable distance from the flames. She took one and he seated himself in the other, then quickly got up again.

"May I get you something to drink?"

She smiled at him, amused by his bumbling eagerness. "You don't even know what I've come for."

"It doesn't really matter. . . . I mean, whatever it is, you are a guest in my house. Perhaps I could bring you a fruit drink? I'm afraid I have no alcohol to mix with it. Alcohol has an adverse effect on my can—my condition."

"A glass of fruit juice would be nice," Julie said. "I am well aware that you do not drink, Dr. Myakovsky."

Stan had already begun pouring from a pitcher on a sideboard near the two armchairs. He looked up.

"Well aware? Why?"

"I've made it a point to find out about you," Julie said. "I am always careful to research my future partners."

Stan stared at her, his lips slightly parted, trying to make sense out of all this. Was she laughing at him? Girls were such unfathomable creatures! Although he was fascinated by them, Stan had always kept his distance, conscious that he was not the athletic, glib, casual sort of man that women liked. And here was this beautiful and exotic creature already talking about becoming partners with him?

"Please explain," Stan said, with what he hoped was dignity. "You say you've studied me?"

"Probably better than you've studied yourself,"

Julie stated. "For example, I know about your first date. You were fifteen."

"Do you know what was special about it?" Stan asked.

"I do indeed," Julie replied. "You never showed up for it. You got cold feet at the last moment. And that, Doctor, could be said to characterize all your dealings with the opposite sex."

Stan remembered the incident. He wondered if he had revealed it in some memoir he might have published at the invitation of a computer magazine. How else could she have found out? And what did she want to know that sort of thing for, anyhow?

"I don't get this." Stan looked at her. "What have you come here for? What do you want?"

"Stan," Julie said, "I'll make it short and sweet. I'm a thief. A good one. No, I'm a lot better than just good. I'm one of the best who ever lived. Unfortunately I can't bring you press clippings. Really good thieves don't get written up. You'll just have to take my word for it."

"All right, let's say I accept it," Stan said. "So?"

"I've made a lot of money in some of my enterprises," Julie went on, "but not as much as I'd have liked. Stan, I want to be rich."

Stan laughed without humor. "I suppose a lot of people want that."

"Certainly, but they don't have my qualifications. Or my desire."

Stan acknowledged this. "I take it you have some ideas on how to realize that goal?"

She nodded. "I have thought of a way you and I could make a fortune."

"A fortune," Stan mused. "How much is that in dollars?"

"Don't laugh at me," Julie said. "I don't know exactly how much it would be. But it would come to millions of dollars, perhaps even billions, and we'd neither of us lack for anything ever again."

"Nothing?" Stan asked, looking at her and thinking how pretty she was.

"We'd have it all," she told him. "That's worth something, isn't it?"

She slipped off the severe trench coat. Beneath it she wore a nylon, military-style jumpsuit. The tight-fitting clothes set off her well-shaped bosom and fine shoulders to advantage. Stan thought she looked great. He wondered if Julie was one of the things he'd also have if he made a deal with her. He liked the idea but kept that thought to himself as well. Although he was extremely susceptible to beauty, he had culti-vated a brusque manner around women so they would never think he was coming on to them and then reject him. He had had a lot of rejection in his life, and he wasn't going to have any more if he could avoid it.

"Tell me your idea," he said.

Julie reached into a small purse she carried, took out a package, and handed it to him.

Stan looked at her questioningly.

"Do you know what this is? Open it and find out."

The package was wrapped in thick manila paper and was held together with tape. He tried to pull the paper off, but there was no place for his fingers to take hold. He went to his desk and found the paper knife, and managed to saw through the tape. Then he slit the paper carefully and opened the package. Within was a plastic box. Inside it, padded with foam rubber, was a stoppered test tube.

Stan held it up to the light. It was a heavy viscous liquid, with bluish lights in it. He unstopped the tube and sniffed. The aroma was unmistakable.

"Royal jelly," he said.

She nodded. "Do you know what this stuff is worth?"

"As a matter of fact, I do. It is one of the most val-uable substances in the galaxy."

She nodded. "And the stuff is in even shorter sup-ply now that we've got the aliens on the run. That's part of what makes it so expensive. And it's a monopoly. The big bionational research companies have it all tied up. They've got places out on other planets where they get the stuff from the aliens. It's all a closed transaction."

"Which is all well-known," Stan said. "Tell me something new."

"Suppose I tell you that I know where we can lay our hands on an entire shipload of the stuff. At least a hundred tons. What about that?"

"Who does it belong to?"

"Whoever gets it."

"Who did it used to belong to?"

"A freelance honey-collecting expedition. But it came up lost, and has never been heard of again."

"So what makes you think they struck it rich?"

"Before vanishing, they sent out one signal by sub-space radio. It was intercepted by a certain Bio-Pharm official. He never got around to using it. I guess he was going to take it to the grave with him, but I persuaded him otherwise."

Stan didn't ask her how she had managed this. At that moment her face looked quite sinister. But it was no less beautiful because of that.

"So you know where it is?"

"I know approximately."

Stan studied her for a while and pursed his lips thoughtfully. Then he said, "And you think it's as simple as walking in and taking it?"

"Flying in," she corrected.

"There might be objections to our appropriating this cargo," Stan said.

"So what? It's not illegal. Salvage rights belong to whoever gets them. The stuff's ours if we can get it."

"And we're dead if we don't."

Julie shrugged. "It's a lot of money, so there's going to be a lot of risk. I don't know about you, Stan, but I'm tired of being small-time. Just once I want to go for all the marbles. Don't you feel that way sometimes?"

Stan could feel the pains of his condition eating

away at him through the haze of the medication. He knew he was sick as hell.

But he also knew he was still alive.

"I think I'm ready for a big one, too," he said slowly. "But there's still a difficulty. Where there's royal jelly, there'll be aliens. How are we going to get through them?"

"The same way your ant, Ari, got through the enemy ant nest, Stan. That's how."

Stan stared at her. "You know about Ari?"

"Of course. I told you I researched you. And I read *Cyberantics*."

"You think I could make a cybernetic or robotic alien and he could get through an alien ant nest?"

"I know you've been working on such a robot," Julie said. "Why don't we find out if it works?"

She looked at him challengingly, and Stan felt his heart lift. At last something was happening to him, an adventure with a beautiful woman.

"Then there's the question of a ship," he said.

"You have one."

"Had. The government just seized it."

She looked at him levelly. "Let's worry about getting the ship later. What we need even worse is a spaceship pilot who's willing to do something illegal."

"I can think of one man. . . ."

"Who's that?"

"Just someone I know. Julie, you flatter me by coming to me with this partnership offer. But evidently you don't know my full situation."

"I don't? Tell me, then."

"Julie, I used to be quite a wealthy man. One of the youngest millionaires on the Forbes list. I have several key patents in bioengineering, and the plans for my cybernetic ant, Ari, are a standard for the field of medical miniaturiation."

"I know all this, Stan."

"Sure. But did you also know that all that has changed? Did you know the government has put a lien on my assets? It seems that Bio-Pharm, one of the biggest of the international pharmaceutical houses, has filed suit against me for patent infringement. What a laugh. They stole most of their processes from me! But it's not easy to prove, and in the meantime they've got me on the run. I don't own a damned thing anymore—nothing except this house and Ari." He lifted up the cybernetic ant to show to Julie. "I even have to beg my grocer to extend me credit so I can go on eating!"

Julie looked at him without sympathy. "I know all that, Stan. It's tough, isn't it?"

He thought he detected a tone of irony in her voice. "You're damned right it's tough!"

"Granted. But so what?"

He stared at her, uncomprehending. "Did you actually come here to insult me?"

"There's nothing insulting in what I'm saying. I came here to make a deal with you. What I find is you sitting around feeling sorry for yourself. I'm offering you something you can do about it."

"It's not just that I'm broke," Stan said. "There's also . . . my condition."

"Tell me about it," Julie said.

Stan shrugged. "There's not much to say. Melanoma. I've got six months. Maybe a little longer if I want to lie in a hospital bed and breath pure oxygen."

"You look like you're moving around pretty good just now," Julie said.

"Oh yeah, sure. But that's just now. This stuff is the only thing that keeps me going." He took out a vial of Xeno-Zip and showed it to her.

"I know all about that stuff," Julie said. "It's my job to keep track of precious substances that come in small packages. And this is the only stuff that does you any good?"

"That's right," Stan said. "It's expensive even for a rich man. For someone whose assets have been seized . . . Well, I'll run out soon, and I don't know what happens then."

"Tough," Julie said, with no pity in her voice. "So this stuff won't cure you?"

Stan shook his head. "Some doctors have theorized that if I could obtain absolute unadulterated royal jelly fresh from an alien hive, before any by-products were added, and before it had time to lose any of its potency, it might buy me more time. But it's impossible to get."

"Except by going to the source," Julie said.

"Yes, that's right," Stan repeated slowly. "Except by going to the source. To a place where the Aliens actually produce it."

"That's the sort of place I had in mind for us to go," Julie said. "Like I told you, I know where there's a shipload of the stuff."

He stared at her, his eyebrows raised. Then his head slumped and he looked sad and worn. "No, no. It's quite impossible. Even if you knew of such a place—"

"That's exactly what I do know," Julie said.

"You know a place where an alien queen produces royal jelly?"

She patted the sleek leather pouch that she carried at her side. "I've got the coordinates right in here, Stan. They're a part of my contribution to this venture."

"Where'd you get that information?"

She smiled. She was so lovely when she smiled. "Like I told you, I was good friends with a Bio-Pharm executive. We were a little more than good friends, actually. Well, when he died—he was quite old, you understand—when he died, he decided that that particular secret shouldn't go to the grave with him."

"So what is your idea?" Stan asked. "Do you think we can just go there and get it?"

"That's about what I had in mind," Julie said.

"The Bio-Pharm people might have something to say about it."

"I figured we could sneak in, grab the shipload, and get out before they spotted us."

"You think it would be as easy as that?"

She shook her head. "I never said it would be easy."

"Or within the law."

She shrugged impatiently. "There's nothing illegal about salvage. Why don't you think of it as your counterclaim to their lawsuit?"

"What do you mean?"

"They're suing you for patent infringement. Wrongly, you say. Well, prove you mean it. Go in there and take what is yours—then take them to court the way they're taking you."

Stan thought for a long while, then he began to smile. "You know, I think I'd like that."

"Now you're talking!"

"But wait a minute, there are still a lot of problems. We don't have a ship. My alien robot has never had a field test. And I don't have any money."

"We can do something about all that," Julie said. "But there really isn't much time. Not for you and not for me. If we're going to do this, we'll have to start real soon. And once we begin, there's no turning back."

"I understand," Stan said.

Julie leaned forward and took Stan's face in her cool hands. He felt something like an electric shock pass through him. Looking at her, he thought he'd never seen anyone so beautiful and so brave. Yes, and maybe a little crazy, too, but what did that matter?

"I want you to think about it, Stan," Julie said. "Give me your answer tomorrow night over dinner. If you don't want to do it, fine, no hard feelings. But if you do—listen to me carefully."

"I'm listening," Stan said. In fact, he was barely breathing.

"If you do decide to do it, then no more crap about something being difficult or you being sick or any of that. If you're going to do it, simply decide to do it, and we'll go on from there."

"That sounds pretty good to me," Stan said. "Julie, where'd you learn all this stuff?"

"From my teacher, Shen Hui."

"He must have been a pretty wise old egg."

"It didn't prevent him from dying," Julie said. "But while he lived, he really lived. Till tomorrow, Stan."

"Where are you going?" Stan said in alarm as she stood up.

"I'm sure you've got a spare bedroom here," Julie said. "I'm going to take a shower and change, and then look over your library and lab. Then I want to get some sleep."

"Oh, fine. I was afraid you were leaving."

She shook her head. "Play your cards right and I'll never leave again."

3

Julie had always been un-
usual. She'd never known her parents. Her earliest
memories were of an international orphanage in
Shanghai. This was the place from which Shen Hui
bought her, when she was still a very little girl. He
had been very good to her, treating her like a favored
child rather than a slave. But she was still a slave and
she knew it, and it rankled. Shen Hui taught her inde-
pendence of spirit as well as how to be a good thief.
It was inevitable that she would try out her need for
liberty on him, the one who was holding her.

She was devious about it, just as he had taught her.
She put aside money from jobs she did for him. And
she studied and learned so she would know all she
needed when she was ready to cut loose from him.
And then came the question of finding the right time.
It seemed to take forever, and the right moment never
seemed to come.

At last they traveled together to Europe. Shen Hui had it in mind to relieve some of the largest art galleries on the continent of some of their smaller and most prized possessions: miniature paintings, small sculpture, carved objects. They went to Zurich first.

The first night Julie excused herself in the lobby of the Grand Basle Hotel, went to the ladies' room, and never returned.

She had planned well. From the powder room, with a small fortune and a forged passport secreted on her person, she made her way to the airport, and then to Madrid, Lisbon, and London. She made the trail difficult for Shen Hui to follow. And she prepared something else.

He came after her, as she had known he would. He wasn't going to let her get away that easily. He had invested a lot of money in her, and besides, his feelings were hurt. He had thought she loved him. He had forgotten his own advice—never trust a slave. His love was replaced by hatred, all the more powerful because it was based on his own guilt and ignorance in being duped by the illusion he had created and named Julie.

They met up almost a year later. He came upon her in one of the public squares in Paris, near the Seine. Julie was wearing a black sealskin coat and a chinchilla hat. Shen Hui noted sardonically that it hadn't taken her long to outfit herself. He added that she had been silly to expose herself to him in this way.

"What do you mean?" she'd asked.

"I mean if you had any brains, you wouldn't have let me catch up with you. Do you realize how easily I could kill you? And you could do nothing about it, not even with all the skills I taught you."

"I know that," Julie said. "And I wasn't careless. I chose to let you find me."

"What are you up to?"

"I don't choose to spend my life running," Julie said. "I am extremely grateful to you, Shen Hui. You have taught me respect for the deeper law that underlies appearances. I appeal to that law now. Although you legally own me, your investment has been repaid many times and it is time that I went free. I served you well and you know it. I would like to shake hands and have us part friends."

Shen Hui stared at her. His skin had aged incredibly, with a yellow cast to it like parchment that has been dried too long in the sun. She had never seen him looking so old. Even his thin mustache, which dropped down on either side of his face, seemed lifeless. And his eyes were brown and opaque.

She wasn't sure what he would say. She knew that her life hung in the balance. Old as he was, and apparently unarmed, she had no doubt he could kill her anytime he chose.

"You are my greatest creation," he said at last. "How could I kill you? Who would I have left to hate?"

Her life had really begun at that point. She spent several years on her own, accomplishing unbelievable feats of thievery in Europe and America. She made money easily, and spent it easily. Her life was rich and pleasurable, but she began to sense a loss of purpose, a slackness that was beginning to alarm her. It was a question of motivation. Shen Hui had taught her too well for her to be content with mediocre motives. Why was she doing what she was doing? What was she living for?

The only thing she could think to do with her life was to get rich. It wasn't enough, she knew, but it was a start. After she accomplished that, she'd take the next step.

For the present she was here with Stan, and Stan was as good as hooked, if she had any knowledge of men.

For dinner that night Stan had ordered a special Moroccan feast catered by a North African couple he knew. Although it was short notice, he had told them to go all out, and he served the meal himself using his best china and silverware. There were game birds roasted on spits, half a sheep braised in many exotic spices and served with rough tasty Arab bread, platters of fruits and vegetables, several different wines. The Moroccan couple followed instructions, delivering the feast and then leaving. Stan paid for it with almost the last of the cash he had on hand. One way or another, no matter what decision he made tonight, it was going to be a new life for him tomorrow.

Stan hadn't thought about what he was going to say. He didn't need to. He was suffused with a knowledge that he couldn't articulate yet. That would have to come later. For now it was enough to sit across the table from Julie while the strains of a Monteverdi madrigal tinkled in the background.

Julie had found an old ballroom dress upstairs, one of his grandmother's, neatly folded in a fragrant cedar drawer. It fit perfectly, and she had worn it down to dinner with a set of large pearl earrings that had once belonged to Stan's mother.

Stan, noting her preparations, had taken out the tuxedo he had worn to his recent college reunion. He put in the cat's-eye opal cuff links and the diamond pin in the buttonhole. He felt tall and graceful in this outfit, and a little ironic. It was playacting, of course, and he knew that; but it was also in some strange sense real. And Stan knew that there were many costumes he could have worn that night. He wouldn't have felt out of place in the golden mantle of Alexander the Great. Because just like the famous Macedonian, he was on the verge of new worlds to conquer. He was also up against a sea of trouble and pain, and he suspected he was doomed to die gloriously and young as well.

At dinner that evening Julie was radiant in the antique gown, Stan looking handsome in his tuxedo. He had saved a bottle of wine for a long time, waiting for an occasion like this. The bottle had been handed down to him by his parents—a rare St.-Emilion, the great vintage of thirty-seven years earlier. Stan had taken good care of the bottle, storing it on its side in the temperature-controlled basement, making sure the cork was properly intact. He brought it up now and opened it with care, pouring a little into a fluted glass and tasting it.

"Just on the verge of turning," he said. "But still superb. We've caught the St.-Emilion at its peak, Julie. This is probably the last bottle of this stuff in the world."

She tasted the ruby-red liquid he had poured for her. "It's marvelous, Stan. But what are we celebrating?"

"Need you ask?"

"I think not," she said, "but I would like to hear it anyhow."

"And hear it you shall." Stan smiled. Never had he felt so at peace with himself. He didn't know where this course of action was going to take him, but he was satisfied to follow it.

"We're going to go with your plan, Julie. And we're going to follow it all the way. We both know the risks. We discussed them yesterday. We both know the odds are against us. But no more talk about that. I've decided, and I know that you have, too. We'll start in the morning."

She reached across the snowy tablecloth and held his hand tightly. "Why tomorrow morning?"

"Because that's when my bank opens," Stan said. "I'm ready for whatever we have to do."

"I'm ready, too, Stan."

"Well," he said, half as a joke and half seriously, "I guess we've taken care of everything except what to name our alien."

"What would you suggest?"

"What about Norbert, after the great Norbert Wiener, father of cybernetics, the science that gave it birth?"

"Sounds good to me," Julie said. "I guess that just about covers it, Stan. Except for one thing."

"What's that?"

She leaned close to him. He felt dizzy with her face so close to his. She bent closer. Her lips were partially open. He was fascinated by her teeth, all perfect except one small one to the left, an eyetooth. It was a little crooked.

And then he stopped thinking as she kissed him, and Ari the cybernetic ant stood in his box on the mantel and watched, and the flames of the fire lifted and died away, and Stan watched Ari watching and watched himself kissing Julie, not knowing that Ari was watching, and all this from within his frozen moment in time and all of it stained in the blue light of the royal jelly of memory.

4

Next morning he had a chance to show Julie around his house. She admired the fine old silverware he had inherited from his grandparents, and looked with something approaching awe at the portraits of his ancestors that hung on the great staircase that led to the upper rooms. There were dozens of somber oil paintings in ornate gilt frames, showing stern-faced men—some with sidewhiskers and some clean-shaven—and proper-looking ladies in starched black bombazine and stiff Dutch lace. Stan had been lucky that this stuff still remained after the great destruction.

"It's wonderful, Stan," Julie said. "I never knew who my parents were. They sold me before I knew them."

"I've got more than enough relatives," Stan said. "You can have some of mine."

"Can I? I'd like that. I'll take that fat one with the smile for my mother."

"That's Aunt Emilia. You've picked well. She was the best of the bunch."

There were other treasures upstairs. Eiderdowns whose cases were heavy with intricate embroidery; gaudy antique jewelry; massive furniture cut from gigantic tropical trees whose species had become extinct.

"This is such beautiful stuff," Julie said. "I could look at it forever. How do you ever pull yourself away?"

"You know, it's funny," Stan said. "I never liked any of this before. But since you've come here . . . Well, it looks pretty nice to me now."

The next day Stan was pleased when it was the time for action. He felt like his life was just beginning. He was very pleased with this notion, although he also dreaded it, because if his life was beginning, it was also drawing to a close. Which would come first, he wondered, victory or death? Or would they arrive simultaneously?

He refused to think about it. What was important was that he and Julie were in this together. He was no longer alone.

He dressed with special care that morning, humming to himself as he shaved. He selected an Italian silk suit and a colorful Brazilian imported shirt made of a light cotton. He wore his tasseled loafers, even going so far as to buff them up to a high polish. He usually laughed at people who took pains over their dress and appearance, but for this morning, at least, he was one of them. It was a way of reminding himself that he was making a fresh start.

He had been thinking a lot about fate and chance, and how they were influenced by the human will. He had come to the conclusion that what he wanted very badly was going to happen, as long as he willed it hard enough. It seemed to him that he was allied to a universal spirit that determined the course of things.

As long as he wanted what the universal spirit wanted for him, he couldn't go wrong.

Although these were exhilarating thoughts, Stan also had some doubts. He wondered if the fire caused by the Xeno-Zip might be affecting his mind. Was he getting a little ... grandiose? Did he really think he had found a way to cheat death?

Sometimes it seemed obvious to him that death was what was really happening to him. This was the real meaning of the disease rotting out his insides. There were too many details of his everyday life to remind him; the spitting and spewing into basins; the many pills he was continually taking, and their many strange effects.

He knew he was a very sick man. But he thought it represented some ultimate courage in himself that he was refusing to face the facts. He decided that if people really faced the facts, they'd all be licked before they could start.

He was determined to go on. It was not yet time to give up and let go. That would come later, when he found his doom; for Stan sensed a horrible fate awaiting him, one that was presently without a name or a face. Then he shook his head angrily and put those thoughts out of his mind.

He found a fresh daisy from the garden for his buttonhole. It was a bright crisp day outside, a day that seemed filled with infinite promise. He could hear Julie humming from the kitchen. She had come down after her shower and was making breakfast. He went in. She was wearing his long fluffy bathrobe. Her hair was tied up in a Donald Duck towel. Her face sparkled, and she looked very young, ingenuous. It was a nice thing to see, though he knew it was an illusion, and only a temporary one at that.

They had bacon and eggs over easy, toast, coffee. A simple breaking of the fast. And now they were ready to discuss plans.

"The first thing we need," Stan said, "is operating capital. I've got a lot of ideas for how to get this project of ours going. But it's going to take some money. Have you any thoughts on how we could acquire a cash flow?"

"I do," Julie said. "Raising money at short notice is what a thief does best, Stan. And I'm the best thief that ever was. How much do we need?"

Stan made some calculations. "A hundred thousand, anyway."

"And how much money do you have right now?"

"I don't know," Stan said. "A couple hundred, I suppose, maybe a thousand in savings."

"That's not enough, is it?" Julie asked.

"Nowhere near. We need fifty thousand anyway."

"As much as that?" Julie said. "Are you sure we need so much?"

"I'm afraid so," Stan said. "We'll have a lot of expenses to set up what we need in order to get a ship, put Norbert into final working shape, get the equipment we need, and get on with our plan."

"All right, Stan," Julie said. "I think I can be of some use here. Give me what you've got. I'll double it."

"How will you do that?"

"Watch and see."

"Will you use your skills as a thief?"

"Not immediately," Julie said. "There's an intermediate step I need to take."

"Could you be a little clearer?"

"I'm talking about gambling."

"I didn't know you were a gambler as well as a thief," Stan said.

"My real profession is thief, but I'm a gambler also because everyone needs a second line of work. The fact is, I'm lucky at certain games. Like Whorgle. I've been told that I've got latent psychokinetic abilities. I can affect the fall of dice sometimes. But they don't play dice at Callahan's, only card games. Well, Whorgle is a new game that depends on hand-eye coordination. I've got that, and I've also got something else. A certain X-factor that sometimes does the trick."

"Well, I guess you know what you're doing," Stan

said. "Although I've been wanting to see some of this thieving of yours in action."

"Being a good thief costs money, Stan."

"That's a funny thing to say. I thought you were supposed to make money that way."

"That's the result, of course. But when you work in the upper echelon of crime, you don't go in and hold up a candy store. And you don't knock off a bank, either. Those are not what I was trained for. You never asked what kind of thief I was, Stan. Well, I'm telling you now. I'm a high-society jewelry thief. I knock off only the best people. I work at political conventions, movie openings, awards ceremonies, great sports events, things that bring together crowds of people with lots of money. But that requires a setup. Otherwise I'd have to spend too long just trying to dope out how to do it. I buy a ready-made plan from an expert in the field. It comes high. But it's guaranteed to bring me to large amounts of money and jewelry."

"How much does a plan like that cost?"

"If you buy one from an expert like Gibberman, it can cost plenty. I'm going to use your money to win more money so I can pay Gibberman to give me one of his great plans. It may sound like a roundabout way to you, but name me any other profession where you can go from a thousand dollars to around a million in less than three days."

"Sounds interesting," said Stan. "Can I come along?"

"Well, of course you can, at least for some of it, but you have to be real cool. You mustn't even act like you're with me. You see, gambling is hard work. I'm going to have to give it all my attention. Then, assuming I win, there's the next part of the operation, which calls for even more attention."

"Yeah? What's that?"

"That's walking out of the gambling place with your money, Stan."

5

t first Stan didn't want
to show his robot alien to Julie. On the one hand, he
thought it was the best piece of work he had ever
done. But would she realize that? What would her reaction be?

It didn't matter what she thought, of course, Stan
told himself logically. Yet all the time he knew it did
matter, very much. He realized he wanted Julie to
think well of him. He had been alone too long, and he
had hidden from everyone, including himself, just
how lonely and desperate he had been. It would have
been too much to have realized that earlier. But now
that Julie had come into his life, he could no longer
bear being without her. He wanted to make sure that
never happened.

He didn't know what was going to happen. He was
scared. But he was also strangely happy. Over the last
few days the individual moments of his life felt better

31

than they had for a long time. Maybe he'd never felt
so good.

He was thinking about this while he showered and
put on clothes fresh from the dry cleaners. He shaved
with special care, and he laughed at himself for doing
all this, but that didn't stop him. He saw Julie over
breakfast. She was looking radiant, her hair sparkling
in the sunshine.

After breakfast, Stan showed her his lab.

After that, it was time to show off his robot alien.

He kept it in a special temperature-controlled room
behind a locked door. The door was to keep people
out, not to keep the robot in, he told Julie. It stood
perfectly immobile, since it was not presently acti-
vated. Its black, heavily muscled body seemed ready
to lunge. Yet Julie did not hesitate when Stan took her
hand and peeled back the robot's lips to show its
gleaming rows of needle-sharp fangs.

"Your pet looks like evil incarnate," Julie said.

"As a matter of fact, he's suprisingly gentle. I hope
I haven't made a mistake in the circuitry. He may need
to be trained to fight."

"I can be of some help there," Julie said.

6

In Jersey City, lying on a rank bed with a filthy mattress, Thomas Hoban stirred uneasily in his sleep. The dreams didn't come so often, but they still came. And always the same . . .

Captain Thomas Hoban was seated in the big command chair, viewscreens above him, clear-steel glass canopy in front. Not that you get to see much in space, not even in the Asteroid Belt. But even the biggest spaceship is small in terms of space for humans, and you get to appreciate even a view of nothingness. It's better than being sealed up in a duralloy cocoon without any vision except for what the TV monitors can offer.

The *Dolomite*—a good ship with an old but reliable atomic drive, but also recently fitted with tachyonic gear for multiparsec jumps—was currently on a local run within the solar system, tooling around doing a job here, a job there, trying to pick up some money

for the owners. Then they got the signal that took
them to Lea II in the asteroids.

Lea was a fueling base, owned by Universal Obsid-
ian but open to all ships. It was a refueling spot. It
even had a kind of café, only a dozen seats and a
menu like you'd expect at a place that hired their
cooks by how little they would steal and cut costs by
never bringing in fresh provisions. Not that fresh
produce comes easy in the asteroids. It costs too
much to make special runs with your iceberg lettuce.

After leaving Lea, Hoban had taken the *Dolomite* to
Position A23 in the asteroids. That was the location
for the Ayngell Works, a refinery on its own slab of
rock, where a robot work crew purified metals and
rare earths mined elsewhere in the asteroids. A23 was
located in one of the densest parts of the cluster. You
had to navigate at slow speeds and with care, but who
didn't know that? And Hoban was a careful man. He
didn't let his second-in-command do the job for him.
Even though Gill was an android and a top pilot and
navigator, Hoban did it himself, and he did it well. In
any event, no one had any complaints about him before he came to A23.

His job on A23 was to take a big metals hopper
into tow and bring it to the Luna Reclamations Facility. Taking it up was no small job. It was a big mother,
too big to fit into the *Dolomite*'s hold. But of course
the asteroid it was perched on had negligible gravity,
so there was no difficulty in pulling the hopper away
from the surface once the magnetic clamps that held
it to its massive base plate were released. Hoban's
crew, by all accounts, were trained men; it should
have been a piece of cake.

The trouble was, they weren't really a trained crew.
There were three Malays aboard who spoke no English and only understood the simplest commands.
That usually worked out all right, but not this time. It
had never been proven, but one of those Malays must
have gotten confused working in the lowest bay.
Somehow he or someone had missed the towline en-

tirely and had locked a fuel-line feeder into the coupling winch. The next thing Hoban knew, the feeding mechanism had been jerked out of the atomic pile, which had shut down automatically, leaving him floating in space without main power.

This wasn't the first time a spacecraft had lost a main engine. Gill estimated six hours to repair it. Meantime the backup accumulators and the steering jets would provide enough propulsion to get back to A23 so they could pick up the five crewmen who had gone down to manhandle the cargo ties into position.

At least that's what should have happened, or so it was claimed in the court inquiry later.

Instead, Hoban had turned the ship toward Luna and got away as fast as he could. He claimed afterward that there was a lot more wrong than just losing an engine. Down on A23, an inexperienced crew member had accidentally pulled the interlocks on the atomic pile that kept A23 running. The damned thing was going critical and there was no time to do anything but run for it. . . .

Leaving the five crewmen on A23 to their fate.

Hoban had had to make a quick decision. He calculated that the pile was going to blow up in three minutes. If he stayed around or moved in closer, the blast would take him with it. Even a class-four duralloy hull wasn't built for that kind of treatment. And anyhow, nonmilitary spacecraft were usually built of lighter-gauge metal than the fighting ships.

It was pandemonium aboard the *Dolomite*. There was a crew of twenty aboard, and five of them were down at A23 with the blast coming up on them in minutes. Half of the remaining crew had wanted the captain to ignore the lapsed-time indicator, ignore the risk, and go back to pick up the men; the other half wanted him to blow off what remained of battery power and get out of there as fast as his jets would take him.

The crew had burst into the control room, hysterical and entirely out of order, and they had begun to

come to blows right there while Hoban was trying to
con the ship and Gill into attending to the navigation.
Letting those men in there had been the captain's first
mistake.

Crewmen were not allowed in officer country except by specific invitation. When a crewman tres-
passes, shipboard code says he should be punished
immediately. If Hoban had ordered Gill to seize the
first man to come in and put him into the crowded little locker belowdecks that served as jail space, the
others might have had second thoughts. Crews obey
strong leadership, and Hoban's leadership at this
point was decidedly weak.

It was in the middle of that shouting writhing mass
of people that Hoban had come to his decision.

"Open the accumulators! Get us out of here, Mr.
Gill!"

That had shut everybody up, since the acceleration
alarm had gone off and they had to get back to their
own part of the ship and strap down while the faux
gravity was still in operation. It was Hoban's hesitation that had almost set off the men, but once he'd
made up his mind, things were better.

The question was, had he made the right choice?
The jury decided there was reason enough to believe
that Hoban had panicked, had not thought through his
position, had not properly calculated the risk. The
jury's report said that he had had more than enough
time and could have gone in for the men without un-
due risk to the ship. It would have been cutting it a
little fine, but in the atmosphere of the trial, men
didn't think about that. They didn't really ask themselves what they would have done in Hoban's shoes.
They just knew that five crewmen were dead, and the
company was liable.

But the question was, under which clause of the insurance contract was the company liable? If what had
happened was beyond anyone's power to change, that
was one thing. But if it was due to pilot error or poor

judgment, then the company had less direct liability. Guess which the jury went for?

Spaceship pilots were important men, like star athletes, and most of them had, in addition to solid abilities, good-to-excellent connections. Hoban didn't have any of that. Just top marks in his class throughout the university and Space School after that. He was the corps' token poor boy; proof that anyone could make it in the corps if he was smart and diligent. But when it came right down to it, after the accident, the company didn't want to pay out on the higher figure of the insurance and Hoban didn't have any friend in high places to keep a watch over his interests. Juries had been known to be bribed, and Bio-Pharm had been known to bribe them.

The case had faded quickly from the news. There were lots of other things to get excited about. No one was even interested in doing a vid special on the Hoban case. But if they'd looked into it, they might have been surprised.

7

Callahan's Sporting Club near Delancey Street was an illegal club. The authorities were always closing it down, but Callahan's always managed to open again in a day or two. Many city mayors and police commissioners had sworn to close the place once and for all, but somehow they never got around to it. Too much money changed hands. It was nice to know that some things, like the power of bribery, never changed.

A panel slid open in a reinforced door, and a face looked out. "Whaddyaa want?"

"I want to gamble," Julie said.

"Who do you know?"

"Luigi."

"Then come on in."

After they were inside, Stan whispered to her, "Who's Luigi?"

"I have no idea," Julie said. "In a place like this,

looking like you know someone is worth almost as much as really knowing."

Callahan's was filled with well-dressed, prosperous-looking people, most of them crowded three deep around the horseshoe-shaped bar. The general depression and malaise that seemed to grip so much of America didn't operate here. Here, things were booming. Stan could see people sitting in the adjoining dining room, eating as though there were no food shortages. It looked like they were eating real steaks, too. From beyond the dining room he could hear the excited sounds of people betting. The gaming rooms would be right down there, and that was where Julie led him.

"What game are you going to play?" he asked.

"I'll try Whorgle," she said.

She pushed her way into the circle, and they made way for her. There were a dozen men and three women betting on the action. They waited while she set out her cash. Then the game went on.

Stan found he couldn't figure out how Whorgle was played. There were cards, of course, and a small ivory marker, and something made it spin and jump between the numbers painted on the table. How long it resided in a square seemed to decide who won, but the cards had something to do with it, too. There were also disk-shaped markers with odd symbols on one side. The money, thrown down on the painted stake lines, passed back and forth too quickly for Stan to figure out what was happening. He knew he could work it all out if he just applied his mind, but right now he was feeling light-headed. It had been quite a while since his last shot of Xeno-Zip. The artificial fire that had enlivened his nerves and dulled his senses was fading out of his system. He was beginning to feel very bad. The pain was simply too hard to handle without something to help it like essence of royal jelly.

At last the pain became too much for him. He had to go into a nearby room and lie down on a couch.

After a while he fell into a troubled sleep and dreamed of grinning skulls dancing and bobbing in front of him.

After a while Julie came and woke him. She was smiling.

"How did you do?" Stan asked her.

"Nobody beats me at Whorgle," she said, riffling through a stack of greenbacks. "Let's go home and get some sleep. Then I need to see Gibberman."

8

Gibberman was a small man who wore a tweed cap pulled low on his forehead and crouched behind his Plexiglas-protected desk in his Canal Street pawnbroker's office, looking for all the world like an inflated toad. He wore a jeweler's loupe on a black ribbon around his neck and spoke with some indefinable Eastern European accent.

"Julie! Good to see you, darling."

"I told you I'd come," Julie said. "I'd like you to meet a friend of mine."

"Delighted," said Gibberman. "But no names, please." He shook Stan's hand, then offered Julie a drink from a half-empty bottle of bourbon beside him.

"No, nothing," she said. "Look, I'm going to get right to the point. I need plans for a job, and I need them quickly."

"Everybody's always in a hurry," Gibberman said.

"I've got places to go and things to do," Julie said.

"Rushing around is the curse of this modern age."

"Sure," Julie said. "You got anything for me or not?"

Gibberman smiled. "A good job is going to cost, you know."

"Of course," Julie said. "Here, check this out."

She took an envelope from her purse and put it down on the desk in front of Gibberman. He opened it, looked inside, riffled the bills, then closed the envelope again.

"You got it there, Julie. All you've got, that's the price."

"Fine," Julie said. "Now what do you have?"

"A piece of luck for you," Gibberman said. "Not only have I got a first-class job, probably worth a million or more, but you could do it tonight if you want to move that fast."

"Fast is just what I want," Julie said. "You're sure this is a good one?"

"Of course I'm sure," Gibberman said. "There's an element of risk in all these matters, as you well know. But with your well-known talents, you should have no particular difficulty."

Gibberman twirled around in his chair and pushed a wall painting out of the way. Behind it was a small safe set into the wall. He twirled the combination, blocking Julie and Stan's view with his body. Reaching in, he pulled out half a dozen envelopes, looked through them rapidly, selected one, put the rest back, then closed the safe.

"Here's the job, my dear. Set for New York, and on a street not too far from where we are just now."

"This had better be good," Julie said. "That's every cent we've got in the world."

"You know how reliable I am," Gibberman said. "Together with my accuracy goes my well-known discretion."

9

"What is this?" Stan asked. They had gone back home and had opened the manila envelope that Gibberman had given her. Inside was a map, a floor plan of an apartment, several keys, and a half-dozen pages of notes neatly printed in a tiny handwriting.

"This, my dear, is what any successful thief needs—a plan."

"That's what you got from Gibberman?"

"I've used his plans for several years," Julie said. "He's very thorough."

"So who are you going to rob?" Stan asked.

"A wealthy Saudi oilman named Khalil. He arrived in New York two days ago. He's going to the Metropolitan Opera tomorrow night to watch a special performance of *The Desert Song*. While he's away I'll relieve him of certain items he usually keeps in his apartment."

"Where is this to take place?"

"He's staying at the Plaza."

"Wow," Stan said. "I never thought I'd be doing this."

"You're not," Julie said. "I am. You'll have to wait for me at home. I always work alone."

"But we're partners now. We do everything together." He looked so crestfallen that Julie felt a pang of sorrow for him.

"Stan," she said, "you know that robot you've built? Would you trust me to do micro-soldering on his interior circuits?"

"Of course not," Stan said. "You haven't had the training. . . . Oh, I see what you mean. But it's not really the same thing."

"It's the exact same thing," Julie said.

"I just hate to see you going into this alone."

"Don't worry about me. Nothing ever goes wrong with my plans. And if it does, I can take care of it."

10

The Plaza Hotel had suffered some damage during the recent time of the aliens, but had since regained at least a semblance of its former elegance. Julie went there that evening wearing a stunning red cocktail dress. She looked, if not exactly like a celebrity, then definitely like a celebrity's girlfriend. The doorman opened the door for her, bowing deeply. She entered the big, brilliantly lit lobby. The reception desk was straight ahead. She didn't want to get too close to it yet. She glanced at her watch as if she was expecting to meet somebody. All the time she was taking in the details.

People were very well dressed. This was a place where money was in very good supply.

To one side a small orchestra was playing a quaint song from olden times called "Smoke Gets in Your Eyes." People were coming in and out of the bar with its glowing mahogany paneling and its soft indirect lighting. She would have liked a drink now, but she had an unbreakable rule: no alcohol or any other kind of drug while she was on a job.

She looked around the bar and then the lobby. Her practiced eye picked out the security men, two of them near the potted palms. She could always tell who they were. They just didn't look like the guests, no matter how well they dressed. She counted five of them. They gave her admiring glances but there was nothing suspicious in their looks. So far so good.

The big hotel was in full swing. There were lights everywhere, and elegant people, and the accoutrements of success. You could smell it in the five-dollar cigars and the expensive perfume on the white shoulders of the women; in the aroma of roast beef, the real thing, wafting out from under silver servers as black-coated waiters brought the well-laden plates around; in the very carpet, permeated with expensive preservatives and subtle-smelling oils.

Julie went to the elevators. One was reserved for the penthouse suites. There was a man standing near it, rocking back and forth on his heels as he surveyed the passing crowds. Julie made him for a plainclothes cop, maybe somebody's bodyguard. She walked on past and went through a set of corridors back into the main lobby. She was pretty sure the guy at the penthouse elevator hadn't noticed her. She was also sure a frontal assault on the apartment wasn't the best idea.

Gibberman had taken this possibility into account. Next door to the Plaza was the Hotel Van Dyke. Khalil's apartment was a penthouse in the Plaza. If, for any reason, Julie didn't want to use the elevator, Gibberman had indicated an ingenious alternate way of gaining entry. It involved swinging from an unoccupied top-floor apartment in the Van Dyke, and going in through Khalil's window. A cat-burglar act, but that was one of Julie's specialties. She wished Stan could be here to watch her. But it wouldn't be safe, and it might distract her.

She had no trouble slipping into the Van Dyke with a group of people going to the top-floor restaurant. When they got off at the top floor, Julie got out with them, but instead of entering the restaurant, she ducked into the short flight of service stairs that led to the roof. From there she had a fine view of upper Manhattan, with the dark mass of Central Park directly in front of her and traffic crawling by a long way below on the street. A cutting wind blew her hair around, and she slipped on a knit cap to hold it in place. "Here we go!" she said aloud.

She fixed her ropes and swung over to the roof of the Plaza. From there she tied her rope to a cornice and, taking a deep breath, swung out again into space, bracing herself with one foot so as not to spin. The stars and the street seemed equally distant as she lowered herself to the level of the apartment windows.

They were open, saving her from having to cut through them with a vibrator tool.

She swung in through the billowing white curtains, landed soundlessly inside the darkened apartment, and rolled to her feet. She could see pretty well with the infrared-enhanced goggles she now snapped on. Her feet were set in a defensive pose, but there was no one there. She gave the rope a snap and it came free from the cornice. She wound it around her waist. Now there was no evidence of her means of entry.

She looked around the apartment. It was large, with a drawing room and a separate bedroom. She checked out the kitchen. The refrigerator was filled with a very good brand of champagne, and there were tins of caviar in the pantry. This Khalil seemed to live on the rarest of fare. The question now was where did he keep the jewelry?

She knew that Gibberman had chosen this mark carefully. Ahmed Khalil was renowned as an international playboy. He loved to give expensive gifts to his ladies of the evening. But where did he keep the trinkets? She had already learned from inside sources that he didn't entrust them to hotel safes. He wanted

them close at hand for the moment when he chose to
reward his current lady.

She moved quickly around the apartment. Although
the place was big, it was still only a hotel suite. The
stuff has to be here somewhere. . . .

And then, suddenly, the lights came on.

"Good evening, my dear," a deep, resonant voice
said.

Julie saw a tall, very thin, dark-faced man leaning
negligently against the wall. He was wearing a
checked headdress. He had a short beard and luxuri-
ant mustache. His face was narrow, and he had a
hawk's nose with a large mole in the left corner.
Standing beside him was another man, also an Arab,
but large—in fact, huge—with a full head of fuzzy
black hair and so much facial hair that his features
were all but obscured. Julie, however, had no trouble
seeing the knife he held in his right hand.

"What are you doing here?" Julie asked. "You're
supposed to be seeing an opera."

Khalil, the tall thin man, smiled. "Your information
is reliable, but so was my counterintelligence service.
We always keep an eye on Gibberman when we come
to New York. He's stung us before. We knew when
you visited him to set up the job. Didn't we, Sfat?"

The giant smiled and touched the point of his dagger with the ball of his thumb.

Khalil said, "Gibberman was happy to tell us what
he had set up for this evening."

Julie nodded. Talk about luck.

"You mustn't hold it against Gibberman for talking," Khalil said. "When Sfat takes the knife to somebody, secrets are shouted from the rooftops. His skill
is better than a surgeon's. With that knife he can lay
bare a single nerve, in the arm, for example, and play
on it as if it were the string on a violin. It is an unfor-
gettable experience, my dear, and one I'm sure you
wouldn't want to miss."

Julie thought of how she had told Stan that nothing
ever went wrong. What a laugh! Of course, it was all

bad luck. How could she have guessed that Khalil would find out about Gibberman? She had discounted the efficiency of the counterintelligence corps these rich Arabs employed.

"Well, Khalil," Julie said, "looks like I'm foiled and caught in the act. Have your man step away from the door and I'll leave quietly."

Khalil smiled. "I'm afraid it's not going to be so easy, my dear."

"You're going to turn me over to the police?"

"Eventually. If there's enough left of you. First, however, it will be necessary to teach you a lesson. Sfat!"

The big man took a slow step toward her.

Julie said, "I thought it would be like that. Thanks, Khalil."

"For what?"

"For freeing me of any scruples. If I ever had any, you've put them completely out of my mind."

She turned to face Sfat, and took two steps toward him while Khalil folded his arms and waited for the fun to begin, a small smile on his lips.

Sfat lifted his arms, hands formed into blades. He bent his knees, feet pointed outward, and Julie recognized the typical fighting stance of a Saudi karate fighter. It was a technique that had its limitations. Sfat advanced, mincingly for so large a man, and his bearded face was set in a mask of cruelty. As he came within range his left hand darted out, the finger's shaped like a hawk's head.

She was ready for it, had been anticipating it. She ducked under the swooping blow and, with a short, economical kick, connected with Sfat's left kneecap. He had been turning as she kicked, and some of the force of the blow was lost. Nevertheless, it was enough to take his feet out from under him. He fell heavily, and Julie pounced.

But this time he caught her unawares. Sfat's clumsy fall had been feigned, and as she came leaping at him his arms and legs were drawn up cat fashion, and he lashed out, expecting to catch her in the solar plexus. She had seen her danger a moment before his counterstroke, however, and turning in midair, managed to avoid his flailing limbs. Her stiffened elbow caught him in the pit of the stomach, knocking the air out of him, and in the second it took him to recover, she rolled away and regained her feet.

Khalil had been watching all this dumbfounded. Now, belatedly, he stirred into action. He stepped forward, crouching in a classic knife fighter's pose. The weapon he carried in his right hand and low against his body was a *yata*, a traditional Yemeni dagger, about eight inches long, slightly curved, and sharpened to a razor edge. It was made from a Swedish saw blade, and fitted with an elaborate rhino-horn handle. Arabic letters were engraved on the blade. Julie's eyes widened when she saw the weapon.

"You do well to fear the *yata*," Khalik said, advancing, light twinkling off the point like the gaze of a one-eyed basilisk.

"Oh, I wasn't exactly afraid of it," Julie said. "Just surprised to see it. Rhino horn is not legally traded. Is it genuine?"

"Of course," Khalil said, feinting and then making a lightning stab at her. "I always kill with the genuine article."

"I'm sure glad to hear that," Julie said. "That makes that knife extremely valuable!"

The blade darted toward her midsection. Julie spun, and the thing passed harmlessly along her left side. As it passed, her arm snapped down, trapping the weapon. Khalil began a long and elaborate Arabic curse in the guttural dialect of Omdurman, but got out no more than a couple of syllables before Julie's left elbow crashed with piledriver force into the middle of his face.

Blood streaming from his nose and mouth, Khalil stumbled backward, losing his grip on the knife that was still clamped under Julie's left arm.

"I'll just keep this for you," Julie said, slipping the

knife into her belt. "It might reduce its value if we got blood all over it."

A feint to the midsection drew down Khalil's guard. Fingers folded in protectively, Julie snapped a blow. The heel of her hand caught Khalil where the upper lip meets the nose. Four of his front teeth cracked off clean at the gum line.

"You ought to thank me," Julie said. "I've corrected your overbite and haven't even charged you for it."

Khalil fell down screaming. He rolled on the floor clutching his head and whimpering. Bloody foam splattered from his mouth. Julie watched him critically for a moment, then muttered, "That ought to keep you occupied for a while."

She turned to Sfat. He had regained his feet, and although his balance was just the slightest bit off-kilter, he was still formidable. If rage could kill, then Julie would be dead ten times over. He came toward her on the attack. He was about twice the weight of the slender girl and he was containing his fury now as he backed her into an angle of the wall, just to one side of an indifferent copy of Gainsborough's *Blue Boy*. There seemed no way she could get out of this one. Shouting an oath in street Arabic, Sfat launched his attack.

Julie had had long preparation for moments like this. Shen Hui's instructions in self-defense had covered all the basics of unarmed combat. He had not been satisfied with that, however, since he accounted himself no expert in the finer points of self-defense. So he had apprenticed her to Olla Khan, a fat-faced master fighter from Isfahan in central Asia. Khan, beguiled by her beauty, had said, "My arrangement with your master is that you will stay with me and serve me in all particulars until you can beat me at unarmed combat. That might take more than a lifetime, my pet."

In fact it took just five months, and Olla Khan ended up in a hospital for his presumption.

And so, now, with Sfat launching his impetuous

and ill-considered attack, Julie's problem was not how to cope with it, but which of several different methods to choose. She also had to decide to what extent she wished to incapacitate him, and this in turn depended on her estimation of his value to her alive. In the split of a second she decided that this gross hairy-faced man with the bad breath was of no value to her, and indeed could serve her better dead as a message to his master, Khalil, to stop resisting and start cooperating.

She didn't think all that through consciously. Instead, she opposed his charge with a sword hand, fingers stiffened. Sfat crashed into her hand and was stopped abruptly as the fingers took him high between the eyes, shutting down his pineal gland and then going on to break his neck. His eyes rolled up, showing the white, and he crashed to the floor like two hundred pounds of dead mutton.

She turned from him to Khalil. "Ready to go another round?" she asked.

Khalil, his teeth scattered over the floor, had had enough. He mumbled through a bloodstained hand. "Don't hurt me anymore. I'm a dilettante, not a fighter. I'll give you whatever you want."

"That's what I like to hear," Julie said. She took a pillow from a nearby bed and stripped off the pillowcase.

"Fill it with good stuff for me," she said. "Don't put in any worthless crap or I'll have something to say about it."

Khalil, totally unnerved, couldn't even dream of resistance. His collapse was absolute. He opened a compartment concealed in the wall behind the bed and picked several precious bracelets, two handfuls of magnificent unmounted gems in a white chamois bag, and a string of glorious baroque pearls, each the size of a pigeon's egg and no two alike. Soon the pillowcase was bulging. Khalil had other objects he wanted to give her, but she stopped him.

"One bagful is enough. I'm not greedy. Besides, I'd need an extra pair of hands to carry it all."

Khalil recovered sufficiently to say, "If you're finished, then get out!"

"Okay," Julie said. "This is good-bye, then." She moved close to him.

He stared at her. The whites of his eyes went a dirty yellow as she advanced on him. He stumbled away, found himself with his back to a bureau. "What are you going to do?" he asked in a shaking voice.

"Just give you a couple hours' sleep. So I can walk out of here like a lady." She touched a nerve in his neck. He slumped to the floor unconscious.

"Be sure to have a dentist look at those stumps," she said. He couldn't hear her, of course, but she was sure he'd remember anyway.

Julie went to the dressing-room mirror and checked her clothing and makeup. She repaired her lipstick, which had been smeared in the combat, and found an ugly red stain on the shoulder of her red dress.

Luckily, Khalil had a really smart ermine jacket in his closet. It covered the stain nicely. She left by the penthouse elevator. No one stopped her as she walked out, passed through the lobby, and exited the revolving front door onto Central Park South, where she called a taxi.

11

"**H**ow did it go to-night?" Stan asked when she got back to the brownstone.

"Not bad," she said, dumping her loot into the bed. "A dream night for a thief. Unfortunately, it's nowhere near enough to buy a spaceship with."

"We don't need to buy one," Stan said. "I've got a plan that ought to work now that we have some money to play around with. The first thing we're going to need is a spaceship driver."

"I'd love to talk about it," Julie said. "But first I need a bath. And I'm famished! Sometimes stealing can be hard work. Oh, by the way, here's a present." She tossed the dagger onto the bed.

Stan picked it up and admired the gleaming narrow blade and the rhino handle. "Where'd you get this?"

"Just a little trinket I picked up during the evening."

12

Over the next two weeks, Julie converted the loot from Khalil's apartment to cash, and Stan lost no time putting it to work. There was information to buy, people to bribe, and round-the-clock work by hired technicians to put Norbert into full working condition.

Two weeks to the day after Julie's theft at the Plaza, she met Stan for lunch at the Tavern on the Green in Central Park. Since it wasn't a workday for her, she permitted herself a cocktail.

Stan was looking pretty well. A shade paler than usual, but still not bad for a man dying of cancer and sustaining himself on heavy doses of the most addicting narcotic substance known to man. His eyes were a little dreamy, but his voice was firm enough as he said, "Julie, we're ready to make our move."

"Today?"

"That's right. Are you ready?"

She gave him an exasperated look. "Of course. You really don't have to ask me that."

"Sorry, I didn't mean anything by it."

Her voice softened. "No, I'm sorry, Stan. I don't mean to snap at you. It's the waiting. It's hard on my nerves."

"Well," Stan said, "it'll soon be over. If this plan works, we'll have ourselves a pilot."

"And if it doesn't work?"

"We could be dead."

"Fair enough. Where are we going?"

"To look up an old friend of mine and make him an offer he can't refuse."

13

Jersey City, even in its best days, had been a city many people found objectionable. It hadn't improved much since the days before the Human–Alien Wars and the human reoccupation. On the day Stan and Julie went there, half of the streets downtown were awash due to a burst water main from a week before, and the city's repair crews still hadn't gotten around to capping it.

Ragged, mean-looking men and women hung around every street corner. They looked like down-and-outers, but there was something sly and dangerous about them, too. There were soup kitchens set up here and there, and the buildings looked old and delapidated. Even the newly built sections of the city were starting to show wear, their poor construction materials already crumbling. Packs of wild dogs slinked in and out of back alleys; nobody had gotten around to getting rid of them yet.

"It's pretty bad," Stan said, like he was apologizing for it.

"Hey, I've seen worse," Julie said. "Not that I want to hang around this place . . ."

At Central Station, Stan found them a motorized pedicab. The driver was a gnarled old brute, dressed nearly in rags, with a shapeless felt hat on which, incongruously, was the glittering bright medallion that let him legally operate a for-hire vehicle.

Stan peered inside the three-wheel pedicab. Some of these drivers had been known to hide accomplices inside, the better to rob the customers, or so it was said. Stan didn't really know what to expect. He hadn't been outside New York City in years.

He gave the driver the address, and the man grunted. "You sure you want to go there, mister?"

"Yes, I'm sure. Why do you ask?"

"You're going to the heart of the old Gaslight District. Where the space derelicts and the chemheads hang out."

"Yes, I know."

"No place for a lady, either."

"Shut your face and get moving," Julie said.

"Long as you know what you're getting into." The pedicab operator started up the hand-cranked washing-machine motor that ran his little vehicle. Stan and Julie settled back.

Once the driver got up to speed, he gave them a dashing ride. He wove in and out of traffic on Jersey City's wide boulevards, the pedicab dodging in and out of the debris that the striking garbage collectors would get around to picking up once they settled their contract with the city. The street was like an obstacle course, filled with boxes, packing cases, mattresses, wrecked vehicles, even the carcass of a horse. There were also plenty of vehicles, driven by kamikaze drivers who were hell-bent on getting somewhere, anywhere, rushing around and dodging in and out of each other's way like rules of the road were no more than memories. There was a dirty gray sky overhead, the sun concealed behind dark-edged clouds. It wasn't anyone's fault that the day was so rotten, but you felt like blaming someone anyhow. Looking around, Stan thought, To paraphrase Robert Browning, anything so ugly had to be evil.

"How do you like it?" the driver asked, turning back to fix Stan with a hard look.

"The city? It looks like it's fallen on hard times."

"Buddy, you can say that again. This has always been a bad-luck city. Gutted during the Alien Wars. That happened to a lot of cities. Gave them a chance to rebuild. Only crappier."

"Well, things are tough all over," Stan said, wishing the driver would turn around and pay attention to the traffic.

The driver acted like he had eyes in the back of his head. Cars came shrieking at him from every direction, and somehow they always missed and he kept right on talking.

"You're from New York, right? I can always tell. You people didn't get the Pulsing Plague like we got it here in Jersey. Turned whole neighborhoods into madhouses filled with raving lunatics before it did them the favor of killing them. But not all of them, worse luck. There are some plague people still alive, you know. They were infected, but it didn't kill them. But it can kill you if they touch you."

"I've been inoculated against plague," Stan said.

"Sure. But what good will an inoculation do you against the new berserkers you get around here? They're mostly people who recovered from the Pulser, but with something missing. It was like some center of control in their heads just vanished. Berserkers can get into a frenzy over the smallest thing, over nothing at all. And then watch out for them because they start killing and don't stop until somebody stops them."

"I'll watch out for them," Stan said, feeling very uncomfortable. What was he getting himself and Julie into?

"You wanta good restaurant?" the driver said suddenly. "Try Toy's Oriental Palace over on Ogden. They got a way with soypro you'd never believe. They use real spices in their sauces, too."

"Thanks, I'll remember that," Stan said. "Are we close now?"

"You can smell it, can't you?" the driver said, grinning. "Yep, we're just about there."

The driver slowed down and looked for an opening in the traffic, found one that was too small, and decided to make it larger. He propelled the little pedicab into it, suffering no more than a bruised bumper, ducked into a narrow street off the boulevard, took a couple of turns, and pulled up to the curb.

Stan and Julie got out. Stan saw they were in an evil-looking neighborhood, which was just about what he'd expected. Above him, rising above the buildings, he saw a landmark: the spire of the Commercial Services Landing Field, a local service facility where nonstellar spaceships took off and landed. There had been a lot of discussion about it in the newly formed city council. Too close to the city, some said. It could be a source of danger. If one of those things goes down . . . Some people still didn't trust spacecrafts. It was a point, but the other side had the answer. "It'll bring jobs into the city. We'll be the closest full-facility field within a hundred-mile radius of New York. A lot closer than the Montauk Point facility. The business will flock to us." And in Jersey City, where business is king and corruption is its adviser, there was no answer to that.

The spaceport's spire was several miles away, Stan figured. He was in a neighborhood of small ramshackle buildings built against the bulwark of several skyscrapers. He was standing in front of Gabrielli's Meat Market, advertising fresh pork today in addition to the usual soypro steaks and turkeytofu butterballs, and the place stank of blood and chemicals. Next to it was a small newsstand, and what looked like a betting parlor beside that. Betting was legal in the state of New Jersey, an important source of revenue. Most of the state legislature didn't approve of gambling, but money was hard to find these days, even with the giant Bio-Pharm plant recently opened in nearby Hoboken and with MBSW—the Mercedes-Benz Spaceship Works—sprawled out in Lodi.

A young woman, perhaps sixteen or seventeen years old, came up to Stan. She was slender and tall, and she wore a new motorcycle jacket.

Ignoring Julie, she said, "Can I help you, mister?"

Stan shook his head. "I'm not interested today, thank you."

She glared at him. "You think I'm selling sex? Forget it, stupid. I can see you got a lady with you. And besides, you don't have enough to buy me."

"What are you offering, then?" Stan said.

"Advice. Guidance."

Stan couldn't help laughing. "Thanks, but we can do without it."

"Can you really? You people from around here?"

"No, as a matter of fact."

"That's pretty clear. You want to walk out of here alive? You'd better buy a pass."

Stan looked around. There seemed to be nothing much happening on the street. It all looked safe enough. Yet something about her tone of voice chilled him, and he said, "Just out of curiosity, what happens if we don't take a pass?"

She shrugged. "What usually happens to people who stray onto other people's turf?"

"But I'm standing in a public street!"

"It's turf all the same. You're in the territory of the Red Kings. I can sell you a pass that'll keep you out of trouble, or you can take your chances."

Julie had been standing by, listening, letting Stan handle it, but she was getting impatient. "For heaven's sake, Stan, give her something and let's get on with it!"

"I guess I'll take two passes," Stan said. "How much are they?"

Her price of ten dollars didn't seem too bad. Stan paid with a twenty and waited for change.

"For the other ten I'll sell you some advice," the woman said.

Stan hesitated, then decided not to argue. "Okay. What's your advice?"

"When you go into the soup kitchen," she said, "don't forget your pail." And then she turned and walked away.

Stan looked at the pass in his hand. It was a playing card, the five of diamonds. Turning it over, he saw a fine looping scrawl in red Magic Marker. He couldn't read it, but it looked just like graffiti.

"Hey, kin I help?" a voice asked.

It was a vagrant in a shapeless graycloth hat who had spoken to them. He looked fat and stupid and evil.

Julie said to him, "Buzz off, buster."

The man looked for an instant as though he was prepared to take umbrage at the remark. Then, warned perhaps by a sixth sense that told him when he was outmatched, he mumbled something and walked on.

"I should be doing the protecting," Stan said.

"Don't get all bent out of shape over it," Julie said. "I can take care of bums and wise guys, but I don't know how to build robots. It all evens out in the end."

"Yeah, I guess it does," Stan said. "Here we are."

They walked up the crumbling steps of a rotting tenement. An odor of roach repellent fought with the smell of crushed roaches. There was not much to choose between them. Dim yellow lightbulbs burned overhead as they climbed to the third floor.

Stan found the right door and knocked. No answer. He knocked again, louder.

Julie said, "Maybe we should have phoned."

"No telephone." Stan hammered on the door. "I

know he's in there. There's a light on under the door. And I can hear the TV."

"Maybe he's shy," Julie said. "I think we can fix that." With one well-placed kick, she shattered the lock. The door swung inward.

Within, there was a dismal-looking apartment that might have been pretty nice along around the time Rome was founded. It was a hideous place of ancient wallpaper and mildew, and the sound of a toilet running. Smell of frying kelp patties from other apartments overlay the basic odors. There was an overflowing garbage pail, with two cardboard cartons of garbage beside it.

For furniture, there was an old wooden kitchen table. Sitting at it in a straight-backed chair was a strongly made, sad-faced, middle-aged man with iron-gray hair.

This man looked up as they came in. He seemed startled by what he saw, yet uncaring, as if it didn't matter what the world threw at him next. There was a small black-and-white TV on the table, and he turned it off.

"Hello, Captain Hoban," Stan said.

Hoban took his time about answering. He seemed to be reorienting himself in the real world, after a long trip to some unimaginable place, perhaps to the time of his trouble in the asteroids.

At last he said, "It *is* you, isn't it? Why, hello, Stan."

"Hi," Stan said. "I want you to meet my friend Julie."

Hoban nodded, then looked around. He seemed aware for the first time of the apartment's appearance.

"Please, sit down, miss. You, too, Stan. I'll get you some tea. . . . No, I'm sorry, there isn't any left. No extra chairs, either. If I'd known you were coming, Stan . . ."

"I know, you would have had lunch catered," Stan said.

"Lunch? I can fry you a kelp patty. . . ."

"No, sorry, just kidding, Captain. We're not staying. We're getting out of here, and so are you."

Hoban looked surprised. "But where are we going?"

"There's got to be a café near here," Stan said. "Someplace we can talk."

Hoban looked around again, grinned sheepishly. "I guess this place isn't too conducive to conversation."

"Especially not a business talk," Stan said. "Have you got a coat? Let's go!"

14

Danziger's was a Ukrainian café on the next block. It had big glass windows, always misty with steam. There were vats of water perpetually at the boil for the pirogis in ersatz flour gravy that were the specialty of the place. Stan, Julie, and Hoban took a small booth in the rear. They drank big mugs of black coffee and talked in low voices.

Stan was concerned about Hoban's condition. It had been a while since he had last seen the captain, back when Hoban had been captain of the *Dolomite* and Stan had bought the ship. Stan had liked the taciturn, serious-minded captain and had kept him in charge.

Hoban was one of the old breed, a straight-shooting captain, always serious and controlled, whose interests were exclusively in intergalactic navigation and exploration, and who could be counted on to follow orders. Stan had bought the *Dolomite* during his flush period, when the royalties were rolling in from his various patents, before his troubles with Bio-Pharm and the government. In those golden days, it had looked like the sky was the limit.

After the asteroid incident, when Hoban had lost his license, Stan had pulled some strings and managed to get him a temporary captain's ticket. They had all been quite close then, Stan and Hoban and Gill, the android, who was second-in-command. But then Stan's problems with Bio-Therm had begun, and the lawsuits had started flocking in like flies to a flayed cow.

A hostile holding company had taken over the *Dolomite*, and their first act had been to dismiss Hoban, who was known for his loyalty to Stan. They accused the captain of various peccadilloes. That was really a laugh, with a man of Hoban's known probity, but mud sticks when you fling enough of it hard enough, and the licensing board had lifted Hoban's temporary ticket pending an investigation.

The captain had taken it hard. He was reduced in the course of one terrible day from a man who commanded his own little empire to a penniless derelict who couldn't find any work better than washing dishes.

Now they sat together in a Ukrainian café, with the late-afternoon sun streaming in through the windows, and Stan said, "I'm going back into space, Captain, and I want you with me."

"It's good of you to say so," Hoban said. "But no employer would have me without a license."

"I still want you," Stan said. "As for your license, we'll claim it's still in force."

"But it won't be," Hoban said.

"You can't be sure of that," Stan said. "Money talks. I think the courts will find for you, if it comes to an actual trial. And I'll get your case reopened after this trip."

"Can you really do that?" Hoban asked. A ray of hope lightened his heavy features for a moment, then his expression darkened again. "But I have no ship, Dr. Myakovsky. Or do you want me to pilot something other than the *Dolomite*?"

"No, we're going on the good old *Dolomite*," Stan said.

"But, Doctor, you no longer own it! And even if you did, I am no longer allowed to pilot it."

"Possession is nine tenths of the law," Stan said. "Once we're aboard and under way, they'll have to argue with us in court. Their lawyers against ours."

"I don't know," Hoban said, slumping down and shaking his head.

"Money talks," Stan pointed out again. "We'll win your case. After this trip, we'll all have it good."

"Yes, sir. Back into space again ... Excuse me for asking, sir, but do you have any money for this venture?"

"Enough for what we need. And a way to get a lot more."

"Where do you want to go?" Hoban asked.

"Let's get into that later," Stan said. "You don't mind if it's dangerous, do you?"

Hoban smiled sadly and shrugged. "Anything's better than rotting here, with nothing to hope for."

"My sentiments exactly," Stan said. "This is Miss Julie Lish, my partner. You'll be seeing a lot of her on this expedition."

Hoban shook Julie's extended hand. "But wait," he said. "I'm sorry, Stan, you had me dreaming for a moment. I'm afraid it's impossible."

"Why do you say that?" Stan asked.

"For one thing, no crew."

"Okay. And what else?"

"The *Dolomite*'s in geosynchronous orbit above Earth, ready to go on a mining trip in a few days."

"We'll have to act quickly. Who's running the *Dolomite*?"

"Gill, until the replacement captain comes aboard."

"Excellent!"

"I don't think so, Stan. You know Gill. He's programmed to follow the rules. Gill always obeys orders."

"Not to worry," Stan said. "Are you sure the new captain's not aboard yet?"

"Yes, I'm sure."

"Then it's simple. We'll go aboard and take off at once."

"Yes, sir . . . But it won't work, sir. You and I are both proscribed from boarding the *Dolomite*. There are guards. They'll read our retinal prints, turn us back. . . ."

"No," Stan said. "They'll call Gill to make a judgment. He's in charge now."

"But what can Gill do? Androids are very simpleminded, Dr. Myakovsky. They obey orders. Their loyalties are built-in, hardwired."

"Like a dog," Stan suggested.

"Yes, sir. Very much like."

"There's still a chance. Since he was animated, Gill has only worked with you."

"That's right. But it's been a while since we've been together. And anyhow, when they changed his orders, they will have changed his loyalties, too."

"They will have tried," Stan said. "Actually, it isn't quite so simple. Loyalty in an android is formed by long association with a particular human. I think Gill will lean in your favor when it comes to a showdown between following your orders or those of the new owners."

Hoban considered it and shook his head doubtfully. "Android conditioning is not supposed to work that way, sir. And if you're wrong . . . It'll be instant prison for all three of us."

"Let's worry about that when the time comes," Stan said. "Of course it's not dead simple. What is? The thing is, it's a chance for us all. What do you say, Hoban? Are you with us or not?"

Hoban looked up and down, uncertain, frowning. Then he looked at Julie. "Do you know what kind of a chance you're taking here, miss?"

"It's better than sitting around listening to yourself breathe," Julie said.

"This venture of yours, Doctor—I suspect it's not entirely legal."

"That's correct," Stan said. "It's illegal and it's dangerous. But it's a chance to rehabilitate yourself. What do you say?"

Hoban's mouth quirked. His face twisted in an agony of indecision. Then he suddenly drove his fist down on the table, causing the coffee mugs to jump.

"I'll do it, Dr. Myakovsky. Anything's better than this!"

The three shook hands. Stan said, "Let's get moving. There's no time to waste."

"There's just one problem," Hoban said.

"What's that?" Stan asked.

"We don't have a crew."

Stan's shoulders slumped and he sat down again.

Julie asked, "How do you usually get a crew?"

"There's no time to get them on the open market," Hoban said, "and we'd have a hard time getting people for a dangerous mission. In circumstances like this, we requisition them from the government."

"What does the government have to do with it?" Julie wanted to know.

"They allow convicts to put in for hazardous duty in space, in return for reduced time on their sentences."

Stan said, "But this time it wouldn't work. The government won't release any of the cons to me now that I've been barred from my own ship."

"Of course they will," Julie said. "Government is slow, Stan, and one part of it never knows what some other part of itself is doing. Just go in and ask the way you usually do. You're a legitimate owner, you've hired crews before. They have to serve you."

"But what if they do know my ship has been seized?"

"First of all, so what? People have property seized every day. It doesn't put them out of business. They have a suit against you, but you're still innocent until proven guilty. And besides, the people who actually give you prisoners, the guards and clerks, what do you think they know about that? They don't know and don't care. They do what they have to do."

"I don't know," Stan said. "I'll be too nervous."

"It will work."

"Maybe. But I don't feel confident about this."

"Stan, if you want to succeed in what you and I are getting into, you're going to have to learn how to fake self-confidence. Have you ever acted in a play?"

"Sure, in college. I was pretty good."

"Well, that's what you're going to do now. Act the part of Dr. Myakovsky, brilliant young scientist and upcoming entrepreneur."

"Acting a part," Stan mused. "What a novel idea! But I believe I could do that."

Julie nodded. "I knew right away you had it in you to play the Big Con. Stan, if you weren't already a scientist, I think you could make a great thief."

It was the nicest compliment Stan had ever been paid.

"And as for you, Captain Hoban . . ." Julie continued.

"Yes, miss?" Hoban said.

"You're going to have to get that hangdog look off of your face. You're a spaceship captain again, not a washed-up drunk who did something wrong once in his life and is making himself pay for it the rest of his life."

"I'll try to remember that," Hoban said.

15

15

Morning came early to the federal penitentiary at Goose Lake, New York. Almost two thirds of the great gray concrete structure was underground, buried under one of the Catskills. What showed above was a windowless dome, gray as a ghost in sunlight, unrelievedly ugly despite the rows of quick-growing trees that had been planted around its perimeter in an attempt to dress it up. A ten-foot-high electrified fence surrounded the facility, but it was pretty much window dressing. No convict had gotten as far as the fence yet. The prison had its ways of keeping the prisoners docile.

Within the windowless pile, artificial light shone night and day. It was part of standard policy to keep the prisoners disoriented, and therefore less aggressive. Inside, there were the usual sections of prison cells, with catwalks outside them where the guards walked. There were workshops, food and laundry facilities, and a separate room where the inmates did state-approved work and earned a dollar or so a day for it.

It was free time now. All the men not doing solitary were walking around the grounds, exercising, talking.

A loud voice came from the prison loudspeaker. "All men whose names are on the Alpha Volunteer List, report to the auditorium on the second level."

The Alpha Volunteer List contained the names of those prisoners with space experience who were willing to volunteer for a hazardous assignment in return for a reduction of their sentences. It had been a while since the call went out for crew. The prisoners were well aware of the good things this early release could do for them. And anyway, it was easier to escape from a spaceship than from a federal prison.

It was not easy getting on the Alpha List, because only a limited number were permitted even to apply. You had to bribe a guard to have any chance at all. And you were likely to have problems with other prisoners who wanted to take your place.

Red Badger had been waiting for this chance a long time. Now he got up, smoothed down his unruly red hair, checked his shoes, and started for the auditorium.

He was stopped by an inmate named Big Ed.

"Where do you think you're going?" Big Ed asked.

"I'm on the list," Badger said.

"You got it wrong," Big Ed said. "That last place is mine."

"No," Red insisted, "it's mine."

"Sure. But you're going to give it to me, aren't you?"

"No way," said Red Badger. "Now, if you'll just let me get past . . ."

Big Ed stood in the middle of the corridor, blocking Badger's way. "Do like I say," he threatened, "or else."

Red Badger knew he was being challenged, knew that Big Ed had been waiting for this moment a long

time, yet he also knew that Big Ed had picked him fig-
uring he was the easiest guy on the Alpha List to intimidate. Badger already knew what he was going to
do about it.

He was known as Red Badger because of his shock
of coarse red hair. He had the light, easily sunburned
skin that went with red hair, and narrow blue-green
eyes that blinked at you from behind sandy eyelashes.
He was a big man, heavy in the chest. He wore his
leather waistcoat open to show his chest with its grizzled mass of hair. He had large square teeth and a
nasty smile.

Badger was an alumnus of many prisons. He had
gotten his nickname at Raiford Prison in Florida, and
as an act of defiance had taken it for his own. Badger
was doing time for armed robbery and assault. He had
a criminal record that went back a long way. Quick
with his fists, he was also quick with his tongue and
was always looking for a chance to cause trouble.
"Trouble is my real middle name," he liked to say. "Let
me show you how I spell it." And then he'd punctuate
his remark for you with his fists. Like the badger, his
namesake, he was most dangerous when cornered.

The fight was to be held according to the accepted
prison rules: just the two of them, having it out in one
of the washrooms. Whoever was still standing after it
was over would go to the auditorium. The two com-
batants went there silently.

Both men knew it did no good to be brawling in
the corridors. There were stingray projectors with
motion-indicator finders mounted in all the corridors,
turning steadily and scanning in all directions. The
stingers weren't fatal, but they hurt like hell and could
be counted upon to whip recalcitrant prisoners into
line. There were no projectors mounted in the washrooms.

Although it was never talked about, the prisoners figured the authorities wanted to leave them places where they could have things out for themselves, establishing who was top dog and who was underdog. Several of them, noticing where Badger and Ed were going, followed along to watch the fun. It had been known for some time that Big Ed was going to try to take Red's place on the Alpha List.

Big Ed was a seven-foot freak from Opalatchee, Florida. A bodybuilder, he looked like a model for Hercules, all gleaming muscle as he stripped off his shirt. Red Badger, on the other hand, was a solid man, but his musculature was well padded with fat. He looked slow, not formidable.

Stripping off his shirt, he stood in the middle of the shower space, looking fat and sleepy, his hands loose and open at his sides, waiting for Ed to make the first move.

"You sure you want this?" Big Ed asked, moving forward slowly, hands raised like an old-fashioned bare-knuckle fighter. "Ain't going to be much left of you when I get through." He looked at the spectators and laughed. "I'm gonna skin me a badger today, boys."

The men laughed dutifully. Big Ed suddenly lunged forward, and Badger responded.

People said later they'd never seen a big fat man like Badger move so fast. One moment he was standing right there, practically under Big Ed's fists. But when Big Ed attacked, Badger was already out of the way, dancing back. He easily eluded a roundhouse right, and, taking his time, delivered a blow to Big Ed's neck, catching him at a nerve junction on the right side.

Big Ed bellowed and moved back. His right arm was dangling awkwardly at his side. He strained to lift it, but could get no sensation into it. He wasn't hurt; not really. It was just that his right arm wouldn't lift.

"Where'd you learn that stunt?" he demanded.

Badger smiled but didn't answer. What good would

it do to tell Big Ed that his most recent cell mate, Tommy Tashimoto, had taught him the fine art of nerve strikes—getting him to practice for hours, hitting over and over again from all angles until he could strike half a dozen targets unerringly where the nerve bundles were near the surface or rode over bone.

Red Badger hadn't been one for formal education. But when he got a chance to learn how to incapacitate a larger, stronger opponent, all the doggedness of his character came out, and he had worked until he knew what he was doing.

Now he circled around Big Ed's right, hitting him quick hard blows to the face and ribs, coming in over the dangling and useless right arm. Big Ed tried to launch himself at Badger. If he could just get his hands on him, even one-handed, he'd tear the smaller man apart. But Red had a strategy to offset that. He hit again and again at the nerve junction in Ed's neck, and soon the numbness was replaced by a galloping pain that traveled up and down Ed's shoulder, from his face to his groin, filling him with an agony so painful as to be exquisite.

At least Badger thought it was exquisite, because he saw he had his man where he wanted him, helpless but still on his feet. A hunk of meat to which he could mete out punishment.

Badger hit and hit, using the heel and sides of his hands. He knew he had this fight won; he just had to guard now against injuring himself. It wouldn't do to be incapacitated for this spaceship call. Big Ed turned and twisted and floundered, but he couldn't defend himself. A shrewd kick on the elbow brought down his left arm. He stood there, his face a mask of blood, while Badger hammered away at him like a man driving nails into a tough piece of wood. He hit and he hit, and Big Ed groaned with pain but wouldn't go down.

"Hell, I got no more time to waste on this," Badger said. He stepped back and, measuring his man carefully, delivered a kick with his steel-capped work shoe right to the point of Big Ed's jaw. The men watching the fight winced as Big Ed's front teeth came flying out like a spray of broken china, and Ed himself crashed face-first to the floor. Badger turned on a tap and cleaned himself quickly but thoroughly. It wouldn't do to be all sweaty for his interview. He checked himself in the big mirror before he left the washroom to make sure he didn't have any of Big Ed's face hanging on his clothes.

16

"Hi, I'm Stan Myakovsky," Stan said. "These are my associates. I telephoned ahead. I need a spaceship crew for a hazardous mission."

If the guard at the front window of the entry gate was impressed, she didn't show it. She was a squarely built woman with short bristly hair. She put down her biker magazine and said, "What company you with?"

"Sonnegard Acceptance Corporation," Stan said, and showed his credentials.

Back before his troubles began, Stan had taken over the *Dolomite* by buying the controlling shares in Sonnegard, a spaceship holding company. The company was the real owner of the ship, not Stan, who had never bothered to have the ship reregistered in his own name. In fact, he had decided not to; that way, if the ship got into any trouble, he wouldn't be liable.

"You'll find my name on the list," Stan said. He was hoping that the government hadn't gotten around to proscribing his company and red-flagging it on the computer. It was unlikely. As Julie had pointed out, it took government forever to bring their records up to date. The inefficiency wasn't strictly government's fault. There was neither the time nor the personnel available to record all the crimes, arrests, and dispositions that were taking place around the clock in an America more lawless than it had ever been in all its lawless history. Sonnegard Acceptance Corporation would probably be a legal entity for months to come.

The guard punched the name up on her computer. "Yeah, you're on the list. Go on through." She buzzed open the heavy metal door leading to the prison.

"So far, so good," Julie said.

Stan, accompanied by Julie and Hoban, went through into a long, brightly lit corridor.

"Oh, I didn't expect much trouble getting in," Stan said. "It's the getting out that concerns me."

"You worry too much," she said. "Doesn't he, Captain Hoban?"

"He's worrying about the wrong things," Hoban said. "What he should be thinking about is what if one of those men recognizes me?"

"You're not exactly a cover girl," Julie said. "I don't think you need to worry."

Their footsteps echoed hollowly as they went down the long corridor, following the flashing arrows that took visitors to the recruitment center.

There was a door at the end of the corridor. It buzzed open for them.

Within was a large office, plenty of plain metal desks and chairs, and a guard seated at a bigger desk in front of a computer.

"Come on in, Dr. Myakovsky," the guard said. "I've got all the volunteers in a holding tank just behind this room. There are twenty of them. That is as you requested, is it not?"

"It's fine," Stan said. "I'd like you to meet Miss Lish,

my associate, and Thomas Hoban, my captain. He'll be doing the actual selection in my name."

"As you know," the guard said, "we have already made the preselection for you, giving you the top-twenty men on our Alpha List. You may reject any of them, and you do not have to give a reason. If you're ready, I'll have the people sent in."

Stan nodded. The guard pressed a button. A panel slid up smoothly in the steel wall. There was a sound of moving feet, and then the prisoners came marching out in single file. Following the guard's commands, they formed a line across the room, stopped, and turned to face Stan and his party.

Captain Hoban walked up to the men. He paced up and down the line, peering into their faces. He came to one, hesitated, stopped, and stared.

Red Badger stared back.

Hoban said, "Do I know you? Have we ever met?"

"I don't think so, sir," Red Badger said. "But of course I've got a lousy memory."

Hoban kept on staring at him. Badger said, "I'm a good spaceman, sir. I just want a chance to rehabilitate myself."

Hoban pursed his lips, frowned, then turned away.

"Anything wrong, Mr. Hoban?" Stan asked.

"No, everything is fine," Hoban said.

"Do the men look all right to you?"

"Yes, they look fine."

Stan could see that something was bothering Hoban, but now was obviously not the time to ask him about it. Maybe, he thought, the captain was just nervous.

Stan turned to the guard. "I'll accept this lot. I'm posting money to send them out to their ship."

"Okay with me," the guard said. "What ship is that?"

"The *Dolomite*," Stan said, and waited.

The guard bent over the computer. "How do you spell it?" she asked, and Stan knew everything was going to be all right.

They were transporting the prisoners to Facility 12, where they would take the shuttle to the *Dolomite*, their new ship.

Hoban was thinking, Damn it, I know I've seen that man before. He knew who I was, I'm sure of it. So why did I pick him? Because I could tell from his look, if I didn't take him, he was going to tell everyone who I was. It's not just my imagination, I knew what that bastard was going to do. I should never have gotten myself into this in the first place. . . .

Unexpectedly, Hoban found himself regretting his decision to go in with Stan. Some people might have thought it was crazy, but people just didn't understand. He was grateful for this chance to redeem himself, get back on top, prove himself a winner. But another side of his character knew himself for a loser and just wanted a soft place to lie down. Funny to think of Jersey City as a soft place, but it was. Somehow he always got fed, always had a roof over his head. And best of all, nobody expected anything of him. He could relax, take a drink or two, take a lot of drinks. . . . He knew that wasn't how he ought to feel. It was like there were a couple of Hobans, and at least one of them was working actively to undermine him. He tried to remind himself that good things lay ahead: he'd soon be piloting his own ship again. You couldn't do better than that. But somehow, it didn't have quite the savor it ought to. And Captain Thomas Hoban became aware that he faced a greater danger than whatever Stan was getting them into. You can guard against murder, but how do you guard against your own thoughts of suicide?

18

There was one way to get aboard a spaceship without having to produce a pass or wait for a computer check. You could go aboard as part of a tour party. It was Julie's idea. They waited a few hours to give the authorities enough time to deliver the prisoners to the *Dolomite*. Then they came to the Staten Island launch site.

All ships picked up extra income by letting sightseeing parties aboard while they were in port, lifting them up to the ship's orbit in a chemical launching craft. Touring the spaceships was a popular entertainment, as in a bygone year people had gone into New York Harbor to visit battleships when the fleet was in. Spaceships were still novel enough that people paid just to walk aboard one.

With the passengers aboard, the little craft lifted lightly and soon was high above Jersey City. Julie looked through a viewport and saw the earth below looking like a swirly blue-white basketball. Passengers ate hot dogs and talked with each other until the lander arrived at the *Dolomite*'s geosynchronous orbit and locked onto one of the ship's entry ports.

Hoban, with Stan and Julie, came aboard the *Dolomite* with a group of eight other people, just a few of the hundreds who came up here every day from the Staten Island Spaceport. Accompanying them was a guide. He was giving his standard spiel about thruster jets and diosynchronous interruptor-type impellers and standard warp capacities.

"Right this way, folks," the tour guide was saying. He was a large man with pale blond hair, and wore a white vest with lavender polka dots under a crimson blazer. "Right this way you'll find the refreshment stand and, just beyond it, the souvenir booth. They carry official ship's souvenirs. Folks, these items are not sold in stores in the city. You can only get them here. There's a hall of diorama views of approaches to various planets. There's even a snack bar featuring delicacies from this world and many others. Right this way—"

The guide broke off his spiel when he noticed something unusual happening.

"Excuse me, you people there!"

He was talking to three people, two men and a woman, who had moved in the opposite direction from the crowd and now were about to open a door marked NO ADMITTANCE EXCEPT TO AUTHORIZED PERSONNEL in five different languages.

"Did you mean us?" one of the men said. He was short and plump and wore glasses. The woman beside him was a handsome creature, slim and with magnificent chestnut-red hair. She was beautiful even with the livid scar that ran down one cheek. The other man, somewhat older than the first two, looked dazed.

"Yes, you," the guide said. "Can't you read the sign on the door?"

"Of course we can," Stan replied. "It doesn't pertain to us."

"You're not trying to tell me you're ship's crew?"

"Certainly not," Stan said. "I'm the new owner."

"Impossible! I would have been told."

"I'm telling you right now. We're going aboard." Stan pushed at the door. The guide moved to stop him, then stopped abruptly when he felt a hand on his shoulder. The young woman had seized him, and she had a grip of steel.

"Madame, unhand me!" the guide said, trying to make a joke out of it, because people from the tour were staring. He tried to shake free, but Julie's fingers didn't budge.

"I'll be happy to let you go," she said. "Just don't interfere with the new owner."

"I have no proof that he's the new owner!" the guide said.

Julie shrugged. "What difference does it make to you, anyhow, who runs the ship? You've got your concession. You're selling your tickets and your hot dogs. You're doing all right."

The guide considered. He didn't want any trouble. Life was hard enough, why stir up trouble with people who were probably nutcases? The woman with the strong hands was right, what difference did it make to him?

"Do whatever you want," he said, stepping back as Julie released his shoulder.

Stan pushed open the door that led into the *Dolomite* proper. As it opened, an alarm went off deep inside the ship. The lights in the corridor behind the door began to flash. There was a sound of heavy running feet, and then two men in brown security-guard uniforms came hurrying up with carbines at port arms.

"What's going on?" one of the guards asked. "Halt, you people! No one is allowed here."

"We're authorized personnel," Stan said. "I'm the

new owner and these are my associates. Kindly escort us to your commanding officer."

"Back off at once or I'll fire," the guard said. "This weapon is set for immediate paralysis. The company is not responsible for any broken limbs or other injuries suffered while resisting authorized orders."

Julie said, "I warn you not to fire that thing." Her body tensed. She seemed ready to throw herself at the guards.

There was a moment of impasse. The guards weren't sure what to do. The situation wasn't quite serious enough to warrant firing. Not yet. On the other hand, what were they supposed to do? They knew they could get into a lot of trouble if they didn't handle this right.

A tall man in officer's uniform came from a doorway inside the ship. "What is going on here?" he asked.

The senior guard said, "These people are trying to break in, Mr. Gill."

Gill had a long, dark, mournful face. His features were small. His typical expression, in common with those of many androids, was impassive and a little melancholy. He stared at the new arrivals unbelievingly. At last he said, "Captain Hoban? Dr. Myakovsky?"

"And I am Julie Lish," Julie said, holding out her hand.

Gill hesitated, then shook Julie's hand.

One of the guards asked, "Do you know these people, sir?"

"Yes," Gill said. "Stand back and let me handle this."

The guards saluted and moved back against a wall.

"What is going on, Captain?" Gill asked.

Hoban looked unsure of himself, but his voice was firm enough as he answered, "Mr. Gill, I have decided to take command of the *Dolomite* again."

"But, sir," Gill protested, "a duly appointed court

stripped you of this command and gave it to me to
hold until the new captain arrives."

"They had no right to relieve me of command,"
Hoban said.

"Are you sure of that, sir?"

"Of course I'm sure, and I am taking over the ship
again pending a formal hearing."

"Perhaps you have that right, sir. I wouldn't know.
But meantime there is a legal decision against you,
and to the best of my knowledge that has not been re-
scinded."

Hoban looked confused. Stan put in, "We are going
to appeal that ruling. A higher court can be counted
on to reverse the decision."

"I sincerely hope so, sir. But in the meantime—"

"In the meantime," Hoban interrupted, showing a
firmness that Stan had not been sure he possessed,
"things return to where they were before. I will retain
command of this ship until the higher court rules."

"Unfortunately, sir, I am bound by the lower court's
decree."

"Your first loyalty," Hoban said, "is to me."

Gill looked doubtful. "That is not how my orders
read, sir."

"Hang your orders!" Hoban cried. "I am giving you
a direct command."

Gill looked puzzled, worried. "My orders are to fire
on you or anyone else who tries to board this ship."

"I don't believe you'll do that, Gill." Hoban started
to walk toward the entry leading to the interior of the
ship.

"Guards!" Gill called sharply. "Switch to killing
mode."

There was a double click as the guards switched
their pulse rifles to killing mode.

Hoban smiled with a confidence he didn't feel and
walked toward the entry.

Gill cried, "Stop!"

Stan and Julie fell into step beside Hoban, who
continued to advance.

Gill stared at them. There was something like despair on his face. He said, "I must do what I must."

"And what is that, Gill?" Stan asked him.

Gill said, "Guards!"

The guards snapped to attention.

"Meet your new commander."

The guards saluted Hoban, who returned the salute.

"Now turn off your weapons"—another double click—"and attend to the incoming crew. They should be arriving any minute. Then you are dismissed."

"Yes, sir!" Both guards saluted, turned on their heels, and marched off.

"Welcome aboard, Commander," Gill said.

"Thank you, Gill," Hoban said. "I knew I could count on your loyalty."

"It's my conditioning that turned things your way, sir," Gill said. "I could not fire on you, nor ask the guards to do so. After our many tours of duty together, you and I have developed too many bonds. But I still think what you are doing is illegal."

"I know you feel that way," Hoban said. "You may leave when the guards return to Earth, and no hard feelings." He held out his hand.

Gill looked at it for a moment, then shook it. "If you don't mind, sir, I'd like to come along."

"But why, if you think this is illegal?"

"I don't care if it's illegal or not," Gill said. "I was just stating a fact. Since I couldn't fire on you, my conditioning in favor of government authority is canceled. I'm your man again, Captain, if you'll have me."

"It's likely to be dangerous," Hoban said.

"That is a matter of indifference to me."

"Then I'll be pleased to have you, Mr. Gill." Captain Hoban smiled.

"If you two are finished waltzing," Julie said sarcastically, "do you think we could get on with it?"

* * *

They accompanied Gill into the ship and to the control room.

Julie said to Gill, "How did you know what decision to make?"

"I didn't know," Gill muttered. "Androids don't have to make decisions. We just follow our conditioning."

"Lucky androids," Julie said.

"Gill, we're having some baggage lifted up from the space station," Stan put in. "With it there will be a large packing case. Please see that it is handled gently."

"Yes, sir."

"When they arrive, get the crew bundled down in hypersleep. And get all the tourists off this ship. I want us ready to depart an hour after the crew is aboard and bedded down."

Gill looked at Captain Hoban.

The captain nodded. "Accept his orders as if they were mine."

The volunteers for the voyage of the *Dolomite* marched in single file under the watchful eyes of armed guards. They left the olive-drab prison lander and marched into the short connecting tube that led into the ship proper. As soon as they were aboard, they all burst into a cheer. The guards gave them hard looks, but put away their weapons and returned to the lander, accompanied by the two guards from the *Dolomite*. Their job was to see that the prisoners got aboard the ship; once aboard, they were no longer prisoners, though not quite free men, either. The arrangement was that they'd report to the proper authorities after returning from their voyage, and show their good-conduct papers signed by the captain, and receive either a commutation of sentence or a complete amnesty. In practice, many of them never bothered to return, and their names went on a wanted list, to which the authorities gave only minor attention.

There were always plenty of new criminals to deal with; no one had any time for the older ones.

They followed the signs that had been set up to guide them to their quarter. But Walter Glint, a short, dark-haired barrel-chested man from Natchez who was Badger's closest friend aboard, noticed that Red Badger wasn't even bothering to look where he was going.

"Hey, Red! You been on this ship before?"

"You bet I have," Red Badger said. "I know her lay-out like the back of my hand."

"How come you never said anything about it when that Hoban guy asked if you'd met before?"

Badger shrugged. "If he didn't remember, I wasn't going to remind him. It was a pretty bad time for him. I'll tell you about it later."

They went into the crew's quarters. There was plenty of room. The *Dolomite* normally carried a crew of thirty-five, but Hoban had pared it down to the bare minimum after consulting with Stan. There was no trouble finding berths. Badger and Glint claimed their own corner, and were joined by their best friends from the federal facility. One of these, Connie Mindanao, was a diminutive woman, brown-skinned and black-haired and fierce looking, her features showing evidence of her mixed ancestry. She was the unlikely combination of a Moro from the Philippines and a Mohawk from New York's Iroquois Confederation. The only thing the two peoples had had in common was a history of head-hunting. Of the other two, one was a big black man from California named Andy Groggins, and the second was a taciturn Laotian hill woman who didn't say much but whose actions were direct and sudden, and apt to be lethal; her name was Min Dwin.

There were others who were friendly with Badger, and some who downright hated him. They sorted out their sleeping arrangements accordingly.

Badger was used to being the center of attention.

A voice came over the loudspeaker. "All crew! Put

away your gear and strip for hypersleep. Everybody
must be on his acceleration couch in five minutes."

Badger called out, "What's our destination?"

His voice was picked up by a wall monitor.
"There'll be a full briefing immediately upon your
awakening," the loudspeaker voice replied.

"How long we going to sleep this time?" Badger
asked.

"That information will be fed into the hypersleep
machinery. No more questions, people! Get ready."

Connie Mindanao said, "What are they trying to
pull on us? I don't know if I'm going to stand still for
this." She looked at Badger. "What do you think,
Red?"

"Relax," Badger told her. "Nothing much we can do
about it just now. The ship's sealed, and anyhow, the
guards are still outside. We've got no chance of making a run for it."

They all settled down onto their hypersleep
couches. The lights dimmed.

19

The *Dolomite* left its geo-synchronous orbit and proceeded slowly to jump point: a position in space well enough beyond Earth's orbit to permit subspace operation without peril to others. From there Hoban radioed for permission to disembark, and shortly thereafter received an okay from the Coast Guard monitoring station at L6.

Stan and his party strapped down. Hoban looked them over and asked, "All ready, Dr. Myakovsky?"

"Ready," Stan said.

"All right," Hoban said. "Mr. Gill—get us out of here!"

Gill's hands moved across the switches. The lights dimmed in response to the sudden power surge as the tachyonic converters whirled into action, compressing time and space, tighter, tighter, until—

—the *Dolomite* suddenly vanished from normal space.

The voyage had begun.

20

Julie was used to the dark. It was friendly and warm, and she felt safe in it. Only in the dark had she found security and safety, shielded away from men's eyes and their motives. The dark was the place where she had trained, so many years ago, when she had learned those matters of stealth and suddenness that were her protection and her trademark. It was then that she learned to make the darkness her own.

And so it had been for all her young life. But it was different now. This darkness that surrounded her now felt sinister, evil. Maybe that was because she knew something lurked within it, something that was trying to get her.

She stopped for a moment in midstep, trying to get her bearings. Her hearing extended itself through the darkness, searching. As her eyes became accustomed to the gloom she made out vast shapes on either side of her. They were machines, made of dark, glistening metal, and they towered above her. Spots of white light from some unknown source winked off metallic surfaces, and reflected from coils and condensers. They didn't even look like objects. They were like the ghosts of objects because their shapes were indistinct, ambiguous, swathed in a darkness that had gradation and depth, and was textured with the layers of silence.

A voice crackled in the tiny radio bug implanted in her ear.

"Julie? Do you see him yet?" It was Stan Myakovsky, calling from the *Dolomite*'s central control room. He wasn't far away, as distances go, but he could have been in another galaxy for all the good he could do her now.

"Not yet," she answered. "But I know he's in here somewhere."

"Be careful, huh?" Stan said. "I still think we should have delayed this run. I'm still not entirely satisfied with Norbert's control system."

Now was a hell of a time to tell her that. She decided to ignore it. Stan sounded agitated. Was he getting cold feet? Or was he just having an ordinary attack of nerves?

She snapped on a tiny flashlight. Ahead of her, picked up in the thin beam, she could see more profound glooms, silent caves of blackness where awful things might lurk. Some of these horrors were caused by the power of her imagination, but she was afraid that some were not.

It was not imagination that told her something in this great dark place was tracking her. She knew it was there. But where was it? She strained her senses to the utmost, trying to pick up some clue. Nothing. But she could tell it was out there. She had a sense of presence, almost like a sixth sense. It was what a successful thief needed above all else, and Julie was an extremely successful thief.

She thought back now on her years of training with

Shen Hui, the old Chinese master criminal. She first
met him when she was a little girl, the youngest one
in the Shanghai slave market that morning. She remembered peering at the crowd that had come to attend the auction, trying to catch a final glimpse of her
mother. But she had already left, unwilling to watch
her only daughter being sold on the open market. The
men started bidding, men from different countries.
Then one old man had outbid the rest, and had paid
the auctioneer in taels of gold. That was Shen Hui.

He brought her to his house and raised her like his
own flesh and blood. Shen Hui was a master thief, a
master of the zen of thievery. He had taught her to develop her latent senses so that she could register
things without literally seeing or hearing them. That
ability came to her rescue now.

Yes, it was not just imagination. There was something near, and it was situated right over . . . there!

She whirled as a great looming thing detached itself from the deep knot of shadows near a gigantic
machine that lay shrouded in its own dust. She found
it fascinating, the way the shadows moved and grew,
like something not human, the way they resolved into
one, and that shadow suddenly turned solid and
launched itself at her with an explosive hiss.

"Julie! Watch out!" Stan's voice rang in her ears. He
had picked up the sudden movement. But late. Stan
was always late. What good could his warning do for
her now? He never seemed to realize it. Not that she
had expected anything more. She was responsible for
herself. And Julie was already in motion as the thing
came at her.

Her long legs, clad in skintight black plastic,
pumped smoothly as she sprinted down the central
aisle of the *Dolomite*'s great central cargo hold. The
creature, three times her height, colored an unremit-
ting black, with jaws filled with long closely packed
fanglike teeth, came after her. Feeling herself being
overtaken, Julie dodged and swerved around the
faintly delineated center line of the hold. This one nar-

row strip had been set for twenty percent less of the faux gravity that so much resembled the real thing. Running on the light-gravity strip made her feel as though she had wings, so rapidly did she move, dodging fixed objects as they came up to smear her, vaulting over smaller obstacles, always moving, the sound of her own blood pounding in her ears.

The creature came running after her, and a ray of light from a globe in the ceiling picked it up for a moment. It appeared to be a full-size alien, with the typical backward-sloping cranium of its kind.

The thing was as startling as an apparition from hell. Its claws, with their doubled fingers, reached for her. Julie turned and fled down the narrow confines of the hold.

The area she ran in widened, and the creature managed to gain a few steps on her.

Stan, watching the action on a monitor in the control room, yelped in alarm as the creature loomed over her. He asked himself why he had ever agreed to let Julie take this training run. Thinking about it now, he could see that it had been an unnecessary risk. If anything went wrong, it could jeopardize the whole operation.

And aside from that, if Julie got hurt ... But he couldn't let himself think about that.

Julie and the alien dodged around enormous packing cases, cubes of plastic ten feet on a side. There were a dozen or so of them, and they were scattered randomly on the floor, part of the clutter that accumulates in any spaceship. Julie ran her fingers over the edge of a box. With a quick look aided by her flashlight, she had fixed its location. A memory of the placement of the other boxes was burned into her short-term memory. In her mind she could see the zigzag path she would have to follow to get to the next bulkhead. After that, a sally port served as a midpoint connection to the next part of the ship's hold.

She ran full out, counting off step by step. Crossing a crowded room in darkness with speed and silence is one of a thief's most useful accomplishments. Julie continued across the hold, her senses on red alert, trying once again to locate the creature that was stalking her. Norbert was good, he was very quiet, she had to give him that. He had learned how to muffle his body movements, and even to quiet the sounds of his body functions. Good as he was, she still was aware of him, but it was an awareness that flickered in and out of existence.

After the midpoint sally exit, she came to the platform that blocked the way to the farthest exit. It was a prestressed antimagnetic steel plate approximately twenty feet wide by two hundred feet long, and five inches deep. She climbed up onto it. It was drilled with many large, irregularly spaced holes ranging in diameter from two to five feet, where components would be fitted later. Running the length of the plate left you vulnerable to stepping into a hole and breaking a leg, or falling through an unshielded ventilator shaft to the deck below.

She had to slow down to make it across. Julie went down the length of the platform at a half-speed sprint, unable visually to detect the openings in the darkness, relying on memory. Norbert came loping along steadily after her. She noticed that he, too, must have memorized the locations of the holes, because he was moving confidently and quickly. She forced herself to go a little faster, even though it increased her chances of a fall.

She reached the far end and hopped off. Norbert had gained several steps on her. She hoped to make it up in the next stage.

Just ahead were the spare firing tubes, big cylinders of cold-rolled steel, eighteen of them, each a hundred and eighty feet long. Moving by touch, Julie located a pipe with an aperture that would just permit her to squeeze in. Norbert, with his greater size, wouldn't be able to follow, would be forced to walk on top of the slippery pipes, thus giving Julie a brief breathing spell. A good escape could be composed of moments like these.

That, at least, was how it was supposed to work. Norbert stopped and looked at the pipe, started to go around it, then came back and managed somehow to collapse his shoulders and crawl into the pipe after her. She could hear the tortured metal-to-metal squealing as he pushed himself through the pipe.

Then she realized that not only was he in the pipe behind her, he was gaining, collapsing himself down to half his usual size and scuttling along like a giant malevolent insect. A sudden sense of claustrophobia came over Julie as she imagined Norbert's big clawed hand closing over her foot.

She forced herself to remain calm. "You won't go any faster in a panic," she reminded herself. One of the first lessons Shen Hui had taught her was to be extra cool in the face of a crisis, to force herself to slow down just when her senses were shrieking at her to speed up. This lesson stood her in good stead now. Suddenly the darkness came to an end and she was out of the pipe and running, a fraction of a second ahead of the alien.

She dodged instinctively as Norbert's arm reached out for her. In a moment's inattention, she slammed into a precariously balanced cart containing machine parts and ball bearings. Metal objects flew in all directions and clattered against the sides of the hold. Julie came down on a bearing in midstride and both her feet shot out from under her. Catlike, she turned in midair, throwing up a protective forearm before she went crashing to the floor on her face.

As she sprawled Norbert loomed above her, arms spread wide, jaws open in a terrifying grimace. Through his open jaws the little inner jaws came flickering out, more malevolent than a crazed pit viper.

Norbert lunged at her, and she was momentarily unable to do anything to protect herself. He was almost on her. . . .

She had an instant to wonder what he was pro-

grammed to do if he caught her . . . or did he make up
that part as he went along?

And then Norbert slipped on the bearings and lost
his balance.

His taloned feet raked the metal floor as he tried to
gain purchase. He crashed to the deck with a bone-
shattering sound.

For a moment Norbert sprawled there. His resem-
blance to a giant insect was now apparent as his arms
and legs twitched and vibrated, trying to find something to hold. Then he righted himself and was up
again and towering over her.

Unable to do anything, Stan had to watch. His fin-
gernails were already ragged, for he had been chew-
ing at bloody cuticles while monitoring Julie's
progress. He leaned forward, intent.

Julie, at the last possible moment, slipped through
the alien's claws and disappeared through the hori-
zontally closing metal slabs at the end of the hold.
The creature yowled in rage as the door shut in his
face and Julie shot the lock.

Immediately Norbert began wrenching at the door,
then, having no luck with the lock, turned his attention
to the hinges.

Julie meanwhile was streaking through the clut-
tered compartment, sprinting at full stride and manag-
ing somehow to avoid the clutter of machines and
packing cases that turned the place into an obstacle
course filled with cutting edges.

Stan was able to track her progress on his monitor
against a schematic of the ship's hold.

He watched a tiny silver dot, representing Julie,
dodge around objects ahead of a longer blue-black
streak that represented her pursuer.

"Come on, Julie," Stan muttered to himself. "You
don't have to run it this close! Pull the plug! Bail out!"

But Julie kept running. She seemed to be going for
some kind of a record. Never had she been so graceful, so light on her feet. She had reached the far end
of the compartment. The egress port was dogged

down tight. Norbert was less than five feet behind her now. He reached for her with taloned claws, ending in dagger-sharp tips. Julie stood her ground, and Stan couldn't help but admire the game quality of her courage. Then she ducked down and scuttled between the creature's legs, catching it by surprise, and escaping with nothing more than a shallow scratch on her right shoulder.

She was up to her full speed in two bounds, and for a moment she thought she had gained on it. But Norbert had learned something, too. He ignored her dodging run and came galloping up alongside her. His mouth, impossibly crowded with needle-tipped teeth, snarled and opened wide. From his jaw, and protruding through his mouth, came the hateful small replica of these jaws, composed of a small rectangular body part like a tongue, which ended in a mouth filled with white sharp teeth.

This was it. There was no place to go.

The creature moved in for the kill.

"Julie!" Stan screamed. "For God's sake!"

At that final moment Julie screamed at the creature, "Cancel predation functions!"

Norbert froze in midmovement. His feeding tube withdrew into his mouth. His jaws closed.

Julie then said, "Return to standard program."

She turned away from the creature, who stood frozen in position, and walked through the connecting passageway to Stan, who was still in the control room, sitting numbly in the big command chair near the computer.

21

In the control room, where he had been watching her progress on a TV monitor, Stan heaved a sigh of relief. He knew Julie would join him soon, after she had showered and changed. He just had time to check the condition of the men in hypersleep, and then he and Julie would be able to go over their plans.

He walked through a dilating door, down a short corridor, and into the long gray egg-shaped room that was devoted to hypersleep. The lights were low, leaving the place in an eternal twilight. The only sound Stan heard was the occasional short click of a circuit breaker.

The men lay in rows in what looked like large coffins with glass tops. Pipes and electrical lines connected all of the coffins and ran to power boxes on the walls. All this maze of equipment was run through instruments that measured output and indicated sudden anomalous changes, checking for heart rate, respiration, and for the electrical brain activity. Every hour, samples were taken of the sleepers' blood and stomach contents. Trace chemicals could set up strange chain reactions. It was necessary to keep the crew's internal environments very stable. Other meters on the wall showed dream activity; it was important for the crew members to dream as they slept. Dreaming too long suppressed can lead to psychosis.

For now, all was well. The men lay in their gray coffins. Most had their hands at their sides, some had crossed them on their chests. In one or two cases, the fingers pulled at each other. This was not abnormal. Events were occurring on deep levels of the brain that the dials and gauges couldn't read.

It was to be a journey of almost two weeks' duration. Not a long one, as space trips go. The men could have stayed awake throughout without harm. But it was policy on most ships to put the crew into hypersleep for anything longer than a week. For one thing, it saved on food and water—critical things on a spaceship. For another, it kept the men out of mischief. There was little to do on the outward leg of a deep-space voyage. The ship shuttled noiselessly through space, and time seemed to flow like invisible treacle.

Stan was pleased that there was no crew to contend with at the moment. He was somewhat less pleased that Captain Hoban had elected to take the hypersleep with his men. Stan would have enjoyed conversations with Hoban on the long outward journey.

"I'd like it, too," Hoban had said. "But frankly, I need the sleep. I'm badly in need of reintegration."

Hoban had come under severe pressure after being relieved of his ship's command. The charge that he had been drunk while on duty, though untrue, had been tough to fight. Even with all the recording instruments that were continuously running on the ship, it was unclear exactly how drunk he had been, or if indeed he had been drunk at all. There were matters of individual alcohol tolerance to consider. Even witnesses, the ship's officers, had been of two minds about what had really happened and to what extent Hoban bore responsibility.

If all this was upsetting to the investigating authorities, it was even more so to Hoban. He didn't know exactly himself what had happened in that fateful hour when the accident had occurred. His own defense mechanisms blocked his memory, preventing him from seeing a truth that might be damaging to him.

Hoban knew that, and so he couldn't help but wonder what his defenses were trying to block.

The hypersleep was known to enhance psychic integration. It gave you a chance to drop out of the world of actions and judgments, into a timeless place beyond questions of morality. Hoban had welcomed that.

Now Stan looked forward to resuscitating Hoban. It was a little limiting for him, having only Julie and Gill to talk to. Julie was a darling, of course, and he was absolutely mad about her. At the same time he couldn't help but recognize her limitations.

Although abundantly educated in the school of hard knocks, she had little formal training in the sciences. Worse, she had little interest in the arts and humanities. She tended to assume that material things were always the most desirable ones. This was an error in Stan's judgment, for how do you price a sunset or a mountain at dawn? How much for the song of the swallow? Still, he realized that he himself was no doubt guilty of the typical human error of overvaluing what he liked and undervaluing what others liked.

Talking with Gill was also limiting. Gill had formidable training in the sciences and knew a great deal about history and philosophy. This didn't give him judgment and compassion, however. For Gill, the proposition that the unexamined life was not worth living had no more relevance than $e=mc^2$. He wasn't equipped to examine the emotional dimension, though Stan thought he saw signs of promise.

After showering and changing, Julie fluffed her hair and rejoined Stan in the main control room. "How'd I do, Stan?" she asked.

Stan pulled himself together. In a voice that strove to be casual he said, "Quite well, Julie. You shaved fifteen seconds off yesterday's time. Keep on like this and you'll soon break your old mark of three minutes in the hold with Norbert."

"Norbert's getting too good," Julie said. "He's learning faster than I am. I'm sure he's smarter than the real thing."

The real thing, in this case, was the aliens Norbert so resembled, and who had caused such strange and deadly events on Earth.

Despite his appearance, however, Norbert was not an alien. He was a perfectly simulated robot model of an alien, equipped with a number of computer-driven programs, among which was the predator mode that Julie had been testing out. At the moment Norbert was in the control room with them, showing no sign of his former ferocity.

"How are you, Norbert?" Stan asked.

"I am fine, Doctor, as always."

"That was quite a little run you gave Julie. Did you think you were going to catch her this time?"

"I do not anticipate such things," Norbert replied.

"What would you have done if you had caught her?"

"What my programming told me to do," Norbert said.

"You would have killed her?"

"I cannot anticipate. I would have done what I had to do. Without feeling, I might add. But let me further add, if remorse were possible for a creature like myself, I would have felt it. Is there an analogue of remorse that does not involve feeling?"

"You have a complicated way of expressing yourself," Stan said.

Norbert nodded. "These matters require considerable thought and recalculation. And when they are expressed in words, they sometimes come out differently from what was intended."

"I've noticed that myself," Stan said.

Just at that moment a large brown dog came racing into the hold from a corridor. Stan had named him Mac. No one was quite sure how he had gotten aboard, but no one had gotten around to putting him off and now he was taking the voyage with them.

Mac ran to Norbert's feet and released a blue rubber ball he was holding in his jaws. The ball bounced three times and came to a rest at the monster's instep.

Stan and Julie watched to see what Norbert would do. The robot alien bent down and his long black arm, which somehow resembled an ant's chitinous appendage, brushed past the dog and picked up the ball. The monster's arm came back, then forward, and he threw the ball through the open door into the corridor. Barking furiously, the dog went chasing after it.

"All right, Norbert," Myakovsky said, "you've had your fun. Go to the laboratory. I'll want to scan some of your response codes. And get Mac to shut up. The crew is still in hypersleep."

"Yes, Dr. Myakovsky," Norbert said, and walked quietly out of the room.

22

door slid open and Captain Hoban walked through. He had a dazed look in his eyes, and Stan knew he could not have been awake for long.

"You're early out of the hypersleep, Captain."

"Yes, sir. I had my dial set to get me up before the crew so I could pull myself together and have a talk with you."

"I suppose it is time we had that," Stan said. "I want to thank you again for throwing in your lot with me. I don't know where this will end up, but I'm glad to be on this adventure with you."

"Yes, sir. Could you tell me what it is exactly we are going to tell the crew?"

Julie, seated nearby, said, "Yes, Stan, I'd like to know myself."

Stan nodded. "We'll give a slightly altered version of what's going on."

"Are we on course, then?" Hoban asked.

"Yes. I fed the coordinates for AR-32 into the navigational computer."

"AR-32? I think I've heard of the place," Hoban said. "Wasn't there some trouble there a while back?"

"There was."

"Then why are we going there, sir?"

"We're pretty sure there's an alien super-hive on that planet, which apparently won't support anything else. A Bio-Pharm ship has been in orbit around AR-32, and my information is that they have been illegally harvesting royal jelly."

"Yes, sir. I understand. But what does that have to do with us?"

"I have a right to my share in that matter," Stan said. "Julie and I are going to relieve them of some of their plunder. Royal jelly is like pirate's gold, Hoban. It belongs to whoever takes it."

"Yes, sir. I don't have much trouble with that concept, though Gill might. But what bothers me, sir, is, does that mean we'll have to kill bugs?"

"It could come to that," Stan said, "though it is not the primary intention of our expedition."

"And might it not involve killing Bio-Pharm people, if we have to?"

Stan stared at him. "Yes, it could come to that. I don't expect them to be too happy about our taking what they have come to regard as their own, but frankly, I don't much care what they feel. No one gives up pirate's gold easily. If they insist on making a fight of it ... Well, we'll take care of ourselves."

Hoban nodded, though he didn't look happy. "I suppose that follows, sir. But I wish you had told me all this beforehand."

"Would you not have come?" Stan said. "Would you seriously have preferred to stay down-and-out in that crummy boardinghouse I found you in?"

"No, I don't wish to be back there," Hoban said. "I'm just considering the situation."

"Then think about this," Stan said. "This situation

could make you rich. Julie and I intend to share our profits with you and the crew. They'll get a small percentage for the dangers they'll run. It won't be much out of our shares, but it'll be more money than they ever saw before."

"Sounds good, sir," Hoban said. But he was still worried. What good was it to be rich if you were also dead?

The time was nearing to wake the crew from hypersleep. The flight was almost at an end. Their destination, the planet AR-32, was coming up on the screens, a glowing dot in the dark sky. Julie knew this would be her last time alone with Stan for a long time.

There was a lot to do, a lot of last-minute details to attend to, and she didn't know when she and Stan would get some quiet time alone. Maybe not until they had finished the expedition—or to call it by its true name, their raid. And that could take time. And if everything didn't go just right . . .

Julie shook her head irritably. There was no sense thinking about failure. Hadn't Shen Hui instilled that much in her?

23

When Julie came into the control room, Stan was still seated in the big, padded command chair. He had taken an ampoule of royal jelly from a dozen that were nested in the padded box on the nearby worktable. He was holding the ampoule up to one of the arc lights, twirling it between his fingers and admiring its bluish glow in the light.

As usual, Julie was both attracted and repelled by the liquid and what it could do to Stan. Yet she had been hoping they could spend this evening together, doing things together instead of thinking about them. Sometimes she thought Stan allowed himself to have real experiences only for the pleasure of reliving them later, as he was able to do with the royal jelly.

Why did he love that stuff so much? She knew it eased the pain of his disease. But it was more than

just a remedy: he was using it as a drug. And Julie
didn't approve of taking drugs.

She hadn't tried the stuff herself. A well-trained
thief allows nothing to dull her senses. Shen Hui and
life itself had taught her this lesson. And yet, much as
she missed him when he launched himself into the
unknown regions that the drug brought him to, a part
of her went with him, because she knew how Stan
felt about her.

Returning the ampoule to its case, Stan asked,
"What did you think about Norbert's performance?"

"He's ready," she said. "You've done an amazing
thing, Stan. Created a robot alien good enough to fool
the real ones."

"Except for the pheromones," Stan pointed out.

"You've taken care of that, too. With the short-range
zeta fields you've developed, plus the pheromone-
altering qualities of the royal jelly, the aliens will think
Norbert is one of them."

Stan nodded. "Just like it was with Ari." Stan was
referring to how his cybernetic ant, Ari, had been programmed to enter the colony of a similar-looking ant
species, where the other ants accepted him as the real
thing.

"How close are we now, Stan?" Julie asked.

Stan punched up the computer screen in front of
him. Numbers flowed across it, and lines weaved in
and out and then held firm.

"We're nearing the vicinity of AR-32," Stan told her.
"It's time to get the crew out of hypersleep."

"The adventure begins," Julie said softly.

"That's right." Stan took out the ampoule of royal
jelly again. "We need a lot more of this stuff, and
AR-32 has it for us. It's funny how a single substance
can be both more valuable than diamonds and more
necessary for life than water. More necessary for my
life, anyhow."

He swirled the little glass tube and watched the liquid flow. Then he looked at Julie.

"You look very lovely tonight."

She smiled back mockingly. "Pretty as a shot glass, as they'd say in the Old West."

"No, I really mean it," Stan said. "You know how I feel about you, don't you?"

"Maybe I do," Julie said. "But it's not because you ever talk about it."

"I've always been shy," Stan said. Abruptly he swallowed the ampoule. "I'm going to go lie down now, Julie. Let's talk more later."

Without waiting for her answer, Stan shambled off to his small office just to the right of the main-control-room entrance. Within it a folding cot was built into the wall. He lay down on it now, without bothering to take off his glasses.

With Xeno-Zip there was no habituation. Each time was like the first. It always amazed him just how quickly the stuff took effect. It was like no other drug he had ever tried, neither medicinal nor recreational, and Stan had tried them all. Alien royal jelly was neither a stimulant nor a soporific, though it had effects similar to both. Primarily it was a way of gaining instant access to all parts of your own brain, a royal road to your own dreams and memories. With royal jelly you could zoom in on your past like a skilled photographer zooming in on a detail, readjusting focus to bring up those images that had faded out. You could freeze the frame on what seemed like reality. You could see what you wanted to see, as often as you liked, and then step outside the frame and watch yourself in the act of seeing. Nor was that all it did. Royal jelly was a painkiller, too, relieving the throb of the cancer that was shattering his life.

The vial dropped from his fingers. It fell to the floor, taking no more than a fraction of a second to shatter on the deck. And in that microsecond, Stan watched it all happen again.

24

First came the rush. It seemed to move along his arteries, and Stan pictured himself, a tiny man in a canoe adrift on the great red waters of his bloodstream. The vision exploded into a thousand fragments, and in each fragment the scene was repeated. The fragments of his vision came together, like millions of diamond particles striving to become a diamond, and then exploded outward again like firework displays arcing in all directions. He could hear a sound that was accompanying this, and he couldn't tell what it was at first, a deep-throated roar that could have come from no human source. At first he thought it was the gods singing, great choruses of ancient gods wearing strange headdresses, some with the heads of ducks and turtles, some jaguars, some foxes. And near them, suspended in shining space, were other choirs of women-gods, full-breasted Brunhildes and slender Naiads, and their song was full of sorrow and promise.

As the ampoule fell to the floor, Stan was already dozing fitfully. Tiny muscles in his eyelids jerked and twitched: REM sleep, but of a previously unheard-of intensity. Dream sleep, but with awareness. Blue-green lights played across his face. It was a broad face, with the beginning of a double chin. Light glinted off his glasses and threw a shadow on his small chin. He looked far younger than his twenty-eight years; like a schoolboy again, coming back to the big old house where he had lived with his parents before the devastation wrought by the aliens. Again he saw his stern father, the scholar, always with an ironic little Greek or Latin phrase on his lips; and his mother, with her high forehead, flinty gray eyes, and hastily pinned-up mass of dark blond hair.

Then he seemed to be walking down a long corridor. On either side, standing in niches like statues, were replicas of his parents at every age and in every mood. Stan could, in his imagination, freeze the frame, stop his parents in midtrack, and walk around them, inspecting them from every angle, and then start the tape of memory running again. All this while the ampoule was in midair.

The ampoule was still falling from his hand, and he could segue instantly from where he was to another memory, himself after class in high school, walking along beside the little brook that ran behind his home, thinking about everything under the sun except his homework assignments. Stan looked down on the work given him by his teachers. He thought it was beneath his intellectual level, unworthy of his efforts. So disdainful was he of school that his parents feared he would not graduate. But he did graduate—there he was at his own graduation, wearing an English schoolboy's suit his parents had bought him while they were attending a seminar in London. He had always hated that suit; he had looked damned silly next to the casual attire of the other boys.

There were many scenes like that, ready for him to step into, but Stan wasn't in the mood for childhood memories. There were other things he wanted to look at. Other times. Other people, places, things.

And so he moved, the ampoule still falling, moved as a spiritual presence, down the spiraling, faintly glowing corridors of the years. And now he was a man, in his twenties, already a well-known scientist, and he was in the doctor's office, buttoning his shirt, listening dumbly as Dr. Johnston said, "I might as well give it to you straight, Dr. Myakovsky. You were correct in your surmise about those black marks on your chest and back. They are indeed cancers."

"Is my condition terminal?"

"Yes." The doctor nodded gravely. "In fact, you don't have much time left. The condition, as I'm sure you know, is incurable. But its progress can be slowed, and we can ease some of the symptoms. You already have the medicine we prescribe for such cases. And there is also this."

The doctor held out a small plastic box. Within it, packed in foam rubber, were a dozen ampoules of a bluish liquid.

"This is royal jelly. Have you heard of it?"

Stan nodded. "If memory serves, it is produced by the aliens."

"That is correct," Dr. Johnston said. "I must tell you it's no cure. But it should relieve the symptoms. It could be just what you're looking for."

"Does it have much in the way of side effects?"

The doctor smiled grimly. "It has indeed. That's why it hasn't received government approval yet, though many people use it. Indeed, it has become the most-sought-after consciousness-altering substance in existence. It gives some an intense feeling of well-being and competence. Others experience levels of

their own being not normally perceived. Still others
have an orgasm that seems to go on forever."

"At least I'm going to die happy," Stan said.

But of course there were also the bad side effects.
Some people had been known to go berserk on the
drug, or to undergo personality changes so great that
their own families didn't recognize them. Could that
be happening in his case?

And then he forgot his concern as the images
swept him up again. There was so much to look at! So
many memories, all nicely staged and lighted, waiting
for him, the sole audience, to put them into motion. It
was like owning all of the theaters in the world, and
in each of them a different movie was playing, and
each movie starred himself, Stan Myakovsky, in all the
scenes of his life. He glided past them, a ghostly presence in his own memories.

25

Red Badger was one of the first crewmen revived from hypersleep. He stretched and yawned, then carefully unplugged the leads that connected him to the central sleep inducer. He looked around. The rest of the crew was starting to revive. Cheerful music was playing over the PA system. There were sounds of coughing and spitting as men cleared their throats for the first time in almost a month.

Coffee was available at a little table. Crew were always given coffee mixed with a new amphetamine upon first awakening. It was needed to help them throw off the effects of hypersleep.

Badger sipped at a black sweetened cup of coffee and felt his head clear.

"You okay, Red?" It was Walter Glint, his sidekick.

"Yeah, I'm fine."

"Min?"

The Laotian hill woman grunted her assent.

"Connie?"

"I'm great, Badger," Connie Mindanao said. "You figure this might be a bonus run?"

"For extra-hazardous duty? They haven't said yet."

"I hope so."

"Why?"

"I've got a ranch house in Bangio I'm trying to pay off."

"There just might be easier ways," Badger said. He looked around. "That's funny."

"What's that, Red?"

"They usually post the ship's destination in the crew quarters. But look for yourself—the board's empty."

"Yeah, that *is* funny," Glint said. "But there's a notice there."

Badger said, "I can see it, dummy. General assembly in twenty minutes. The captain and the owner's gonna talk to us."

Glint said, "You've been on these ships longer than I have. That's not the way they usually do it, is it, Red?"

"Nope." Badger scratched his jaw. "I'll bet they're up to something. This might be interesting, Glint."

The loudspeaker said, "All crew! Assemble at once in the main theater."

Stan and Julie walked out onto the raised stage. The crewmen looked up attentively when he rapped a pointer on the lectern to get their attention.

"Our destination is not far away now," Stan said. "It is a small O-type star named AR-32 in the standard catalog. Around it revolves a single planet, with several good-sized moons to keep it company. These moons create violent and unpredictable weather currents on the planet, which has been named Vista. Captain Hoban, do you know anything about this planet?"

Hoban had been sitting to one side of the stage. He

cleared his throat now and said, "I have heard of the place, sir. They used to call it the Festerhole, back when there were still a lot of pirates and privateers operating in the space lanes. There was once a jelly-gathering operation there involving one of the bionationals. That was some years ago. To the best of my knowledge it has been deserted since."

Stan thought, Good old honest Hoban telling the crew more than they need to know! Still, they'd have to find out sometime what this mission really involved.

The crew stirred and looked at each other. This talk of the Festerhole was making them uneasy. What was this assignment, anyhow? What was it the powers wanted them to do this time? No one had spoken about a bug-hunting expedition. That called for extra pay!

There was a rising murmur of protest from the crew. The greatest menace of recent times were the aliens, those big black monsters who had been pushed off Earth with difficulty, and elsewhere continued to show their murderous abilities in the face of everything Earth had been able to throw against them.

Badger rose to his feet and said, "Sir, this wouldn't by any chance be a bug-hunting expedition, would it?"

"Not exactly," Stan said.

"Then what exactly is it . . . sir?"

Stan ignored the red-haired crewman's insolent tone. "This is basically a salvage operation," he said. "We'll be taking a load of royal jelly off a wrecked freighter."

"Yes, sir," Badger said. "And aren't the bugs going to have something to say about that?"

"Our information is that there are no bugs on the wreck. We'll go in fast, take what we need, and be out of there again. There's also the possibility we'll find an abandoned hive on the planet. The jelly in that could be worth millions."

Walter Glint said, "Nothing was said about bugs when we volunteered, sir."

"Of course not," Stan said. "My information is secret. If I told you back on Earth, half the freelance salvagers from Earth and the colonies would be there now."

"Bugs can be dangerous," Glint said.

"Not when you take precautions," Stan quickly put in. "You were warned that this was hazardous duty. You're not getting time off your sentences for sitting around in some holiday spot. And remember, there's bonus pay in this for all of you. It could come to quite a lot, if the salvage is as rich as I think it is."

"How much?" Badger asked.

"That's impossible to calculate before we have it," Stan said. "Don't worry, there is a standard formula for crew shares. I intend to double it."

The men cheered. Even Badger smiled and sat down. This was interesting, he thought. He wondered what would come next.

26

Stan rapped for attention. But before he could get started again, a door opened and a man came in. He moved rapidly and with a strange grace, a cross between a glide and a lope. His face was expressionless. Although all of his individual features were human, the total result was not human at all. The crew knew at once, even before the introduction, that this man was a synthetic. Captain Hoban's introduction clinched the matter.

"People, this is Gill, an artificial man from the Valparaiso People Factory. He's the second-in-command."

"Sorry to be late, Dr. Myakovsky," Gill said. "I just finished the energy readings."

"No problem, Mr. Gill. Take a seat."

Gill sat down by himself in the back of the room.

Gill was a solitary. In recent years the People Factory in Valparaiso, Chile, where many of the better synthetics were produced, had been doing an im-

proved job on skin colors and texturing. Gone was
that old look of damp putty that had once character-
ized synthetic people and had provided a basis for so
many jokes by bad comedians. Now the only reliable
visual gauge for detection of an android was the
speed of their comprehension responses. That and a
certain mechanical jerkiness to their movements,
since the final stage of fairing the input levels and
ranges of the synthetics' operating systems was a
slow, expensive process, and many employers didn't
care if a synthetic's hand trembled as long as he didn't
drop the test tube or light stylus—or whatever.

Despite their artificial origins, synthetic men were
full-fledged members of human society, with voting
rights and a sexual program.

Stan was about to go on. But just at that moment,
from an outer corridor, Mac the dog came trotting
into the room. He had a bright blue rubber ball in his
mouth, and he looked around expectantly.

Someone in the crew laughed. "Fetch it here, boy!"

And then something else came into the room behind the dog.

It came loping in on all fours, and at first glance it
looked like a beetle the size of a rhinoceros. It was
colored a shiny, unrelieved black. Its skull was very
long and curved back over its shoulders. It was
toothed like a fiend and taloned like the devil itself. It
was Norbert. And he looked like he had just come
from hell.

There was silence for one long straining moment.

And then pandemonium broke loose.

The crew scrambled to their feet and started running for the exits. Their work boots clattered on the
metal deck as they surged toward the exit door, trying
to push each other out of the way.

Stan grabbed the microphone and shouted, "Just
stay where you are! Do not make any aggressive
movements! Norbert will not harm you, but he is programmed to resist aggression. Just stay calm!"

It was not a calm-making situation. Yet even now

catastrophe could have been averted. The crew was quieting down, coming out of its panic, starting to make jokes. Norbert was just standing there, making no sign that he was going to attack anyone. And then he was bending, slowly picking up the dog's rubber ball, throwing it back to him.

It could have ended right there. But there was always a wise guy around, someone who had to push things a little too far.

This time it was a crewman known as Steroid Johnny, an overmuscled hunk in a skimpy T-shirt, tight jeans, and lineman's boots, who carried an unlicensed pressor rod in his boot and liked to cause trouble.

Steroid Johnny saw his chance now. "Come on, Harris," he said to a lean, grinning blond man lounging beside him. "Let's take this sucker down. Shouldn't be no aliens here anyhow."

The two men advanced on the motionless robot alien. Steroid Johnny winked at Harris, who went slinking around to the right, picking up a crowbar from a toolbox as he went. The robot's head swiveled, keeping both men under surveillance. Johnny feinted to his left, then went straight in at Norbert. Five feet away he stopped and turned on his pressor beam. He directed it at Norbert's back-sloping head.

Norbert was pushed back hard—for a moment.

Then the big robot shrugged his way around the pressor beam, ducked under it, and was moving toward Johnny. Johnny backed up and tried to get the pressor beam into a blocking position, but Norbert moved faster, lunged forward, his jaws opened, the inner jaws shooting out of his mouth. The pressor beam fell to the deck. Johnny tried to get out of the way, but Norbert already had one big hooked claw clamped on his left shoulder.

Johnny screamed as he was lifted straight into the air by the skin of his shoulder. He hung there in Norbert's grip, screaming, struggling to break free. Norbert's inner jaws, impelled with all the energy of his powerful crysteel-mesh throat muscles, drove through Johnny's chest, splitting him like a side of beef. Norbert dropped the red dripping thing to the deck and turned, ready for the next one.

Harris, seeing the way things were going as he ran to attack Norbert, tried to pull up in midstride. Too late. Norbert swung around like a grotesque yet graceful ballet dancer and struck out with one of his taloned feet. The blow landed high on Harris's sternum. Norbert's talons made an audible hissing sound as they cut through the air, driven by the force of his heavy shoulder muscles. The talons ripped Harris apart from the left shoulder blade to his right hipbone. Harris opened his mouth to scream, but no sounds came out. His lungs had been punctured in the blow. He made an ugly squishing sound as he fell to the deck.

The rest of the crew took this in and froze in position. They had never seen anything move as fast as Norbert, when he was aroused.

Norbert halted, looking around. He seemed about to attack again. Just in time, Stan shouted out the shutdown order: "Priority override! Code Myrmidon!"

Norbert froze in position, awaiting further orders.

It was a moment of balanced possibilities. The crew seemed on the verge of panic, ready to run out of the control room screaming.

Captain Hoban gulped hard and felt nausea at the back of his throat, but he knew he had to control the men. He got hold of himself and said coldly, "Two of you there, get pails and mops and clean up that mess. See what comes of not following orders? This didn't have to happen. Now get a move on. . . ."

There was an awkward, sullen moment, and then the crew obeyed. And the ship *Dolomite* hurtled on toward its rendezvous with AR-32.

27

Subdued, the crew returned to their quarters. The men seemed dazed, unsure of what to think. All of them except Min Dwin, the Laotian hill woman. She went directly to her bunk and pulled out her spacebag. From it she took out a long object in a flat leather sheath. She pulled it free. It was a machete, sharpened to a razor edge.

Badger said, "What are you up to, Min?"

"Those bastards killed Johnny," Min said. "I'm going to get me some officer meat."

"With that? They'll cut you down before you get within ten feet of them."

"Maybe I can pick up a gun. One of those that fires the softslugs. I'd like to see that weird doctor with the glasses take one in the gut." She started toward the passageway leading back to the main ship's stations.

"Hold on a minute, Min," Badger said.

She stopped and turned. "Yeah, what is it?"

"Johnny was your man, huh?"

"Yeah. It was a recent thing. Now it's over. What about it?"

"Come over here and sit down," Badger said.

Reluctantly she complied, sitting on a locker with the machete balanced on her knees.

"Min, I understand you're plenty pissed off. I am, too. I wasn't all that fond of Steroid Johnny, or his friend Harris, but I wouldn't have wanted what happened to them."

"Right. So?"

"So this. It was Johnny's own fault, Min."

"It would never have happened if that professor guy hadn't brought that thing along."

"Sure. That thing he calls Norbert is obviously dangerous. But so what? We work around dangerous stuff all the time. That's what we volunteered for."

"I know. But Johnny—"

"Johnny disobeyed a direct order. He thought he knew better. I hate to say it, Min, but him and Harris got what they deserved."

"I never thought I'd hear you saying this, Red," Min said. "Who's side you on, anyhow? You suddenly turned into a company man?"

"I'm just telling it like it is," Badger said. "It's like somebody told Johnny not to stick his hand into a buzz saw, and he went and did it anyway. Who would you kill then?"

Min twisted her fingers together in an agony of indecision. "I don't know, Red. It doesn't seem right just to leave it."

"You're right about that," Badger said. "But now's not the time to do anything about it. You go walking out of here with that machete, they'll put you down fast and ask questions later."

"Aren't we going to do anything?"

"Sure we are. But not now."

"When, then?"

"Look," Badger said, "don't push it with me. I know you're sad over Johnny. You'll get over it soon and find someone else. As for what we're going to do, we're going to wait and see how things develop. When we make a move—if we do—they won't be expecting it. Is that fair enough?"

"Yeah," Min said. "I guess it is. You got any drugs on you, Red?"

"Walter here takes care of my supply. What have you got, Glint?"

Glint had a first-rate stock of assorted chemicals. He was the crew's supplier and he always had plenty to sell.

"Try this one," he said, taking a pillbox out of his spacebag and shaking out two into his hand. "This'll make you forget Johnny ever existed. If you like them, I'll make you a good price for a hundred. But these two are on the house."

"Thanks, Walter," she said.

"Hey, what are friends for?" said Walter Glint.

28

Gill sat at the control board, his fingers playing sensitively over the buttons. A telltale above his head gave a readout on orbit and showed a digital display of gravity vectors. Another telltale showed electromagnetic activity. AR-32, the planet itself, had come up rapidly and now filled most of another larger screen.

The planet was colored a dusty yellow and gray, with occasional black and purple markings indicating barren mountain ranges. Large livid splotches showed dead seabeds. A faint shadow darkened the upper right hand corner of the screen; it was cast by Ingo, second largest moon of AR-32, made of nearly seventy-percent telluric iron.

While Gill set up the orbiting procedure, Captain Hoban slid into a control chair beside him and ran up a readout on electrical and solar phenomena on the planet's surface. His sad face creased into a puzzled frown.

"I'm getting some strange signals," he told Stan.

"Where are they coming from?"

"That's what's strange. I can't get a fix. They keep on shifting."

"Can you derive any information as to their production?" Stan asked.

"Beg pardon, sir?"

"Is someone making these signals, or are they natural phenomena?"

"At this stage I can't tell," Hoban said. "We have no definite data on any other ships in the area."

"There's a lot of solar debris around, though," Stan said. "No telling yet what it might be."

Gill punched up another set of numbers. "The weather down there on the surface is even worse than you expected, Dr. Myakovsky."

Julie came into the control room. She had already changed into a plasteel landing outfit. The cobalt-blue plastic form-fitting clothing with its orange flashes looked stunning on her. Stan's heart was in his mouth as he watched her.

"Are we ready to go down?" Julie asked.

Captain Hoban said, "I wouldn't recommend it, Miss Lish. The surface phenomena are worse than we were led to believe. Perhaps if we give the weather time to settle down a little . . ."

Julie shook her head impatiently. "There's no time for that. If our worst peril is from the weather, Captain, we're doing very well indeed!"

"I suppose that's true," Hoban said. He turned to Gill. "Are you ready to accompany the party, Gill?"

"I am, of course, ready," the synthetic man said. "I have taken the liberty of asking for volunteers for this. There are five of them, and they are waiting for your orders."

He stood up from the control panel. He was tall, and even with his mismatched features, he was good-looking. If he had been a true man, you would have said there was something haunted about his expression. Since he was only a synthetic, you had to figure there'd been something amiss with his facial mold.

"Captain Hoban," said Stan, "can you show us our target in more detail?"

Hoban nodded and fine-tuned the controls. AR-32's surface sprang up into high magnification. Fractal-mapped shapes blew up in size and complexity. Hoban adjusted the magnification again. A tiny dot on the landscape grew quickly, until, at extreme magnification, it turned into a low dark earthen dome that rose up from the flat plain, showing up well against the rugged landscape.

"That's the hive," Hoban said. "Not easy to miss it. It's the biggest thing in this part of the planet."

"Looks pretty quiet," Stan mused.

"We're still a long way from the surface," Gill reminded him. "Things could change by the time we get there."

"True enough," Stan said. "But what the hell, this is what we've come for. Julie? Are you ready?"

"Ready, Stan," Julie said. "It's going to be a walk in the park."

Stan wished he shared her confidence.

"Why are you going to the surface?" Hoban asked. "I thought we were coming to look for an orbiting wreck."

"All in good time," Stan said. "Right now we've got the hive below us and no sign of life around it. If we can get a load of royal jelly from there, we can take care of the freighter later."

"Right on," Julie said. "Let's go for all the marbles."

Stan felt encouraged by the beautiful thief's cheerfulness and determination. Maybe this thing was going to go all right, after all.

29

The number-one lander was in its own bay, stacked parallel to the backup lander, just behind the big hold where Julie had made her last training run with Norbert. Now Norbert walked behind Stan and Julie, holding Mac the dog in his arms. There was something doglike about the robot's posture; in a sense he was a mechanical watchdog, ferocious when challenged, utterly loyal to his master, Stan. Behind Norbert, and keeping their distance, were the five volunteers for the landing party. They had been promised a sufficient bonus for this undertaking, enough for avarice to overcome common sense. But, of course, if they'd had common sense, they wouldn't have been in space on the *Dolomite* in the first place.

Captain Hoban, who was already at the number-one lander waiting for them, initiated the hatch-opening procedure. The lander, nestled in its bay, was almost a hundred feet long. It contained a miniature laboratory and was fully equipped with the telemetry needed for the mission.

Norbert was proceeding to the hatch when Mac the dog came streaking out of the corridor, the rubber ball in his jaws. He raced into the lander just ahead of Norbert.

"We'd better get that dog out of there," Hoban said.

"Let him stay," said Stan. "He may be of some use accompanying Norbert once we're on the surface."

"Just as you wish, sir," Hoban said. "I wish I were going with you."

"I wish you were, too," said Stan. "But we need you here on the *Dolomite*. If anything goes wrong, we're absolutely dependent on you for backup."

"Don't worry, Stan, nothing's going to go wrong," Julie said. Her smile was brilliant. "Don't you agree, Gill?"

"Optimism has not been factored into me," Gill said. "I am constructed to understand situations, not to have feelings about them."

"You're missing the best part," Julie said. "Having feelings about stuff is what it's all about."

"I've often wondered about that," Gill said.

"Maybe someday you'll find out. Are we ready?"

"After you," Stan said.

She made a mocking little salute and stepped into the lander. The others followed. Captain Hoban waited until he heard Stan report on the voice channel that the lander was well sealed and all systems were on-line. Then he returned to the control room and initiated the takeoff procedure.

The lander fell away from the *Dolomite*'s hull and dropped toward the swirling surface of AR-32. Stan adjusted his restraining harness and called out, "Everybody secure?"

The five volunteers from the crew were strapped down in the forward cabin. They were carrying weapons that had been issued to them by Gill: pulse rifles and vibrators. All had been given suppressors. These state-of-the-art electronic machines, about a meter long and weighing less than a pound, were clipped to their belts. The suppressors emitted a complex waveform that confused an alien's vision, rendering the wearer invisible.

Julie and Gill were lying on deceleration couches in the main cabin behind Stan. Norbert was crouched all the way in the rear, holding a stanchion in one clawed hand and cuddling Mac with the other. There was no seat aboard the lander large enough to hold the big robot alien. But his strength was such that it was likelier the stanchion would move than his grip be torn loose.

Then Captain Hoban's face appeared on the screen. "Dr. Myakovsky, are you ready for release?"

"Ready, Captain," Stan said. "Open up and turn us loose."

There was a powerful humming noise from the *Dolomite*'s interior motors, a noise that could be felt inside the lander as vibration. The *Dolomite*'s bay doors slid open revealing the star-studded sky as seen from AR-32's upper atmosphere. There was a click as the doors locked in the open position. Then a bright green telltale on Stan's control board came to life.

"You've got control, Stan."

Stan felt his stomach turn over as the lander pulled away from the *Dolomite*. G-forces twisted at his gut. Sudden sharp flashes of pain went through his chest. A haze of pinkish red enclosed his vision, with blackness beginning to form on the edges.

"Stan!" Julie called out. "We're coming down pretty fast."

Gill said, "Hull ionization is beginning to be a factor."

Stan got himself under control. His fingers danced on the controls. "Okay, I've got it. Gill, give me a landing vector."

They were deep into AR-32's atmosphere. Long, thin, ragged yellow clouds, twisting and turning into fantastic shapes, whipped past the Perspex viewing

window. There was a rattle of hailstones striking the
hull as they passed through a temperature inversion
layer in the atmosphere.

The image of Captain Hoban jumped in and out of
focus on the screen. But his voice was steady as he
said, "Dr. Myakovsky, this planet has a heavy radia-
tion belt. Better kick on through it at best speed."

"What do you think I'm doing?" Stan gritted. "Sight-
seeing?"

"Are you all right, Doctor?" Hoban asked. "You
don't look so good."

"I feel great," Stan said through gritted teeth. Black
dots were swimming behind his eyes as he fought to
hang on to consciousness. His chest burned with a familiar agony. He could feel the straps of the restraining harness tug at his shoulders as he cut down
power and started to bring up the ship's nose. The atmosphere lightened and darkened as they went
through more cloud layers. On the computer screen,
the flight path for their landing came in glowing am-
ber.

Gill said, "We're on the final approach now. Good
going, Stan."

Stan forced himself to concentrate, though he
was none too sure he could remain conscious. The
g-forces eased as he pulled the lander into position
for its landing run.

There was more visibility near the ground. In the
tawny yellow light Stan could see house-sized boulders strewn across a tilted plain. They were fast approaching an old riverbed, wide and level, and that
seemed a good place to make the final landing.

Stan adjusted the trim tabs and began the landing
procedure. The lander put her nose up and steadied.
Wind gusts shook the ship just as it touched down.
There was a crunch as they smacked the ground, then
a bad moment as the lander soared into the air again.
Then it came down again, hard, and this time it stayed
down.

When the lander had come completely to a stop, Julie looked around and said, "Welcome to AR-32, everyone. It may not look like much, but this planet is going to make us rich."

"Or dead," Stan muttered, but to himself.

30

Back on the *Dolomite*, Captain Hoban watched the lander spin away on the viewscreen. He felt hollow, useless. There was nothing for him to do at the moment. Gloomy thoughts began to invade his mind.

Captain Hoban had continued to think about suicide. This didn't surprise him. He only found it strange that he hadn't thought of it before, during all the bad days of the trial.

He shook his head. Back then, something had buoyed his spirits, some belief that he was going to come out of this all right. And then his opportunity had seemed to arrive when Stan visited him in Jersey City and made his offer, and here he was in space again. But he had a bad feeling about it. His thoughts were full of foreboding images, and the men torn apart by Norbert hadn't helped his mood any. He suspected there would be a lot more deaths ahead, maybe even his own. Maybe he wouldn't have to commit suicide after all.

On the other hand, he could do it now. Gill could handle the ship all right. Stan and Julie didn't really need him. . . .

Somewhere in his mind, Hoban knew this was a crazy line of thinking. He was a valuable person with reasons for living. He had nothing to be ashamed of. And yet the shame was there, constantly bubbling up from the depths of his mind, a seemingly automatic process that he couldn't shut off.

It obsessed him that he had been dismissed from his own ship. He still burned with shame when he remembered how the authorities had revoked his license. It was all so terrible, and so unfair. Probably there was no hope of real reinstatement. He had let Stan talk him into joining this crazy venture without thinking it through. When he got back to Earth—if he got back—the authorities would be merciless with him. Maybe he'd gone far enough.

He was preoccupied with his thoughts, and so was not pleased when he heard a crisp knock at the door of his stateroom. Now that the lander was away, he'd been hoping for a few minutes alone so he could get caught up on writing the ship's log.

"Who is it?" he asked.

"Crewman Badger, sir."

Hoban sighed. He still didn't know why he hadn't rejected Badger at the prison, when he had the chance. He had finally remembered where he'd seen him. Badger had been one of the crew of the *Dolomite* when he'd had his accident in the asteroids, one of the men who had witnessed his disgrace.

Damn, damn, damn.

He didn't like Badger, thought he was sly and untrustworthy. But he had to admit, the man hadn't given him any trouble before. He did know Badger's type. Hoban had looked over the comment sheets on the crew, sheets compiled by other captains on other flights. The word on Badger was that he was cunning,

insubordinate, and a troublemaker. There was no specific charge against him on the evaluation sheets, but
the implication was clear enough. "Come in, Crewman
Badger. What do you want?"

"I have the latest report on the debris in this area
of space, sir."

"Why didn't you just put it on the computer, as
usual?"

"I thought you'd want to see this one before it was
opened for general access, sir."

"Why? Is there something unusual about it?"

"I'd say so, sir. Our new radar overlays show
there's more than just space junk out there in orbit,
Captain. I'm pretty sure there's a wreck in orbit near
us."

"A wreck? Are you sure?"

"Can't be absolutely sure at this range, sir," Badger
said. "But the pictures show smooth metal surfaces
that must have been machined. It looks to me like a
Q-class freighter, sir. Or the remains of one."

Hoban took the radar printouts from Badger's hand
and carried them over to his desk. He studied them
under infrared light, then, using a grease pencil, outlined an area.

"You mean this bit right here?"

"That's it, sir."

Hoban studied the readouts more closely. He had
to admit that Badger had a good eye for this sort of
thing. It appeared to be a ship's remains, floating out
there in an orbit around AR-32, along with a lot of
other stuff, mostly stellar debris.

This, he decided, might be the wreck that Stan
Myakovsky had been looking for. Hoban decided to
find out and have the information for Stan when he
returned.

"We're going to have to check it out," he said.
"Badger, I want you to take one man, suit up, and go
to the wreck's location. See if you can find its flight
indicator."

"Yes, sir!" said Badger.

"And don't go talking about this with the rest of the crew. That wreck has probably been there a very long time. No need for them to get excited too soon."

"Right, sir. No reason to alarm the crew over something like this."

Hoban nodded, but he didn't like agreeing with Badger. It seemed more natural that he should be on the opposite side of anything Badger felt. But he decided that perhaps he was being unfair. All that anyone had against Badger were rumors, and the man's unfortunate personality. No charge against him had ever stuck. And his decision to bring the wreck immediately to Hoban's attention had been quite correct.

Badger went back to the crew quarters. His sidekick Glint was drinking a cup of coffee at one of the wardroom tables. He looked up quizzically when Badger came in.

"Come on," Badger told him. "We got a job to do."

Glint swallowed the rest of his coffee and stood up. "What sort of a job?"

"There's a wreck out there. It's going to take spacesuits."

"Yeah? What's up, Red?"

"I'll tell you about it as we go," Badger said.

31

Stan had brought down the lander within viewing distance of the humped-up mound that was the alien hive, which he was able to inspect closely through the viewscreen magnifier. Gill and Julie stood behind him as he manipulated the views.

The hive was not only the largest nonnatural feature on this planet; it was also larger than any natural feature Stan had yet seen there. Even the mountains were no more than a few hundred meters in height. The hive, standing over a thousand meters above the windswept plain, was huge, imposing, with a dark majesty. The winds scoured it, grinding it down, and there was constant activity from the aliens, who stood out as little black dots at this distance, building the hive up again like ants repairing an anthill.

Aliens, so soon! But, he reminded himself, he had been expecting them ... hadn't he?

"I hope you're taking note, Ari," Stan said, holding the cybernetic ant on his fingertip so it could get a good view.

"I don't know if Ari is," Julie said, "but I sure am. I didn't know the hive would be so big. And I didn't know we'd run into aliens so soon."

"We've got the suppressors," Stan reminded her.

"Sure," Julie said. "But are they reliable? It's pretty new technology." She sighed and looked out across the plain again. "That's one big hive."

"This one could probably be classified a super-hive," said Gill. "It's far bigger than any other recorded in the literature on the aliens."

"Why do you suppose?" Stan asked.

"This is only a conjecture, of course, but it seems to me the odds against survival on this planet are so great that the aliens had to concentrate their forces, keep one big hive going rather than a lot of smaller ones."

"Saves us from having to make a lot of choices about which hive we plunder," Julie said. "Let's get to it, shall we?"

Gill shook his head. "I advise you to wait until the storm activity on the surface has abated somewhat."

Outside, through the Plexiglas, they could see the raging gale that was the usual weather on this planet. The wind had whipped itself into new heights of frenzy. Sand and small stones were blown across the plain like exploding shrapnel. Larger rocks, swept from the low crags in the distance, tumbled across the plain like steamrollers gone berserk. Lightning forked and crashed in vivid streamers of electric blue.

Beneath the lander, the ground shook and heaved in a nausea-inducing motion. Stan thought: Volcanic activity, just what we need. But he wasn't really worried. He had taken an ampoule of Xeno-Zip before leaving the *Dolomite*. He felt strong and confident, and the pain was gone.

There was a burst of high-pitched static from the speaker, and then Captain Hoban's voice came on.

"Dr. Myakovsky? Are you reading me?"

"Loud and clear, Captain," said Stan. "What do you have to report?"

"We spotted some debris in orbit near us," Hoban said. "Upon further inspection, I have found the wreck of a space freighter, just as you predicted. It's broken into several pieces, but there's a main section that could even contain human life. I doubt that'll be the case, however. This wreck looks like it's been there a long time."

"Do you have any identification on it yet?" Stan asked.

"I've sent two men over to check it out," Hoban said. "With a little luck we'll pick up a flight recorder and find out what happened."

"Contact me as soon as you have it," Stan said. "That could be very important information."

"I'm well aware of that, sir. I'll let you know first thing. Sir, ship's telemetry and remote survey equipment tells me you've put down the lander on potentially unstable ground."

"Everything around here is unstable," Stan said. "Except for the rock outcropping the hive stands on. You wouldn't want me to put down right beside the hive, would you, Captain?"

"Of course not, sir. I was just pointing out . . ."

"I know, I know," Stan snapped. He took a deep breath and tried to get control of himself. He was getting weird flashes now from the drug. It seemed to be taking him on an elevator ride; one second his mood was up, the next minute down. And too soon, the pain was coming back. Take it easy, he told himself.

Still, his breath sobbed in his throat as he said, "I'm going to sign off now, Captain. We have to wait until the storm calms down before we can carry out the next step. I will use that time to get a little rest."

"Yes, sir. Over and out."

Captain Hoban's face faded from the screen. Stan closed his eyes for a moment, then opened them again. Julie and Gill were both standing nearby, watching him. Stan felt a sudden shame at his own weakness, and at the pain that was mounting in intensity throughout his throat and chest. At a moment like this the only thing he could think of was the next ampoule of Xeno-Zip, nested in its padded box with the few others he had brought along.

He shook his head irritably. It was too early for another ampoule. He hadn't planned to take one just yet, he didn't know what it would do to him, but the pains were getting very bad, perhaps even affecting his judgment.

"I'll see you both later," Stan said. Even before they turned to leave the control room, Stan's fingers were at the table drawer where he kept the box of royal jelly ampoules.

32

Julie and Gill returned to the aftercabin. They were alone except for Norbert, who stood silently against the curving wall like a futuristic basilisk, with Mac the dog asleep in his arms.

"Well, Gill," Julie said, "what do you think of all this?"

Gill looked up from his inspection of the armament they had brought. His expression was mild, quizzical. "To what, specifically, do you refer?"

"Stan and his mad trip for royal jelly. This planet. Me."

Gill took his time before answering. "I do not ask myself that sort of question, Miss Lish. And if I did . . ."

"Yes?"

"If I did, my conclusions would have no value. I am not like you humans. I am a synthetic."

"How do you differ from real people?"

Gill looked disturbed, but managed to smile. "No soul, for one thing. Or so they say."

"And for another?"

"No feelings."

"None at all, Gill? Yet you look like a man."

"Appearances can be deceiving."

"Don't you even find me attractive?" Julie asked.

Again there was a long pause. Then Gill said, "There is an old saying of your people. 'Let sleeping dogs lie.' I would advise that here."

"Why is that?"

"Because synthetic people with feelings are something the human race wants no part of."

"That must be some other race," Julie said. "Maybe I'm not part of it. I wouldn't mind it at all if you had feelings. You could tell me about yours and I'd tell you about mine."

"Our feelings would be nothing alike," Gill said.

"Are you so sure?" Julie said. "Sometimes I've felt that I've been set up to follow some program written by someone else. 'The Beautiful Thief,' this one is called. I sometimes wish I could just rewrite my programming. Do you ever wish that?"

"Yes," Gill said. "I know what you mean." Then he shook his head irritably. "Excuse me, Miss Lish, but I must go finish checking out these weapons. Dr. Myakovsky is going to need us at any time."

"Do what you have to do," Julie said. She walked away, and Gill watched her go.

33

Starlight glittered on his space armor as Red Badger left the *Dolomite*'s air lock and soared weightlessly toward the freighter wreck. Behind him came his backup man, Glint, illuminating the wreck with a powerful duolite beam.

Badger gestured, though their destination was plain enough: the gray mass of the wreck, lying in several distinct parts, blocking the stars.

Getting there was simple: both men, on a signal from Badger, opened squirt cans that propelled them across the intervening space.

Badger said into his helmet radio, "You reading me okay, Glint?"

"Loud and clear," Glint said.

They landed on the hulk's largest section with a clank of magnetic boots. Badger's power wrench opened the airtight door that led into the ship.

A lot of the freighter's metal covering had been

peeled back by strong explosions. It was no trouble at all, once they were past the external armor, to slip in between two structural girders and make their way to the interior.

The searchlight picked out the bodies of men, trapped in the sudden inrushing vacuum when the ship's side had been pierced. Exploded bodies lay across girders and floated unsupported in the zero gravity.

Badger and Glint moved slowly, clumsy in their airtight space armor, their searchlights throwing brilliant swords of light through the gloom. A corpse, hanging over a loop of high-pressure hose, seemed to reach out and touch Badger's helmet, lightly, as if just saying hello. . . .

The redheaded spaceman laughed and pushed the thing aside. The body floated slowly across the shattered compartment, its arms held out loosely in front of it like a swimmer doing the dead man's float.

They reached the flight deck. Here there were more bodies, some terribly mangled by the pieces of flying machinery that had taken on the power of exploding shrapnel as the ship had come apart, others looking strangely peaceful, as if they'd never known what hit them. Death had had a busy few moments here before the eternal silence of space had entombed them all.

"Here's the control section," Glint said over the little space-helmet radio that connected the two men.

"Good enough," said Badger. "Let's find what we came for and get the hell out of here."

They floated past an operations console that looked as good as new. The ship's name was still stenciled on the bulkhead, and the paint looked almost new.

"*Valparaiso Queen,*" Glint spelled out. "She won't be going Earthside no more."

"Tough luck for her," Badger said, his tone flat and unemotional. "Here's what we're looking for."

Under the command console was a panel with

three fingertip-sized indentations. Badger pressed
them in counterclockwise order, starting at twelve
o'clock. The panel slid away. Badger directed Glint to
shine the searchlight inside. Using wire cutters from
the tool kit strapped to his waist, Badger cut the leads
inside and withdrew a small heavy box made of a
metalized plastic substance.

"This is what we came for. Now let's get out of
here."

34

Back aboard the *Dolomite*, Badger and Glint passed through the air lock and removed their suits. Glint started walking toward the elevator that led to the ship's command territory. He stopped when he saw that Badger was not following him.

"What's up, Red? Aren't we going to give this to the captain?"

"Of course we are," Badger said. "But not just yet." He led the way down a passageway to a door marked WORKSHOP D—AUTHORIZED PERSONNEL ONLY. Glint followed him.

"What're you doin'?" Glint asked. "You going to fix that gizmo?"

Badger stopped and looked scornful. "You really are some kind of a moron. No, I'm not going to fix the gizmo. Why do you think I volunteered us for this job?"

"I was wondering about that," Glint said.

"I want to get a look at what's on this flight recorder before I give it to the captain. Fat chance Hoban would ever tell us."

Glint looked admiringly at his partner, then hurried to catch up as Badger pressed the stud that operated the door to Workshop D.

35

The lander was too small to have separate staterooms. There was a cubbyhole in the rear with a deceleration couch that pulled down from the wall. Stan had lain down there. When Julie came in he was asleep, his glasses still on, his round face momentarily untroubled. Julie bent over to shake him, then hesitated. Stan looked so peaceful there. His large face was calm, and quiet handsome. She noticed what long eyelashes he had, and what delicate skin, fine-pored like a young boy's.

The most recent ingestion of Xeno-Zip had taken Stan's spirit far away, into the limitless perspectives that were the psychic environment of the drug. He was traveling through a place of pure light and color, and he smiled at the friendly shapes around him.

Julie stared at him almost in awe. She knew that Stan was moving down the visionary trail in some impossible dreamtime, walking down a hall of memory

filled with all the images of everything that had ever
been or would be. And these images were melting like
wax in the warmth of the soul's embrace. Stan was a
sorcerer forcing time itself to stand still and be ac-
countable to the moment. He had found eternity in an
instant, and he was balancing it on a needlepoint.

He was in his own time now, a time that had no duration and no limit. He was in a place she could never
get to. But, she wondered, out here in the world of
solid objects and fiery forces, how much time did he
have left? How much time was at Julie's disposal, for
that matter? Could Stan see their time lines in that
strange place where he was?

"Stan," she whispered to him, "what are you dreaming about? Am I in the dream with you? Are we
happy?"

Stan mumbled something but she couldn't catch
the words. She reached out and touched him on the
shoulder. His eyes snapped open, as if he had been
waiting for this signal. She watched his face tense as
pain returned to his consciousness. Then he had himself under control and said, "Julie ... What is it?"

"Captain Hoban wants to speak to you again. He's
pulled a flight recorder from that wreck."

"Okay, fine." Stan sat up, then got somewhat unsteadily to his feet. Julie's slender, hard arm was
around him, supporting him, her warm fragrant hair
was at his shoulder, and he breathed her fragrance
gratefully.

"Thanks," he said.

"Hey, don't mention it. We're a team, aren't we?"

He looked at her. Her eyes were enormous, brilliant, with dark pools at the center. He felt himself
melting into them. A wave of emotion came over him.

"Julie ..."

"Yes, Stan, what is it?"

"If you're doing this for my sake ... please don't
stop."

36

The voices on the flight recorder were very clear.

"What ship is that?"

"This is the Valparaiso Queen, *Captain Kuhn commanding, thirty-seven days out of Santiago de Chile. To whom am I speaking?"*

"This is Potter of the Bio-Pharm ship Lancet. *Do you realize you are trespassing?"*

"I think you exaggerate, Captain. There's no trace of your claim in the recent issues of StarSwap."

"We haven't chosen to go public with it just yet. But there are electronic warnings posted at the beginning of the quadrant. Surely you intercepted those warnings?"

"Oh, those!" Captain Kuhn laughed. "An electronic warning hardly constitutes a legal claim! No, Captain Potter, unless you publish your intent with the

federal Department of Interplanetary Claims, it can't be said to exist. I have as much right here as you."

Potter's voice was low, and hoarse with menace. "Captain Kuhn, I am a man of little patience. You have already used up my entire store. You have about one second to go into retrofire and get your ship out of there."

Kuhn replied, "I do not take kindly to peremptory orders, Captain, especially from one who has no legal right to give them. I will leave this vicinity in my own time, when I'm good and ready. And you may be sure I will file a complaint with InterBureau over your attitude."

"You will have more to complain about than an attitude, Captain Kuhn, but I doubt you will ever file that report."

"Do not try to intimidate me!"

"The time for words is past. The torpedo that puts paid to your pretensions is now coming toward you at a speed well below that of light, but fast enough, I think you'll find."

"Torpedo? How dare you, sir! Number two! Full power to the screens! Take evasive action!"

And then Badger had to turn down the volume as the recorded sound of the explosion shook the walls of Workshop D.

37

"What's the latest on the storm?" Stan asked.

Gill looked up, his long melancholy face half in a green glow from the ready lights on his control panel. On the screen above him, data waves danced in long wavering lines, the numbers changing with a rapidity that would defy the computational abilities of any but a synthetic man with a math coprocessor built into his positronic brain. Gill was such a man, and his computational abilities were enhanced by the rock-steadiness of his mind, which was not subject to the neurotic claims of love, duty, family, or country. Yet he was not completely emotionless. It had been found that intelligence of the highest order presupposes and is built upon certain fundamental emotional bases, of which the desire to survive and continue is the most fundamental of all. The designers of artificial men would have liked to have stopped there. But the uncertain nature of the materials they were using—in which minute differences in atomic structures eventually spelled big differences in output, as well as the inherent instability of colloidal structures—made this impossible. Gill was standard within his design parameters, but those parameters expressed only one part of him.

"The storm is abating," Gill said. "There's been a twenty-percent diminution in the last half hour. Given the conditions here, I think that's about the best we're going to get. In fact, it's apt to get a lot worse before it gets better."

"Then let's get on with it," Stan said. He turned to Norbert, the big robot alien, who still crouched patiently in a corner of the lander. Mac the dog, growing impatient, whined to be put down, and Norbert obliged. The dog investigated the corners of the little lander and, finding nothing of interest, returned to curl up at Norbert's taloned feet.

"You ready, Norbert?"

"Of course, Dr. Myakovsky. Being robotic, I am always ready."

"And Mac?"

"He is a dog, and so he is always ready, too."

Stan laughed, and remarked to Julie, "I wish now I'd had more time to talk with Norbert. His horrible appearance belies his keen intelligence."

"You are responsible for my appearance, Dr. Myakovsky," Norbert said.

"I think you're beautiful," Stan said. "Don't you think so, Julie?"

"I think you're both pretty cute," she said.

38

In the forward cabin of the lander, the five volunteer crew members were sitting as comfortably as they were able in the cramped confines. Morrison, big and blond, an Iowa farmboy, had unwrapped an energy bar and was nibbling at it. Beside him, Skysky, fat and balding with a walrus mustache, decided to eat an energy bar of his own and fumbled it out of his pocket. Eka Nu, a flat-faced Burmese with skin a shade lighter than burned umber, was mumbling over the wooden beads of his Buddhist rosary. Styson, his long face as mournful as ever, was playing his harmonica, monotonously repeating one phrase over and over. And Larrimer, a city boy from New York's south Bronx, was doing nothing at all except licking his dry lips and brushing his long lank hair out of his eyes.

They had been excited when they volunteered. It was a chance for some action, after the confines of the ship. They'd heard stories about the aliens, of course, but none of them had seen one. They hadn't even been born at the time of the alien occupation of Earth. Aliens now seemed an exotic menace, a weird kind of big bug that would fall easily to their guns.

Morrison was fiddling with his carbine. He decided to insert a new feed ramp. He stripped the receiver and replaced the ramp, then snapped the connector into place. The ramp toggled through a diagnostic code and then clicked into place. He shoved a magazine into the carbine, touched the bolt control, and cycled a round into the firing chamber. The magazine's counter showed an even one hundred antipersonnel rounds ready to go.

"Hey, farm boy," Skysky said, "you planning to shoot something?"

"If I get the chance," Morrison said, "I'm going to bag me one of them aliens and bring home his horns."

Eka Nu looked up from his rosary. "Aliens no got horns."

"Well, whatever they got, I want to bring a piece of it home. A piece of skull maybe. Wouldn't that look good mounted over the mantel?"

Styson said, "You better just hope one of them critters doesn't nail your hide up over the mantel."

"What're you talking about?" Morrison asked. "Them creatures ain't civilized. They ain't got mantels."

Just then Stan's voice came over the loudspeaker. "You men! Get ready to embark into a pod. Check your weapons."

"Okay," Morrison said, getting to his feet. "Time we had ourselves a little hunting."

The men were all on their feet, checking their weapons and talking excitedly. They were clumsy, some of them seeing modern weaponry for the first time. Morrison—who was their natural leader due to his size and self-confidence, though he was of the same rank as the rest of them—had to show Styson how to release the safeties. He was beginning to wonder if the guys would be all right, but he figured as long as they knew which end to point and what to pull, they'd be fine. What creature could stand up against military caseless ammunition?

39

The number-one lander had three escape pods. These were used for close-up maneuvering, in order not to jeopardize the lander itself by piloting it around poorly mapped ground features. This standard-model pod was shaped like an enormous truck tire. Its circular form allowed for the miles of complex wiring that took up most of its interior and allowed it to ride the planet's electromagnetic currents with some success.

Norbert fitted himself in, and Mac nestled up to his chest.

"Comfortable?" Stan asked, peering in.

"The question has no relevance for me," Norbert replied. "When your body is electronically operated, one posture is as good as another. But Mac is fine, Dr. Myakovsky."

"Glad to hear it," Stan said. "Good luck, Norbert. I'll be sending down the five crew volunteers in a separate pod. This moment brings us to the whole point of this operation—getting you and Mac and the men to the surface of AR-32 near the alien hive. Have you got all the stuff you'll need? Did you remember to check the charge in the inhibitors?"

"Of course, Dr. Myakovsky. They should give me enough time to do what I have to do."

"Okay," Stan said. "Good-bye, Mac. You're a nice little dog. I hope I see you again one of these days."

"Not likely, Doctor," said Norbert.

Suddenly Stan was furious.

"Just get the hell out of here!" he said, slamming the pod's hatch shut. "I don't need your comments. Did you hear that, Julie?"

"Take it easy, Stan," Julie said. "Norbert didn't mean anything. He only states facts. Anyway, what's the big deal?"

Norbert's voice came over the radio. "I am ready for the descent, Dr. Myakovsky."

Stan turned to Gill. "Cut the pod loose. And then get the volunteers into their own pod."

Gill, seated at the control panel, turned a switch. The pod came loose from the landing platform with a soft explosive sigh of power. It ejected straight into the air, dipped for a moment, then its electromagnetic receptors came up to full and the pod darted across the stormy landscape of AR-32 toward the distant hive.

40

Badger and Glint left the workshop and entered crew country from the corridor into the crew's commissary. A wave of sound and smell hit them. The sound was of fifteen men and women, mostly young, celebrating their arrival at AR-32 with song and booze, hamburgers and pizza (these latter accounting for the smell), and a level of noise that had to be heard to be believed.

Celebrating landfall was an old custom among ship's crews. Columbus's men had celebrated in the same way, their arrival in the New World offering them a good excuse for a spree. That's what the arrival at AR-32 meant to the crew of the *Dolomite*, too: a chance to cut loose and tie one on in the secure surroundings of the commissariat, where officers were not permitted and where scanning procedures were prohibited by the strong Spacemen's Union.

Here the men could say what they wanted, and

there were no ship's officers nearby or at the end of an electronic listening device ready to take their names and report them for summary discipline. The union wouldn't allow it, and Red Badger had counted on that when he made his entry.

Long Meg, a wiper third class from Sacramento back on Earth, slapped Badger on the back and pushed a bulb of beer into his face. "Where you been, Red? Not like you to miss a spree!"

"I been out to the wreck," Red said.

"What wreck? They didn't tell us about no wreck."

"No, they didn't," Red said. "That's very like them, isn't it?"

Meg pushed her face close to Badger's. "None of your bullshit. What wreck are you talking about?"

Badger grinned at her easily. "That's what the captain sent me and Glint here to investigate. It showed up on the radar and he sent me to get the flight recorder."

"Oh. Is that all?" Meg asked. "I guess the captain will tell us what was on it all in good time."

"I don't think so," Badger said. "If we knew what was on that recorder, it might change our minds about a few things."

"Come out with it, Red! What are you talking about?"

"Suppose that flight recorder showed a freighter just like ours, poking around here just like we are, then being blasted to hell by someone who didn't want them here? What about that, huh?"

"That would be serious," Meg admitted, and several other crewmen nodded agreement. "Are you saying that's what it said?"

"I'm not saying nothing," Badger said. "You can decide for yourselves."

"You took the flight indicator?"

"I listened to it in the workshop. And now I'm going to play it for you. Once you've heard it, you can come to your own conclusions."

"I hope you know what you're doing, Red," Meg said. "I'm sure the captain is expecting you to give that to him immediately."

"Don't worry," Badger said. "The message on it is pretty short."

41

The pod, with Norbert and Mac aboard, was dancing around like a leaf in a storm. Norbert had lost contact with the other pod containing the five volunteers. Wind force threw his pod up into the air, and crosscurrents spun it like a top. Mac howled, and Norbert just clung tight.

"Hang on, boy!" Norbert called. Mac, cradled in his arms, was whimpering, his eyes rolling, in a paroxysm of fear.

Norbert had brought along some extra equipment in case of distress to the dog. The trouble was getting to it. Norbert was practically compressed into the space of the pod, and his size made him take up more room than an Earthman. The little ship was swinging around violently, but Norbert did not suffer from vertigo. He managed to reverse one of his wrist joints and grabbed a large piece of felt he had brought along. He managed to wrap this around Mac, cushioning him. The dog gave a little yelp as the cloth came around him, but he seemed to appreciate it. His spastic movement became calmer, and he began to adjust to the violent movements.

The pod, descending on automatic, danced and veered in the wind. Norbert was tempted to manually override the pod's controls and see if he could ease out the movements. But he decided against it. The pod's autopilot had been designed with a program that softened out its jerks and slides. He couldn't hope to do better. He concentrated instead upon providing a firm platform for Mac and keeping the felt wrapped around the shivering beast without smothering him. Norbert himself didn't breathe, and he had to remind himself that all other creatures did.

The ground was coming up fast now to meet them. Wind shear, this close to the ground, added another factor to the dangerous uncertainties of the descent. (The pod's own pulsar beams had to slow them and absorb the shock as the ground rushed up to meet them.) Then they were bouncing across it, and finally, spinning, they came to a halt.

Then Dr. Myakovsky's voice: "Norbert, are you all right?"

"Perfectly all right, Doctor. And so is Mac."

"Was the landing very difficult?"

Norbert had something new in his vocabulary, learned from Julie, and he hastened to use it now. "A piece of cake, Doctor. A walk in the park."

"Hurry up and get the job done," Stan said. "We want to get rich and get out of here."

42

After Badger played the recorder for the crew, there was an utter silence for a brief moment. Spaceship crews, with their volatile mix of people from all walks of life, tend to have low boiling points. The crew of the *Dolomite* was no exception, particularly since it included a high percentage of criminals.

"What the hell does it mean?" Meg asked.

"It means that a ship like ours was fired upon and destroyed. If they did it to them, then why not to us?"

"Wait a minute!" one of the crew said. "They aren't allowed to do that!"

"What does it matter what they're allowed?" Badger said. "People with power do what they please."

The crew began quarreling among themselves. Badger waited for them to sort it out. He was pretty sure what conclusion they'd come to. And if, by a remote chance, they didn't, he'd steer them toward it.

He knew that cons were always open to the charge that they were being exploited, a supposition that had proven true too many times in the past. The crew had listened to the flight recorder from the *Valparaiso Queen* and, aided by Badger's comments, came to their own conclusions.

It was obvious that there was danger out there. Danger that Captain Hoban would soon know about. Danger that impinged directly on the lives of the crew. So what would Hoban do about it?

After a while the first babble of talk died down, and Walter Glint said to Badger, "Captain Hoban will see this soon. What do you think he's going to do about it?"

"I'll tell you what he'll do," Badger said. "Nothing, that's what he'll do! Hoban is paid by the crazy doctor. The one who's always zonked out on fire. The one who's got the robot alien that killed two of our shipmates. Hoban will do what the crazy doctor tells him to do, because he's gettin' paid plenty to take the risks. But what risks are you being paid to take? Tell me that, huh?"

It was easy to get a spaceship crew angry, less so to drive them to action. Excited and desperate though they were, it still required work to goad them into taking the law into their own hands. But they were halfway there, Red thought.

Badger was starting a rebellion, but he didn't know quite what he would do next. The quirks of his own mind had perplexed him since childhood. Although he was starting this revolt, paradoxically he felt a strong sympathy for Captain Hoban. At one time he had thought he was going to help him. After all, Hoban had gotten him out of prison. But that was before he saw the tapes, before he realized the extent of the danger they were running, before he decided to do what he could to prevent it.

It's necessary to get them moving, Badger thought. Before there are more deaths.

43

"**D**r. Myakovsky? This is Captain Hoban. Do you read me?"

"The atmospherics are difficult, Captain, but I am able to understand you. Please note that just a few minutes ago we launched the pods containing Norbert and Mac and the volunteers. We have them now in distant visual range."

"Excellent, Doctor. I'm glad that part of the operation is going according to plan."

With his sharpened senses, Stan caught the note of uncertainty in his captain's voice. "Is something the matter, Captain?"

"I'm afraid it is, sir. It concerns the flight recorder that we salvaged from the wreck I reported to you about. Before saying any more, let me play it for you, sir."

"Okay, go ahead," Stan said.

44

Stan, Julie, and Gill listened in attentive silence as the tape ran. They heard the exchange between Kuhn of the *Valparaiso Queen* and Potter of the *Lancet*. Although they knew the tape was going to reveal some kind of trouble, they were unprepared for the explosion of the *Valparaiso Queen* as she received the *Lancet*'s torpedo amidships.

"Let me just make sure I've got this straight," Stan said, when the tape ended. "The recorder shows that *Lancet* blew up *Valparaiso Queen*?"

"There seems no doubt about that, sir," Hoban said.

"Well, so what?" Stan said.

"There seems good reason to believe that *Lancet* is still in the vicinity."

"And you think we are in danger?"

"Given Potter's record of violence, it is entirely possible, sir. Even likely."

"Let me point out, Captain, that we are not a defenseless freighter. We have the normal armament against piracy. If *Lancet* should attempt anything against us . . ."

"I will point that out, sir."

"To whom?"

"The representative from the crew. They are sending him to ask what I intend doing about this situation."

"Are you telling me that you played the tape for the crew?" Stan asked.

"No, sir. They took the liberty of listening to it before turning it over to me."

"Well, damn their presumption." Stan turned to Gill. "Have you ever heard anything like it?"

"Unfortunately, yes," Gill said. "The annals of space exploration are full of accounts of insubordinate crews."

Stan said to Hoban, "You must point out to them that *Lancet*'s action was illegal and exceptional. Our situation is not more hazardous because an overzealous captain performed an illegal deed. Nevertheless, I think that in view of the men's feelings we propose a special bonus to them."

"I agree, Doctor," Hoban said. "I was going to make the suggestion myself."

"Do what you can with them, Captain. We'll talk again later." Stan signed off.

"What do you think is going to happen?" Julie asked.

Gill said, "Obviously there's trouble. But I'm sure Captain Hoban can handle it."

"I hope so," Stan said. "We have a few problems of our own to take care of down here."

He turned back to the screen. The others looked now, too. They were viewing the landscape of AR-32 through Norbert's visual receptors. Norbert's head was turning, checking out the landscape as he walked forward. Ahead of him, Mac suddenly started barking and ran toward a little hill. They heard Norbert say, "Come back, Mac. Wait for me!"

Then the view began to shake as Norbert broke into a run. For a moment they could see nothing but jagged brown-and-yellow lines. Norbert was watching the uneven ground, struggling to keep his balance. Then he went over a little rise. There was a sudden red-yellow explosion and his screen went into a wild array of colors and test patterns.

"Just what we needed," Julie said. "Stan, can you clear up that view?"

"I'm working on it." Stan turned the controls. "Gill, you got any ideas?"

"Let me just try this," Gill said. His hand probed the front controls on the computer. "I think that's getting it, sir. The view is beginning to come back. . . ."

The confrontation on board ship flared up suddenly. One moment Captain Hoban was talking with the crewmen and apparently getting somewhere, then the whole thing blew up.

Badger had rapped at the door to the control room. "Sir. Permission to speak to you about a grievance."

"Now is not a very convenient time, Mr. Badger."

"No, sir. But the union laws state that grievances of a serious nature are to be settled on the spot."

"And who determines whether they're serious?"

"A duly authorized shop steward, sir. Me."

"All right," Hoban said. "Come in. Let's get this over with quickly."

Badger entered the control room followed by Glint and four other members of the crew. They looked ill at ease in the officers' area, with its soft lighting and flickering wall scanners. The helmsman stood alone in a little fenced-off enclosure to one side, scanning the ship. Two engine-room officers were also present. None of the officers was wearing sidearms. In the inquiry that later followed, Captain Hoban was faulted for this omission.

"What seems to be the problem?" Hoban asked.

"As you know, we took the liberty of viewing the

ship's log that I brought back from the rest. You've seen it, sir?"

"Of course," Hoban said.

"What did you think, sir?"

"They caught *Valparaiso Queen* napping. They won't find us so easy."

"Yes, sir. But what has that got to do with us? We're not soldiers, sir."

"We are going about our peaceful and lawful business," Hoban said, hoping it was true. "We aren't out looking for trouble. But if it comes, they'll find us ready. That is a perfectly normal situation in space, Mr. Badger."

"Sure, a crew has to be ready for trouble. But it doesn't have to go out of its way to find it."

"We don't have to run from it, either," Hoban said. "But it is an unusual situation and additional compensation would not be out of order. I will make an announcement shortly, granting the crew extra hazard pay."

"That's not good enough," Badger said. "We want some assurances now that this Potter isn't going to blow us out of space."

Hoban knew it was time to be firm. "I don't care what you want, Mr. Badger. You're a troublemaker. This situation will be resolved and we will let you know what our disposition of it is."

"That is not good enough, Captain."

"Well, it's just going to have to be good enough! You are all dismissed."

One of the engineers tugged at Captain Hoban's sleeve, trying to get his attention. Hoban turned, and saw that Glint had sneaked over to the weapons locker and helped himself to some of its contents. He had pulled out a Gauss needler. This weapon, with its big side magazine of steel slivers, had not been allotted in the standard issue, where favor was given to primitive slug throwers and the newer beam weapons. Glint may just have been fascinated by the handgun's deadly lines, and by the bulbous housing that contained the magnetic impulse equipment.

"What do you think you are doing?" Hoban shouted. "Put that down!"

One of the engineers reached for the weapon. Glint fired, perhaps by reflex. Steel splinters drove through the engineer's left shoulder. There was a moment of shocked silence. And then all hell broke loose.

The second engineer was diving for the weapons locker even as the first was going down. The first thing his hand encountered was a Wilton tangler. He swung it at Glint and pressed the release stud.

Glint managed to duck out of the way. The tangler bolt, with its rapidly expanding core of sticky plastic, soared over his head like a gray bat and wrapped itself around one of the crewmen behind him.

The man screamed and tried to tear the stuff away from himself. The tangler held him tight and began to contract.

He fell, still inextricably caught in the mess.

Suddenly it seemed that everybody in the control room had picked up a weapon. Threads of light from beam throwers glanced off metallic surfaces and glowed against the Perspex windows. Solid projectile loads ricocheted off the ship's walls, darting around like angry hornets. Explosions rocked the control room, sending up dense, greasy clouds of acrid smoke.

The second engineering officer had the presence of mind to bar the entry port, thus stopping any reinforcements coming from crew country.

Hoban ducked down behind a spare-parts case bolted to the floor. The crewmen found shelter in various parts of the control room. The officers were dug in at various locations. Most of them had managed to pick up arms.

For a while there was a strenuous exchange of small-arms fire, its intensity in that confined space enormous. Hoban thought it was like being inside a snare drum that some madman was attempting to play.

45

"It's gettin' too close for comfort!" Badger cried as his refuge in a corner of the room was zapped with blue-white flame.

"You can say that again," Glint said. "We better get out of here!"

"I'm thinking about it," Badger said. "We might need to regroup, reorganize. . . ."

Machine-gun bullets stitched across the ship's walls above their heads, showering them with fragments of metal. There was more noise as a concussion grenade, thrown by Hoban, landed just outside of effective range.

"Okay," Badger said. "Time we got out of here."

The normal egress port was barred, but an elevator to other areas stood with its doors open. Badger and Glint and the remaining crewmen beat a hasty retreat, and managed to shut the doors and get the elevator moving.

Captain Hoban, wounded in the arm by a beam weapon, refused medical attention and led the pursuit.

Most of the crew had not joined the rebellion. Those who had been wavering now decided they'd had enough.

Only Badger and Glint and their close friends, Connie Mindanao, Andy Groggins, and Min Dwin, were irrevocably committed.

All together now, they moved down one of the corridors, maintaining a rolling fire to keep the pursuing officers at a distance.

Glint was saying, "Where we going, Red? What we going to do now?"

"Shaddap," Badger said. "I've got it all doped out." He led them through the now deserted commissary and out to the rear hold. "Where we goin'?" Glint asked.

Badger didn't answer.

"There's no place to go!" Glint said.

"Don't worry, I know what I'm doing," Badger said. "We're going to get out of here."

"Out of here?" Glint looked puzzled.

"Off this ship," Badger said. "We'll take one of the escape pods and leave this death ship behind. We'll go down to AR-32."

"Yeah, okay," Glint said. Then he thought of something. "But where'll we go after that, Red? There's no civilization down there!"

"We'll then make contact with *Lancet*."

Glint turned it over in his mind. *Lancet*? Dimly he remembered that that was the name of the Bio-Pharm ship that had nuked the other ship, the *Valparaiso* something. The one they had gotten the flight recorder from.

"Red, are you sure we want to do that? Those people are killers!"

"Of course I'm sure. We're on their side now. They'll give us good money for turning our information over to them. They're going to be very interested to hear about Captain Hoban and the doctor and what they're up to. We'll be heroes."

"I don't know," Glint said.

"Trust me," Badger said. "Anyhow, what else can you do?"

"I guess you're right," Glint said. You could tell from his voice that it was a load off his mind, letting Badger make the decisions for both of them.

The others in the party weren't interested in asking questions. They wanted to be led, to be told what to do, and that was what Badger liked to do, lead people. It made him feel strong and good, until something went wrong, which, unfortunately, it did all too often. But not this time. This time he knew what he was doing.

"Come on," Badger said. "We've got to get the spare lander."

Andy Groggins said, "They're apt to be waiting for us there, Red."

"If they are," Badger said, "then so much the worse for them."

46

Stan sat in the lander and watched through Norbert's viewing screen as the robot's view of AR-32 swayed precipitously and began to slide off the screen. The lander was still vibrating after its bobsled descent through AR-32's turbulent atmosphere. Stan felt battered and bruised: sitting at the controls trying to steer all that liveliness and power to a safe landing was like going fifteen rounds with the Jolly Green Giant. Stan still wasn't sure which had won.

He fine-tuned the knobs on the viewing screen, trying to focus on the images Norbert was sending back from the surface of AR-32. The picture lurched with each of the robot's footsteps, and jumped in and out of focus.

Stan hated out-of-sync pictures like that. They seemed to trigger some long-dormant primeval recep-

tor in his brain stem. He found the oscillations of the
picture upsetting his own psychic balance.

He tried consciously to steady himself. He didn't
want to go freaking out now, but the way that picture
jumped was going to do it to him yet, and they'd have
to scrape him off the wall.

Then the picture stabilized and the focus locked in.
Stan was looking at a pile of wind-polished boulders
in various shades of orange and pink. When Norbert
raised his head, Stan could see ahead of him a narrow
valley of stone and gravel. The swirling clouds of dust
made visibility difficult after about fifty feet.

"Look at this place," Stan remarked to Julie. "We
haven't seen a green thing since we got here. I
wouldn't be surprised to learn that this place has no
natural vegetation. None on the surface, anyhow."

"If plants won't grow here," Julie remarked, "how
are the aliens able to sustain themselves?"

"I said there was no vegetation on the surface,"
Stan said. "Belowground it could be a very different
story. There's an ant species that practices underground gardening. The aliens might have followed the
same course of evolution."

"This isn't their home world, is it?" Julie asked.

"I doubt it very much. It's extremely unlikely that
they evolved here. No one knows the location of their
original home planet."

"So how'd they get here?"

"I have no idea. But however they did, they must
have brought their culture with them. And their nasty
habits."

Norbert's picture began to bounce again.

"He's going uphill," Stan said. "Have you spotted
Mac yet?"

"He ran on ahead," Julie said. "He's out of the picture now."

Gill said, "There's something in the viewer's top
right quadrant."

Stan studied it. "Yes, there is. Norbert, magnify that
quadrant."

Norbert did so. The object sharpened, resolving from a black dot to a blocky shape of lines and angles.

Gill said, "It looks like a cow skeleton, Doctor."

Norbert walked over to it. Up close, it did turn out to be a cow skeleton, though the head was missing. Norbert panned the remains. Mac had found it, too, and had pulled loose a thighbone. The animal's rib cage had been exploded outward under great pressure from something inside.

"What could have done that?" Julie asked.

"Probably a chestburner," Stan said, alluding to the young of the alien species.

"I doubt that cow creature came here naturally," Gill put in.

"Of course it didn't," Stan agreed. "If those bones could speak, I think we'd find that cow and a lot of her sisters were brought to this planet from Earth."

"As hosts for the alien young?" Julie asked.

"No doubt. That's what Neo-Pharm was up to back in those days. And as T-bone steaks for the crew of the *Lancet*."

"Speaking of *Lancet*," Julie said, "I wonder when we're going to run into them?"

"Soon enough, no doubt," Stan said. He studied the image Norbert was sending. "Hello, what's that? Another cow skeleton?"

"Lower left quadrant, Norbert," Julie said, spotting it.

Norbert turned obediently and walked over. Within twenty yards he came across the body of an alien.

It lay facedown in the gravel, its long black form alternately concealed and revealed by the windows of dust that blew incessantly across the valley floor.

At Stan's instruction, Norbert viewed it through an infrared scanner, and then an ultraviolet, to make sure the body wasn't booby-trapped.

It appeared to be free of danger. He approached and bent over it, with Mac—hair bristling and teeth barred—coming along at his heels.

"What can you see?" Stan asked.

"It is an alien," Norbert replied. "There is no doubt of that. It is perfectly motionless, but not dead. There is no sign of life, but also no sign of damage or decay. It looks almost as if it could be asleep. I'm switching to ultrasonic scanner to conduct a survey of the internal organs."

After a short delay Norbert reported again. "It's internal organs are functioning, but at a very slow rate. It's like it's asleep or unconscious. There are several more tests I could try—"

Whatever Norbert had in mind, it didn't happen, because Mac chose that moment to sense movement on the other side of a nearby hill and ran there, barking. Norbert got up and followed.

When he reached the crest of the hill and looked over, the first thing he noticed was the small, fat-bellied little spaceship, resting on its supports, nose pointed skyward, ready for takeoff.

The second thing he noticed was the aliens, a dozen or so of them, lying motionless on the ground, just like the one he had left.

And the third thing he noticed were the humans, three of them, bending over the unconscious aliens.

47

For the men from Potter's ship, the *Lancet*, it had begun as a normal day's harvesting operation. This three-man work crew had been down on the surface of AR-32 for half of their five-hour shift.

After relieving the previous crew, their first task had been to inspect the suppressor gun. It was mounted on top of the spaceship, where it could be powered by the ship's batteries.

It was a jury-rigged contraption, thrown together by a clever engineer from Potter's ship, a man with a knack for coming up with useful inventions on the spur of the moment.

Suppressors were a new technology in the continuing war against the aliens. They had resulted so far in small modules worn on a man's person. But Potter's engineer had taken the suppressor principle one step farther. He had theorized that the aliens would be sus-

ceptible to a stunning effect from certain vibratory
impulses if they were narrow-band broadcast at sufficient intensity. He based this hunch on his study of
alien anatomy. It seemed to him that the aliens had
developed a great sensitivity to electrical cycling
pulses. These could excite or stupefy them, depending
on the velocity and amplitude of the waves broadcast.
He experimented with electromagnetic bombardment.

Now, from its mount on top of the spaceship, his
cannon turned like a radar dish, blasting electronic
impulses that kept the aliens stupefied while the crew
of the *Lancet* milked them of their royal jelly.

It was not difficult duty, as Des Thomas had remarked to Skippy Holmes, with whom he was working. "I mean, if you forget they're aliens, it's much the
same as taking honey from bees."

"Big bees," Skippy said.

"Yeah, very big bees, but it's the same thing. Hey,
Slotz!" Thomas called to the third man of their crew,
who was on top of the spaceship, working with the
bracing that held the suppressor in place. No matter
how well you put those things up, the incessant wind
eventually worried them loose.

"What is it?" Slotz said, pausing with power wrench
in hand.

"You almost finished up there?"

"I need some more bracing material. A flying rock
tore some of the support away."

"We'll radio it to the ship. The next shift can bring
the stuff out. We're nearly out of here."

Slotz turned back to his work. Holmes and Thomas
took up positions around the recumbent alien. Together they heaved the big creature over on his side.
Arnold took up the scraper, working quickly around a
leg joint. He packed the sticky, light blue residue into
a canvas bag. From here, it would be transferred to a
glass container within the potbellied little harvester
ship. As Des Thomas finished milking his alien he
heard a barking sound and looked up. He was amazed
to see a large brownish-red dog running over the top

of the hill. Given the circumstances, he couldn't have
been more amazed if it had been an elephant or a
whale.

"Come here, boy," he called. "I wonder where
your—"

It was at that instant that Norbert came striding
over the crest of the hill and down into the harvesting
area.

There was a brief tableau: three human crewmen
frozen like dummies, Norbert striding forward like a
fury from the deepest hell, and Mac, all innocence,
barking and capering along like he was on an outing.

Holmes came unfrozen first. "One of them's come
awake!" he shouted. "Get that sucker!"

Slotz got off the top of the spaceship rapidly. The
three men dived for their weapons. These were always kept handy because, although no alien had
woken up suddenly like this before, no one really
trusted the new suppressor technology—especially
when you took into account how goofy looking its in-
ventor was.

Holmes got his hands on the carbine he had
propped against a rock outcropping. He slipped off
the safety, aimed hastily, and pulled the trigger. A
stream of caseless forty-caliber slugs streaked toward
Norbert, who was no longer there to receive them.

The threat toward him instantly pushed Norbert
into predator mode. You could almost hear the new
program click into place.

Softslugs bouncing off his carapace, Norbert slid
under the fusillade of projectiles from Des's Gauss
needler. A fragmentation grenade bounced off his
chest and exploded as it was bouncing away. Norbert
was showered with white-hot fragments of metal, but
they didn't have the force to penetrate his metallized
hide.

Although he wasn't hurt, Norbert was not pleased.
Skippy Holmes was the closest, and the crewman just
had time to scream as Norbert hooked his face at the

temples with two curved talons and tore it off in one economical move.

It was a moment of gratuitous horror, though Norbert didn't view it that way. Just doin' my job, sir.

Skippy buried the raw meat of his face in his hands and fell to the ground, gurgling, blood bubbling from his shattered skin. He didn't suffer for long; Norbert's spurred foot hooked out the man's stomach and a good selection of his internal organs.

Seeing this, Chuck Slotz gagged and took to his heels, sprinting toward the harvester's open entry port, closely followed by Des.

Norbert came racing after them, and almost made the entry port. It closed in his face, and Norbert slammed into it with a force that shook the harvester on its six slender legs and caused the radarlike suppressor apparatus on its roof to topple over and fall to the ground in a crackle of sparks.

Slowly, very slowly at first, the aliens lying on the ground began to stir.

48

Gill gasped as the scene of carnage was played over Norbert's visual receptors and relayed to the screen aboard the *Dolomite*'s lander.

Norbert, standing in front of the harvester's sealed door, was saying, "I am awaiting further orders, Dr. Myakovsky."

"Yes," Stan said. "Just stand by for a moment." He turned to Gill. "What's the matter? Why are you looking that way?"

"I—I wasn't prepared for the violence, Doctor. I had no idea Norbert was programmed to kill."

"How could you have thought otherwise? What do you think we're out here for? A sight-seeing trip? Gill, we're all programmed to kill."

"Yes, Dr. Myakovsky. If you say so."

"You, too, are programmed to kill, are you not?"

"In defense of human lives, yes, I suppose I am. It

is just that I didn't know we were going to exercise that option so . . . lightly."

"We're here to get rich," Stan said. "Whatever it takes. Right, Julie?"

"That's right, Stan," Julie said, then turned to the artificial man. "You'll share in the money we get, too. Even an artificial man can use money, right?"

"All sentient beings need money," Gill said dryly.

"That's right," Julie said. "Anyhow, we're in it now, and it's us or them. You know what Potter will do if he finds us? The same thing he did to the *Valparaiso Queen*."

Gill nodded but didn't answer.

"Think about it, Gill," Stan said. "Don't get humanitarian on us too soon." He paused, then added, "If it's really against your principles, perhaps you'd like to wait in the back bay until this phase of the operation is over? I wouldn't want you to do anything foolish."

"Do not worry about me, sir," Gill said. "I have no sentiment about matters of killing. Sentiment was not programmed into me. I was surprised, that is all, but now I understand. I am ready to do whatever is necessary to protect you and Miss Julie."

"Glad to hear it." Stan wiped his forehead. He looked like he himself was having a little trouble getting used to killing. Only Julie showed no signs of upset.

Gill hesitated. "Sir, we have no visual contact with the crew volunteers."

"Damn it!" Stan said. "Does everything have to go wrong at the same time? Norbert! Can you get into the harvester?"

"The door is locked, Doctor," Norbert said.

"I doubt it's a very advanced locking mechanism. Give me a close-up of the lock."

Norbert leaned forward, focused on the locking mechanism and switched to the X-ray mode.

Stan studied the picture for a moment. "It looks like pretty standard stuff. Tell you what, just rip off the keypad and you'll be able to turn the handle manually."

"Yes, sir."

"Better hurry up about it. It would be best to prevent those guys from getting in touch with Potter."

49

Inside the harvester, Slotz and Thomas fell over each other getting to the radio. Thomas got there first and flipped the transmission switch

"*Lancet?* Come in, *Lancet!*"

Slotz, standing just behind Thomas, heard a banging sound on the entry port and made sure he had his carbine.

"Hurry up, Thomas! I don't know if the door will hold him!"

"I'm trying," Thomas said. "But I've come up with nothing so far."

"The antenna!" Slotz said. "It came down with the suppressor gun when the alien slammed into the ship."

"That's just great," Thomas said. "So we can't transmit. And it's two hours before the next shift comes down."

"Maybe we can hold out." Slotz found a fresh magazine in his pocket, ejected the spent one from his carbine, and snapped the new one into place.

The hammering suddenly stopped. The men heard a sound of metal ripping.

"He's tearing off the lock cover!" Slotz cried.

"Nobody can do that," Thomas said.

"Trust me," Slotz muttered. "He's doing it."

There was silence for a moment. Then a clicking sound.

"He's through the cover! He's working the unlocking mechanism!" Slotz shouted.

"Whaddaya want me to do about it?" Thomas said. Into the radio's dead transmitter he shouted, "Mayday, Mayday!"

Then the door slammed open with great force and Norbert was coming in, a towering black fury. Slotz tried to level the carbine, managed to get off one round that glanced off Norbert's shoulder and ricocheted around the cabin like an angry bee. Then Norbert was on him. The robot alien caught the back of Slotz's head, leaned forward, mouth open, second jaws extending through his slavering mouth. Slotz, eyes wide and wild, tried to pull himself out of the way, but there was no budging Norbert's grip. The second jaws shot out like a piston and smashed through Slotz's open mouth and continued through, snapping the man's spine like a dry stick.

Seeing what had happened, Thomas scrambled away from the radio. He had a pulse rifle in his hand and he triggered it. A tongue of brilliant light licked out against Norbert's chest. It had no apparent effect on the robot, but at that close range the heat was reflected back into Thomas's face. He shrieked as his hair caught fire. And then Norbert was on him, two taloned hands on his shoulders, hind legs raking the man's middle with razor-sharp claws. Simultaneously fried and eviscerated, Thomas fell to the floor, dead before he landed.

In the ensuing silence, Mac came trotting into the

harvester, looked around, seemed unimpressed by the blood and gore that coated the walls, and trotted up to Norbert.

The robot alien patted him once on the head, then said, "That's all for now, Mac. I have to report."

The interior of the harvester was a shambles. There were bits and pieces of crewmen scattered all over the struts and inner bracing members. Bright arterial blood lay in puddles on the metal floor. Blood lapped at the corners of the room, and the self-cleaning units were clogged with it.

Mac sniffed around, whimpered, then barked excitedly. He was getting a lot of mixed signals. Finally he decided something was wrong, but he'd have to let somebody else figure it out. He found a corner and lay down with his muzzle on his paws. Norbert came along behind him, stopped, and surveyed the damage he had caused.

Stan, back on the lander, was following visually. His voice was low. He was coaching Norbert.

"You're doing fine, Norbert. We want to check out the whole ship for possible damage. You're really quite violent once you get started, aren't you?"

"Not intentionally, Doctor."

Julie leaned over Stan's shoulder. "What's that in the background, Stan?"

"I'm not sure.... Norbert, make a hundred-and-eighty-degree turn and do a slow pan. That's it. Now freeze. And magnify. Okay, freeze it right there. And correct the color. Good!"

Julie said, "Plastic storage units. Each of them would hold—what? Five liters?"

"More like seven," said Gill.

"There are hundreds of them stacked there," Stan said. "More on the other side of the hold."

"Are they royal jelly?" Julie asked. "Can we be absolutely sure of that?"

Stan replied, "There really seems no doubt. What

else would they be filled with? Cloverleaf honey? The harvester is packed with the stuff. They must have been just about ready to take off back to *Lancet.*"

"Good thing we got here when we did." Julie laughed. "They've done our work for us, Stan. We're rich!"

Stan grinned. "We'd better not start trying to spend it just yet. Norbert, have you completed your assessment of the damage yet?"

"Yes, Dr. Myakovsky."

"Any problems?"

"I'm afraid that in the fight this unit here was destroyed." Norbert indicated the interior suppressor gear, which was strewn around the cabin, most of it broken into fragments of crystal and plastic.

"Ah well," Stan said, "Can't make an omelette without breaking eggs, as some famous man once remarked. Do you know who said that, Gill?"

"I'm afraid I don't," Gill said.

"And here I thought you knew everything. Well, well ..." Unexpectedly he began to giggle.

"Stan," Julie said, "what's the matter?"

Stan pulled himself together. "Whom the gods would destroy they first make mad. I don't suppose you know who said that, either. Well, never mind. Of all the stuff you could have destroyed, Norbert, I'm afraid you picked the worst. I think that's the interior equipment for the ultrasonic suppressor."

"Are you certain?" Julie asked. "How can we know for sure?"

"There ought to be a serial number here somewhere." Stan examined the bits of twisted metal. "Yes, as I thought. Now we need to go to the next step."

"Is that difficult?" Julie asked.

"Easy enough ... Norbert, give me a picture through one of the portholes."

Outside, Stan could see a yellowish-brown haze with dark shapes moving through it. Half the aliens were up, the others were reviving swiftly. They moved sluggishly at first, then with increasing vigor, toward the harvester.

"Clear up the focus," Stan snapped.

"Sorry, Doctor . . ." With the focus cleared, Stan could see the distinct dark alien shapes milling around outside the ship.

"Okay," Stan said. "The suppressor is kaput and the aliens are awake. That's okay. Basically, our job is over. We've got the harvester. It was a little messy, but we got it. We need only pilot it up to the *Dolomite* and get out of here. Norbert, check the controls."

The robot alien moved to the control panel. After a moment he said, "I'm afraid we've got trouble, Doctor."

Stan could see for himself through Norbert's visual receptors. The battle inside the harvester had wrecked some of the controls.

"Oh, Stan," Julie said, "can Norbert fly that thing out of there?"

"Sure, if conditions were right," Stan said. "But I'm afraid it's not going to be as easy as that. The controls are all screwed up."

"Can't he fix them?"

Stan shook his head. "Sure, given time, but we don't have much of that. First we're going to have to get into communication with the *Dolomite* again. Gill, have you had any luck in raising Captain Hoban?"

"I haven't gotten him yet, sir," Gill said. "Something serious seems to have happened to the *Dolomite*."

"That's just great," Stan said. "I wish he'd call."

"He will," Gill affirmed. "I know Captain Hoban. He would make contacting us his first priority."

"Well, it gives us a little time. A chance to do something I've long wanted to do."

Julie looked at him. "Stan, what are you talking about?"

"I want to take a look inside that hive." He looked hard at Gill, as if daring him to challenge him. Gill felt momentarily uncomfortable and glanced at Julie, who gave an almost imperceptible shrug. Gill reminded himself that it was difficult to assess the situation and impossible to pass judgment on humans.

"Just as you say, sir," Gill said at last.

"Norbert, are you standing by?" Stan demanded.

"I am, Dr. Myakovsky."

"Okay. I take it all your systems are functioning properly?"

"All my readings are in the green," Norbert reported.

"Is your suppressor working properly?"

Norbert checked. "It is, sir."

"And Mac's?"

Norbert bent over the dog. "It is functioning correctly."

"Then turn it off and open the harvester port."

"Sir?"

"Norbert, are you having synapse failure? Didn't you hear me?"

"It is such an unusual order, Doctor, that I wanted to be certain I understood it correctly. When I turn off Mac's collar, that will render him visible to the aliens."

"That's exactly what I had in mind," Stan said. "We're going to make the aliens a little present of Mac."

"Give him to the aliens?"

"That's right. You aren't going soft on me, are you, Norbert?"

"No, sir. But is it necessary?"

"Of course it is. They'll probably take Mac directly to the queen. They give the queen all the best stuff first, don't they?"

"I think so, sir. So it is reported in the literature."

"That's right," Stan said, with a laugh. "For a moment I forgot you weren't one yourself."

Gill and Julie looked at each other. Gill frowned slightly and looked away. Julie pursed her lips. She didn't much like what was happening. But what the hell, it was no business of hers.

Stan explained. "Mac will represent food to them. A tasty little morsel fit for a king. Only in this case it's a queen. That's who they'll take Mac to. And you, my dear robotic friend, will follow them. Protected by your own suppressor, they won't even see you. Without suspecting a thing, they'll lead you through the labyrinth to the royal birthing chamber. Through your eyes I'll get the first pictures ever taken of the queen of this hive. I'll be doing a unique service to science. That's worth any number of little dogs like Mac. He's just a common mutt. But you, Norbert, are unique."

Stan turned to face Julie and Gill. Light glinted off his glasses. His face was drawn. His voice, high and strained, rose as he asked, "Does anyone here have any objections?"

Gill looked away and didn't answer. Julie looked faintly annoyed as she said, "Give them Mac or a kennelful of mutts, it makes no difference to me. But would you mind telling me, just to satisfy my own curiosity, why are you doing this?"

"It's the only way I can be sure of getting Norbert into the hive quickly without him having to spend God knows how long looking for a way in. The outside of the nest is sealed against the weather, as you might have noticed. Did you check that out? The aliens must have a whole system of tunnels for getting in or out. There must be a hundred miles of tunnel in something that big. This way I'll have Norbert lay down an electronic path."

Gill said, "What purpose will that serve, Doctor?"

"Two at least," Stan said. "First, with Norbert videotaping as he goes, we'll provide science with an invaluable record of life inside an alien hive. And second, we can come back here whenever we like to collect more jelly."

"Now you're talking, Stan," Julie said. "I knew you weren't just antidog."

"Of course not. As a matter of fact, I'll have Norbert try to rescue Mac when they've reached the queen's chamber."

"That might not be possible," Gill said.

Stan shrugged. "Let's get going. Norbert, do it!"

50

"Nope," Morrison said. "I can't get a reading."

"Let me try," said Larrimer. He fiddled with the controls. But it showed no trace of the first pod, the one with Norbert and Mac aboard.

Almost as soon as the five volunteers from the crew had entered the second pod, they lost visual contact with the first, and found themselves flying blind into a whirling sandstorm. Overhead, purple-black ranks of clouds had formed, and soon their visibility was further cut by heavy, driving rain. After the rain let up, the ground below steamed, and a thick mist arose from the land.

Definitely not flying weather. But the pod was equipped with autopilot and a landing program. Their direction finder was slaved to the first pod's beacon. All they had to do was sit tight and the pod would take them to Norbert.

In theory.

In practice, the autopilot was unable to compensate for the driving wind, a wind that roared loudly enough to be heard inside the pod. The autopilot's little computer had all it could do to keep them from piling up on the ground below. It brought them down safely, then the comedy of errors began.

First Larrimer, who had been entrusted with the radio, found out that it would not transmit or receive. Not enough power, maybe, or maybe interference from the electrical storm overhead. Maybe it had even taken one bang too many during their hectic descent.

"Well," Morrison said, "they can probably find us even if we can't find them."

"Are you sure of that?" Skysky rubbed his bald head nervously.

"Sure I'm sure." Morrison spoke with a confidence he didn't feel. "They'd want to retrieve the pod, anyhow. Those things cost money."

Eka Nu looked up. "No," he said. "Pods are considered expendable. So are crew, sometimes."

Not a cheering thought.

"Anyhow," Morrison said, "all we have to do is find Norbert. The professor is not about to abandon his favorite. toy."

That cheered them up a little. Morrison brought out an electron detector and tried to tune it to the trail Norbert was supposed to leave. The little machine buzzed steadily, but showed no sign of a direction. Morrison turned it in every direction. It still didn't indicate anything.

"Maybe the hull shielding is stopping the signal," Morrison said. "We've got to go outside anyway, so maybe it'll be better there."

"Go outside in this?" Larrimer asked, jerking his thumb at the mist that rolled in a slow wave across the plain.

"We can't stay here," Morrison said. "If they did try to find us, they wouldn't stand a chance. Our only hope is to find Norbert and await pickup with him and the dog."

"Great," Styson exclaimed. "What about if we run into aliens?"

"We've got our weapons," Morrison said, "and we have suppressors. What more could you ask for?"

The others grumbled, but it was obvious that they had to make a move. First Morrison told them to check their weapons, and there was a clatter of metal on metal as they shoved magazines into their carbines and set the plasma burners on standby.

"Ready?" Morrison asked. "Okay, here we go."

He cracked the hatch. It opened smoothly, and they stepped out one by one onto the plain.

The first thing they discovered was that they couldn't see worth shit. It wasn't quite as bad as that, actually. About three feet visibility, Styson estimated.

Cautiously they stepped out of the pod and tested out the land. It was solid underfoot. Moving only a few feet away from the pod, they formed a circle around the electron detector and tried to get a reading. The thing buzzed, and the needle swooped erratically, but there was no definite and unambiguous signal. At last Morrison decided to follow the biggest needle deflection and hope for the best.

"It's this way," he stated. He didn't know where he was going, but he knew they had to go somewhere. He was beginning to think this volunteering hadn't been such a good idea. The bonus had sounded good, but you don't get to spend it if you're dead.

In single file, staying close to each other, the volunteers moved across the plain. All five men had weapons at the alert. The mist billowed around them like white waves in a sea of clouds, sometimes covering them completely, which was like walking through a sort of impalpable white cotton candy. Sometimes the mist would begin to dissipate, and then the men could see each other's heads and shoulders, rising ghostlike out of the whiteness, with wisps of mist clinging to them. But then the mist rose again and buried them.

Morrison, in the lead, was following a compass course he had set after taking his best guess as to what the electron detector was indicating. It didn't occur to him that it might not mean anything at all. That would be too unfair.

Styson, bringing up the rear, kept on turning around and trying to look behind him. He was sure something big and terrible was going to materialize out of the mist and snap him up. It was a crazy, kid's sort of thinking—he knew that—but he couldn't control his fear. His hands tightened on his carbine. He wished he was holding his harmonica. That always gave him confidence. But it was in his pocket, because he needed both hands to hold his carbine. Now his fingers tightened on the weapon, and he checked to make sure all safeties were off. He missed his harmonica, but he knew it was a lot more important to hold on to the weapon. Stood to reason . . .

And then the mists closed down again and the men lost all visibility. Styson staggered along, carbine held out in front of him like a blindman's cane, trying to peer into the numbingly white world in which he found himself. What a rotten job this had turned into!

And then he bumped into something.

Styson stumbled, then regained his balance. Larrimer had been next in line. He called out, "Larrimer, is that you?"

There was no answer. Whoever was ahead of him was just becoming visible, a dark shadow in the pale glimmer of the surrounding mist.

"Whoever it is, try to keep the pace up," Styson said. "We need to get out of here. . . . Who is that, anyway?"

He reached out and poked what he thought was Larrimer on what he thought was Larrimer's shoulder. There was a movement, and the shape ahead of him turned. The mists started to dissipate, and Styson saw something too tall to be Larrimer or any other man,

something so tall that he had to crane his neck back
to see it.

No mistaking what it was now. It was an alien, and
there was something about its quick, questing movements that decided Styson that this was not Norbert.
This was the real thing.

He tried to get his carbine up, but the sling had
somehow gotten tangled around his left arm. And the
massive creature was too close to him, anyhow. He
closed his eyes and made a quick, fervent prayer.

Moments later he opened his eyes. The alien had
walked right past him, brushing against him as it did
so. It continued to move away, still looking around as
if seeking something.

"Hey, fellas!" Styson called out. "We got company!"

The men ahead of him were aware of this. They
had spotted aliens before Styson did, but had kept
quiet in order not to alert the creatures. Aliens were
primarily visual hunters, but no one knew to what extent they could also use their hearing. This didn't
seem the time to find out. Now, as Styson caught up
with them, they shushed him into silence.

Morrison continued to lead. The mist thinned, and
soon they could see black shapes moving through
white cotton. Aliens, moving in the same general direction the men were going, walking singly or in small
groups. They passed the men and paid no apparent attention to them. One went by within a foot of
Morrison and never turned its head. Morrison was
starting to feel a modest confidence. . . . And then it
happened.

The mist closed down again. The men fumbled
their way forward, fighting to keep their balance, and
then there was a loud gurgling sound followed by silence.

"What was that?" Morrison asked.

"Damned if I know," Larrimer replied.

"Is anyone missing? Call out your names, but not
too loud."

Three men responded to Morrison's request, but the fourth, Skysky, did not answer.

Morrison risked shouting. "Skysky? Are you there, Skysky?"

Nothing.

"Watch yourselves, boys," Morrison said. "I think we got trouble."

It made no sense, Morrison thought, but it seemed like an alien must have grabbed Skysky, broken his neck before he could do any more than gurgle, and taken his body away.

The suppressors were supposed to hide them from the aliens.

But Skysky was definitely gone.

So, one of two things. Either Skysky's suppressor had failed, or he had walked right into an alien, and that close, it had been able to figure out what Skysky was.

A six-foot breeding organism.

Don't think about that.

"You gotta really watch hard," Morrison said, as if the men needed to be told. "Skysky must have gotten careless. The mist is lifting again. Maybe we can find someplace to hide."

The mist dissipated swiftly. The men could see about fifty yards on all sides of them. The visibility continued to improve, and Morrison told them to fan out. The men complied and, following Morrison's lead, continued to move steadily toward something that looked like a brown breast on the horizon.

They were passing groups of aliens, but now were able to keep a better distance. The aliens continued to ignore them.

Until one alien stopped ignoring them.

It stopped in midstride, swiveled, turning its huge head slowly, and then locked in on something. It turned toward it and began to run.

When Styson looked to his left, he saw an alien coming straight for him—not for anyone else in the group, but him. He threw up his rifle and fired. The caseless round broke through the alien's shoulder, almost severing the arm at the shoulder joint. It just seemed to make the creature angrier than it already was. Aliens start out angry and build from there.

Ignoring the arm dangling from its side, it grabbed Styson around the waist with its good arm. Styson screamed and tried to get the carbine into line. The alien opened its jaws. The secondary jaws looked out for a moment, then rammed into Styson's face.

Styson had tried to duck at the last instant, so the secondary jaw caught him in the left eye rather than the mouth. The tooth-lined mouth punched through to Styson's brain, and when it withdrew, it took a fair amount of gray matter along with it.

And then the alien turned away from Styson and revolved its head again.

The other four men had frozen into position, not daring to move while the alien was prowling around Styson, unable to shoot without hitting their comrade.

It turned out that shooting wasn't necessary. Not at that moment, anyhow. The alien turned and loped away, rejoining the group it had left earlier.

Morrison got the men moving again.

51

Their breathing space was short. Aliens continued to stream past the three crewmen. But now, some of those closest to the humans were slowing down, turning their heads this way and that. Morrison prayed that they had stiff necks or something. But no such luck. Two of the aliens turned away from the stream and started toward the group. After a moment a third one joined them.

"Shit!" Morrison said. There was no doubt where that bunch were going. Straight at him. He started firing when they were still thirty yards off, then pushed the selector and fired a grenade. In fact, he fired off all his grenades, something he hadn't meant to do, but he wasn't used to these weapons, which were military style. The grenades went lobbing in the air, and most of them came down behind the aliens. Morrison's last one hit an alien in the chest and, a moment later, exploded in its face. The alien was thrown backward by the force of the explosion. He picked himself up, but his face, such as it was, was ruined. His mouth was gaping open, and through his jaws protruded the smaller secondary jaws. They hung limp at the end of their muscular tube. The tube appeared to have been bitten through. The alien was not out of it yet, though. Shaking its head, it moved again toward Morrison, limping but still deadly.

Morrison didn't have time for that one yet. The two closer ones were coming up fast. He took the one to his left, blasting caseless projectiles into its chest. He could hear firing near him. It was Eka Nu, who had moved up to join him. Farther away, Larrimer tried to join them, but a long black arm came out of nowhere and caught him in midstride. He jerked around like a trout on a hook as the alien brought him close to his face. Then it released the facehugger, and Larrimer fell to the ground, moaning and twitching. The alien hoisted him to his shoulder. Larrimer knew he was going to have the worst death he could have imagined, hanging just barely alive from a wall in the hive while a newborn grew within him, getting ready to eat its way out.

Morrison and Eka Nu had their hands full with the two aliens, who were coming at them at a full charge. Morrison saw his projectiles slam into the alien, and still it kept coming. He fired until the magazine was empty. He fired the last rounds with his eyes closed. When he opened them, the alien was dead at his feet. Eka Nu hadn't been so lucky, however. The alien on his side had kept on coming on all fours, had grabbed Eka Nu around the shoulders, hugged the crewman to him, then turned him. The two stared face-to-face for a moment, then the facehugger hit and Eka Nu knew no more.

Morrison found himself alone. He was panting, exhausted, trembling. The guys were all gone. He looked around. He didn't see any aliens. Maybe they had left. Maybe he could still find . . .

Then something moved on the ground. It was the

alien he had winged. He was still coming, crawling. And behind him, half a dozen others were starting over.

Yes, Morrison thought, I guess you could say the suppressors had failed. No other explanation.

I did the best I could, he thought as he turned the carbine so its muzzle faced him. He preferred a slug in the mouth to a facehugger.

The harvester's entry lock gave way under repeated blows from the outside. The door flew open. Big-bodied, ghastly, and weird, three aliens crowded into it, their eager, evil faces turning at all angles on short powerful necks, checking out the place, alert for danger. They ignored Norbert, protected by his suppressor. The dead crewmen from the harvester required no attention.

Stan, watching from the lander, said, "All right, Norbert. Do it now."

Norbert lifted Mac, removed his collar into which a suppressor was built, and handed him to one of the aliens. The alien showed no surprise, quietly accepted Mac from Norbert's arms.

Handling the dog carefully, the alien turned, left the ship, and joined the others outside. Then, as if in response to an inaudible signal, they all started marching across the plain. Stan, Gill, and Julie watched on their screen as Norbert fell into line behind the group of aliens carrying Mac. Watching from the lander through Norbert's vision sensors was uncannily like being within the robot alien himself, feeling his body sway and move as it negotiated the uneven ground. Stan had to adjust the audio because the wind out there on AR-32's plain had risen swiftly after the mist dissipated and now was shrieking like a banshee, pushing and pulling against the line of aliens, slowing but not stopping them as sand was alternately pushed into mounds in front of them and then suddenly scoured away.

They were moving toward the hive, which was now and then revealed as Norbert changed the angle of his vision from the ground immediately in front of him to the hazy horizon line. The hive was still quite a long way away, perhaps a hundred yards, when the aliens stopped and began looking around.

Stan leaned close to the screen and stared but he couldn't tell what they were looking for: a specially coded pheromone signal, perhaps, because they fanned out and continued searching, their heads turning back and forth like hounds following a scent.

At last one of them found something. A silent signal seemed to pass between him and the others, and they all moved together to a piece of ground that looked no different to Stan's eyes than any other. Rooting in the soil, the leading alien dislodged a large flat piece of stone, revealing a shallow tunnel leading into the earth.

The tunnel sloped downward for perhaps twenty feet, then leveled out. It had been made with some care. The light, friable soil was held in by flat rocks, some of which were highly phosphorescent.

"Look at how the roof is shored up," Stan remarked to Gill.

"That's more technical skill than we ever gave the aliens credit for."

"It is possible, sir," said Gill, "that their tunnel-building abilities are genetic, as is the case with the ants you have studied."

"Yes," Stan said. "Can you see what they're doing, Ari?" He lifted the cybernetic ant on his fingertip and moved his hand toward the screen. "These are like big cousins of yours, aren't they?"

Ari raised his head, but it was impossible to tell whether or not he was thinking anything.

Down in the tunnel, Norbert was reporting that the passageway was widening as they moved closer to the hive. Soon other branchings appeared as the aliens moved; as if by instinct, making their way through the increasingly complex maze without hesitation.

"Norbert, you've been laying down an electronic trail, haven't you?" Stan asked.

"Yes, Doctor. Ever since we were on the outside of this tunnel. But I'm not completely sure the job is getting done."

"I hope it is. It could come in handy. Don't you think so, Julie?"

"Sure, Stan," Julie concurred. "But I don't understand why you're sending Norbert in there. We've already got what we came for."

"You mean the harvester full of royal jelly? Yes, that was the purpose of our mission, and we have accomplished it. But we still have some time on our hands until Captain Hoban gets back into communication. So why not choose this moment for the advancement of science? It will profit all of mankind to know what the inside of a hive really looks like."

"That's true enough, Stan," Julie said. "I didn't know you cared that much about science, though."

"Julie, there's a lot I care for that I don't put into words. You ought to know that."

"I guess I do, Stan. You're not really interested in getting rich from this mission, are you?"

"Not as interested as you, my dear. But that is because I may not have much *tiempo para gastarlo*, as the Spanish say. But doing this is better than staying home trying to argue the doctors into giving me a better prognosis. At least here I can be with you, and I can't tell you how much that means to me."

Stan coughed, self-conscious for a moment, then glanced again at the screen. "Norbert is getting deeper into the hive and we still haven't heard from Captain Hoban. I think this might be a good moment for me to take a brief nap." Without further ado, he got up and went to the cot in the lander's rearmost living area.

Julie and Gill watched for a while in silence as Norbert, on the screen, continued to penetrate deeper into the hive. At last Julie said, "What did it mean, that thing he said in Spanish?"

"Tiempo para gastarlo," said Gill. "It means 'time to enjoy it.' "

Julie shook her head. "Stan's got a lot of knowledge."

"Yes," Gill said. "But perhaps not much time."

There were four crew members with Red Badger as he set up his next plan. Walter Glint was there, of course, and Connie Mindanao, limping from a beamer scorch in the side, and Andy Groggins and Min Dwin, both unwounded. That was a pretty good force to match against the five or six loyal men Captain Hoban probably had available.

That was the good news. On the bad side, they had been forced back to a rear area of the ship. It would be difficult to mount an attack through the corridors, with Hoban and his officers now armed and ready for them. And probably the rest of the crew would come in on Hoban's side, now that the first attempt at a takeover had failed. Things might have been different if Hoban hadn't responded so quickly. Badger, who had thought the captain to be a burned-out case, had to reevaluate the situation now.

Red was annoyed that his first plan hadn't succeeded. His people hadn't moved fast enough, and Hoban had been unexpectedly decisive. Now the best move was to get off the *Dolomite* and plan to contact Potter on the *Lancet.* Trouble was, getting off the ship wasn't going to be quite as simple as he'd like it to be.

There was just one lander left, the backup, now that Myakovsky and his people had gone to the surface of AR-32. It was sure to be guarded. Captain Hoban would have radioed the crew guarding the rear facilities, putting them on the alert. How many were there? Two or three, including the sergeant of the guards? Badger knew they'd have to get around or through them somehow.

"When we reach the storage bay, no firing until I

say so," Badger told the others. "I've got a little plan that just might work."

"Whatever you say, Red," said Glint.

Badger led them down the gleaming aluminum corridor, over deep-piled carpeting that seemed to soak up sound, past flickering lighting fixtures. The ever-present hum of the ship's machinery sounded in the walls like somnolent wasps. The only thing that told of the recent action was a faint smell of propellant and burned insulation in the otherwise antiseptic air; that and the labored sound of Connie Mindanao's breathing as she waited for the antipain shot to take effect.

At last they reached the transverse corridor that led to the pod bay. A faint hum warned Badger that all was not well here. He looked carefully and noted the violet-edged nimbus that extended from the walls.

"They've turned on the beam restraints," Badger said.

Glint came up from the rear and examined the situation. "They sure did, Red, but they don't have them on full."

Badger looked again. "You're right, Walt. They must not be running full power through the ship's net. Probably because of the damage we caused in the control room. Those beams should be visible to a distance of six inches from the side of the wall."

Min Dwin looked the situation over and reported, "Their circle of interdiction will extend beyond their visible range."

"Sure it will," Badger said. "But there'll still be a hole we can get through."

The entrance to the corridor was like a tall O. The violet flame burned on all sides of it, surrounding it entirely, but leaving the middle of the hole open.

"We'll have to dive through," Glint said. "Make sure not to touch the sides or the bottom."

"Shouldn't be too difficult," Badger said.

"Maybe not for you," Connie Mindanao said. "But

I've been wounded. How am I going to take a good jump through?"

A cruel little light glittered in Red Badger's eyes. "We'll take care of it for you, won't we, Glint? Grab her other arm."

Although she protested, the two big crewmen grabbed Connie. They swung her back and forth and, on the command from Badger, threw her headfirst through the corridor. Connie gave a shriek of protest as her foot trailed in the violet glow, but landed safe on the far side.

"Now the rest of us," Badger said. "The lander is just around the next bend. We're almost there!"

52

"Do you ever get sick of us so-called real people?" Julie asked suddenly.

Gill looked up, startled. He had been intent on the screen, watching as Norbert followed the group of aliens through the tunnels. Gill wanted to be ready to report to Dr. Myakovsky when the doctor awoke from his nap. But Julie's question seemed worthy of serious thought and he gave it, though not taking his eyes off the screen that showed Norbert's progress.

"I'm afraid," Gill said at last, "that I do not understand the question. It implies a precondition: that there is something in human behavior that I might get sick of. To what are you referring, Julie?"

"Wow!" Julie laughed. "I didn't expect to get that much out of you. But it isn't an answer."

"I am asking you to define your question, Miss Lish."

"You know very well what I mean," Julie said.

Gill found himself caught up and bewildered by the complexities of human thinking. It seemed to him that Julie was saying one thing and meaning another. The technical semanticists who had programmed his response bank had not given sufficient attention to the problem of ambiguity. Perhaps they couldn't solve it.

Gill and Julie looked at each other for a few moments in silence. Then Gill spoke. "You are referring, perhaps, to the fact that human actions are not always logical in terms of advantage? That they sometimes appear to be downright self-defeating?"

"Okay, that's one way of saying it," Julie said. "What do you think of that?"

Again Gill paused before answering. "I can only believe that illogic is essential to being human, since it is the one thing we synthetics are not capable of."

"You can't go against logic and programming, is that it?"

"It is, Miss Lish."

Julie didn't answer at once. Presently she reached out and took Gill's hand. Startled, the synthetic man let it go limp. Julie held it like she had never seen a hand before. She studied it, turning it slowly this way and that.

"What an amazing piece of construction this is." She marveled. "How perfectly the skin has been rendered and textured. It's hard to believe that anything as cunning as this could belong to someone not human."

"Yet so it is," Gill said.

"Is it? Or are you just being modest? A very human trait, I assure you."

"I don't know," Gill muttered. "One thing I do know is, Dr. Myakovsky loves you very much."

"Yes," Julie said, "I think he does. It's why he's here, isn't it?"

"I believe it is, Miss Lish."

"But why then am I here?"

"I do not know," Gill said. He hesitated. "It is a difficult way to get rich."

"Do you know of any easy ways?" Julie asked. "Do you know any better ways to pass your time on Earth than doing what I'm doing now?"

Gill shook his head. "I know nothing about these things."

Julie frowned and let his hand drop. "I like you, Gill, though you're very naive about some things. Look, Norbert seems to have reached the queen's chamber."

"You're right," Gill said. "I'll go wake up Dr. Myakovsky."

"I appear to be in an anteroom deep in the middle of the hive," Norbert reported. "I can see the queen's chamber just beyond. These surfaces and angles resemble nothing in my memory bank, Doctor. They seem to have been constructed according to a completely alien system. But that would stand to reason, wouldn't it?"

"You're doing fine," Stan said over the radio. "I just woke up and I'm pleased to see your progress. None of the aliens has sensed yet that you're not one of them?"

"No, Doctor. Though their examinations grow more stringent the deeper we go into the hive."

"I think we have them foxed," Stan said, sounding very pleased with himself. "This anteroom you're in appears to be an interesting place. Can you fix the focus? I can't make out what's on the walls."

"They are large containers," Norbert said. "They appear to be made from a waxy substance similar in molecular makeup to royal jelly. They appear to be filling those containers with jelly."

"Might they be storing water?" Stan asked.

"I don't believe so," Norbert said. "The containers seem to be holding liquids of slightly different colors and densities. The aliens grow quite excited when they go near these containers. They have to be urged by what I take to be the guards to move on. I think that these containers hold royal jelly deposited by certain especially potent queens or queen types. These may be more efficacious than the common run of the jelly, and be prized by the queen accordingly."

"With your equipment," Stan asked, "can you ascertain which is the purest?"

"There's no difficulty in that, Doctor."

"Then draw me off a sample. This sounds like the pure royal jelly I need."

After a moment Norbert said, "It is done."

"Good," Stan returned. "We'll meet up soon. Bring the sample with you. What are they doing with Mac?"

"The alien holding him has brought him into the queen's chamber. He is offering him to the queen."

"That is the queen ahead? The image is not distinct."

"There is a diffracting vapor in this room, Doctor. It is difficult to make out anything clearly. Take it easy, Mac!"

Stan said, "Why did you speak to the dog?"

"To get him to be quiet, sir. We don't want to mar matters as he is presented to the queen. She is receiving him now. Although I am not expert in alien physiognomy, I'd say she finds pleasure in the gift. She's holding him up to her olfactory receptors—"

"You should have killed him first," Julie interrupted.

"I was not instructed to do so," Norbert said. "No matter. He is beyond pain now. Doctor, one of the guards is coming over to me. It is to be another inspection."

"Well, you've passed them before."

"Yes, sir. But there are three guards interested in me this time. It must be because I came so close to the queen. Or maybe it was when I took the sample. I am stepping up my production of pheromones."

"Good idea," said Stan. "Is it helping any?"

"It doesn't seem to be doing much good. They are making odd head movements. I do not know what it means."

"What the hell has gone wrong?" Stan asked urgently. "What are they doing now?"

"They seem suspicious. They have seized me. What do you want me to do, Doctor?"

"Damn it," Stan spat. "I should have gotten you out of there before this! Norbert! Break free and get out!"

"Yes, sir," Norbert said. The big robot whirled, tearing himself free from the aliens' hooked claws. Then, dropping to all fours, he began scuttling down the corridor.

A reverse sensor in the back of Norbert's head clicked on and showed the view: the long winding tunnel curving behind, the three aliens scurrying on all fours after him.

Norbert was running full out. Stan had never seen him go so fast before. A thrill of pride went through him as he witnessed his creation in action. With speed like that, surely . . .

Stan could tell from the jarring movement of his sensor lens when the alien guard landed on Norbert's back. Stan winced as though the blow had landed on him. How could the guard be that fast? he wondered.

To Norbert he said, "Fight him off! Get out of there!"

"I'm trying, Dr. Myakovsky. But there are three of them—"

Abruptly the screen went blank.

Stan cried, "Norbert! Can you hear me? Come in!"

"Nothing," Gill said. He touched a dial, shook his head. "He's off the air."

"He's dead!" Julie cried.

"I didn't want this to happen," Stan screamed. "Not Norbert! Not Norbert!"

Julie said urgently, "Stan, get a hold of yourself."

Stan shuddered and let out a deep breath. He seemed calmer. "Can you get Captain Hoban?" he asked.

"Not yet, sir," Gill said.

Julie had stepped out of the control area for a moment. Now she was back, and her hair was flowing around her head like a network of electrical sparks had gotten into it.

"Stan," she said. "I just checked the short-range weather forecaster in the rear cabin. It's going haywire!"

"Just what we need," Stan groaned.

53

"There's the Bay port, just ahead," Andy Groggins said. He had run ahead of Badger and the rest of the party. He had a slug-thrower with telescopic wire stuck under his arm. Strapped to his waist was a Geiss needle. He'd tied a bit of cloth around his forehead to keep sweat out of his eyes.

"We'll just ease our way in it," Red Badger said. His synthide shirt was torn, revealing his hairy freckled chest and prominent paunch. His small eyes gleamed as he pressed forward. He had a Krag beamer under his arm, its selector pointing to rapid intermittent.

The corridor widened at this point. There were separate passageways leading to "stores" in one direction and to "power" in the other.

As they came out into the wide opened area between corridors, a voice called out, "Freeze, you!"

Badger stood motionless. The others, coming along

behind him, managed to slink into the shadows. But Red Badger felt very exposed. He didn't let his apprehension show, however.

He took two casual steps forward and said, "It's all right, the captain sent us."

"He didn't tell me nothin' about that," the voice said.

Badger had it located now. It was coming from a paint locker on the far side of the corridor. The guard who was stationed here must have taken refuge when the trouble began elsewhere in the ship. But where was his partner?

"I don't blame you for being cautious," Badger said. "But I'm telling you it's all right. We're here to relieve you."

As he talked he peered ahead, trying to figure out how long it would take him to blast through the paint locker and kill the man inside. Too long, he decided. The guard could get him in a single well-placed burst first.

"Stop right there and drop your weapons," the guard called out.

"You're making a mistake," Badger said, and kept on coming. "Captain Hoban told us to secure this area as quickly as possible. Damn it, man, this is serious!"

"Stop right now, or—"

At that moment there was a double burst of slugthrower fire as Glint and Connie opened up almost simultaneously from opposite sides of the corridor. They held down their fire while the paint locker rattled up and down and bounced against the corridor wall, finally letting up only after blowing the door off the hinges and seeing the single guard inside fall out onto the deck.

"Let's go," Badger said, leading the way to the pod. "We're getting out of here."

54

"It's Badger and his men," one of the engineers remarked, reading the terse information that flowed to the TV screen from all parts of the ship. "He's killed the guard."

"Damn it!" Captain Hoban said. "Can you see what they're doing now?"

"They've just entered the pod."

"Seal the ports!" Hoban ordered.

"Too late. They've already opened them."

"Close them again!"

The engineer punched buttons then shook his head. "They've locked them into place. They're blasting off."

Hoban watched on the screen as a schematic came up, showing the *Dolomite*'s landing pod lifting out of its bay and maneuvering away from the ship's side.

"I can still pull them back with the short-range

tractors," the engineer said, his fingers poised on the controls.

Captain Hoban hesitated. At this range, he knew that the tractors would pull the pod apart. Badger and the others wouldn't stand a chance. He didn't want to go that far. There would be a court of inquiry over this. He needed to keep his record clean.

"Book their departure in the ship's log," he ordered.

"I don't know that they'll make it," the engineering officer said. "The weather's really bad out there."

Hoban looked and saw that an entire weather front had moved in while they were dealing with Badger. Long ragged clouds covered the planet's surface, clouds that were whipped and torn apart by the wind's violent action. Lightning flashed, huge jagged blue-violet bolts, several miles long, lancing out of the black-bellied clouds into the naked land below. Although the *Dolomite* was well above it, Hoban gave an involuntary shudder at the size of the storm.

"Try Dr. Myakovsky again," he ordered. "We have to warn him."

"I'm trying, sir," the officer said. "But no luck so far."

55

"I'm getting something," Gill reported.

"Thank God," said Julie.

"Is it Hoban?" Stan asked.

"Yes, I think it is."

Stan swung around in his big command chair and took the microphone from Gill's hand. "Hoban? What's going on there?"

"Sorry for the delay in transmission, sir," Hoban said, his voice echoing eerily around the lander's cabin. "We've had a revolt onboard. It's in hand now, but a group of crewmen have seized a pod and are on their way to the surface."

"Nothing much they can do to us," Stan said. "Listen, Captain, something really important has happened here. We've lost Norbert."

"Your robot alien? I'm sorry to hear it, sir, though I was never that fond of him."

219

"At least he died doing what he was built to do,"
Stan said.

"What about the dog?" Hoban asked.

"Yes, the dog's gone, too," Stan said brusquely.
"Why is everyone so upset about the dog? The dog's
not important. We've got troubles of our own."

There was no reaction to that. Stan cleared his
throat and wondered how soon he could take another
ampoule. Then he brought his attention back to present matters.

"Captain Hoban, we've found what we were looking for. The beekeepers have done our job for us.
Norbert took over a Bio-Pharm harvester ship. It's
packed full of royal jelly. We're rich, Captain."

"Yes, sir. If we can just get out of here now. Can
you get up to our orbit?"

"Negative," Stan said. "We're still in the lander,
which is barely maneuverable in this weather. Taking
shelter in the harvester is our best bet, but it's going
to take some doing to get there."

"Yes, sir," Hoban said. "I copy."

"Secondly, preliminary visual inspection shows the
flight controls of the harvester were badly damaged in
the fighting. I doubt it'll fly, but it'll provide more refuge than the lander. You'll have to come down to us."

"Yes, sir," Hoban said, without enthusiasm. "What
about the volunteers?"

"We've lost touch with them," Stan answered. "As
soon as we get ourselves out of here, they'll be our
first order of business."

Hoban didn't like it, but it didn't seem the time or
place to voice a disagreement.

"It ought to be simple enough," Stan said. "What
you need to do, as soon as the weather stabilizes a little, is send the backup lander down here to pick us
up. Our situation here is none too stable."

"We can't send the backup lander," Hoban said. "I
told you, sir, Badger and his men took it. Can you maneuver at all in your lander, Dr. Myakovsky?"

"I don't know," Stan said. "They weren't made for

that sort of thing. And the weather down here is getting pretty severe."

"It's a major storm," Captain Hoban told him. "The worst of it is heading your way."

"Damn!" Stan spat. "You can't maneuver the *Dolomite* to pick us up, can you?"

"Not in this weather. None of us would stand a chance."

"All right." Stan paused. "Just a minute, let me think."

It was then that the storm front burst in all its fury upon the lander and the unprotected splinter of land it rested upon. Despite its weight, the lander was rocked to its foundations. The earth beneath it rippled and swayed. Lights went out and were replaced by the dull red glow of emergency lighting. Julie screamed as another motion of the storm shot her legs out from under her. Gill caught her before she was slammed into a support.

"Into the pod!" Stan shouted, referring to the small escape vehicle that the lander carried. "Gill, get in there and get power up."

Gill paused for a moment, looking at the five-point steel door separating them from the lander's rear compartment. "Maybe I should stay and try to help the crew?"

"They don't have a chance," Stan said. "We need your help to keep us alive! Now move!"

The three of them, Stan, Gill, and Julie, struggled back to the pod and, during a brief lull, got in. Stan slammed home the hatch and Julie dogged it into place. Gill waited until they were all strapped in, then blew open the lander's exit doors. The storm swept in.

Gill took the pod out under full acceleration. There was a moment of intoxicating freedom as the pod pulled away from the ship, then the full fury of the storm caught the little craft.

Stan just had time to secure himself into a command chair by magnetic clamps, then the pod was launched into the air like a rocket from a launcher. As it turned, Stan could see the land beneath the lander collapse, throwing the vehicle into a deep pit that suddenly yawned beneath it.

Glancing around, he saw that Julie was secured on a deceleration couch. A moment later the internal lighting went out.

The storm blazed at the pod's windows. There were long, stunning lines of force, outlined by a driving rain, lashing in at them. The pods spun around, its automatic stabilizers working hard to keep it on an even keel. The ground came up sickeningly below them, and the pod's jets blazed, avoiding the collision. They were airborne, and the sky through which they tore was colored ocher and purple. It was a world without stability, a place where titanic forces battled as though it were the beginning of time.

"Can't you get her down, Gill?" Stan called out above the deafening clatter.

"I'm trying, Doctor," Gill said, busy over the controls.

"You can do it, Gill!" Julie cried.

"We hope," Stan said.

Gill's long fingers played across the controls. The pod seemed to flutter and skitter like a crazed bat in the luridly lit space between the harsh ground below and the beetling thunderheads above. The little craft spun like a leaf driven by a storm. Julie had to shut her eyes tightly to control the vertigo and nausea that racked her as the pod trembled and shook and rattled like a riveting machine gone berserk.

For Stan the pain was almost unbearable as his tortured lungs strove to replace the air that the violent motions of the storm were driving out of him. He had never known such pain. And yet, paradoxically, he was also experiencing a moment of great exhilaration, a feeling of himself as a conquistador of the new age, persevering through pain and hardship as a new world and new opportunities came into sight.

Yes, he thought, it has all been worth it. The pain

reminds me that I'm alive. This is the way to go. But
I do wish it would stop!

And then, abruptly, they entered a space of quiet
air and Gill was able to maneuver the controls. Suddenly the pod dropped thirty feet and hovered for a
moment on its jets, bare inches above the ground.
Then, with an almost grudging sigh—as though the in-
sensate machine had enjoyed its experience of being
airborne in the midst of fury—it settled to the ground.

Gill set the clamping system that secured the ship
to the bedrock it had settled upon.

He said, "Last stop, Grand Central Station. All passengers prepare to detrain."

Stan unbuckled himself shakily. "Why, Gill, I didn't
know you had a sense of humor."

"I don't," Gill said. "My words were for the purpose
of helping you and the others keep your spirits up."

"Commendable," Stan said. He closed his eyes for a
moment, enjoying the blessed relief of relative silence
and no motion. Then he asked, "Everyone okay? Then
let's take stock."

56

Red Badger and his people sat together on the semicircular couches that almost filled the main section of the pod. Red had remembered to bring aboard a carton of emergency rations, each in a self-heating aluminoplex container. He passed these around now. Walter Glint had a half-full canteen of raisin wine he'd brewed himself in the ship's locker room, before the hypersleep procedure, using copper tubing he'd liberated from the heat circulation system. He passed around the brew, and Min Dwin came up with some narcosmoke cigarettes. In a little while they were quite a cheerful bunch. If only they'd been able to raise some dance music! It was one hell of a party shaping up.

Badger liked to party as well as anyone. But the unfamiliar duties of command distracted him from really letting go. He turned to the little all-wave radio receiver tucked away in one of the pod's storage compartments. He needed to keep his people content, because he was counting on them to see him safely through this.

Although he wouldn't let on to the others, Badger was more than a little disturbed by how things had gone so far. He had counted on seizing the *Dolomite* in his first attempt, when surprise had been in his favor. Back then, taking the initiative had seemed the thing to do.

That was not how matters had worked out, however. Now they were alone, isolated on a savage planet that favored no life except alien. Badger had been thinking furiously, trying to find a way to wrest victory from the jaws of defeat.

Then he thought he had it.

He set the sweep alarm on the radio to wide scanning and began searching the radio waves. It required no master radio operator to find a signal in a place as barren of radio activity as this one. Red locked onto the signal and began transmitting.

57

Adams, the *Lancet*'s radio operator was a tall gangling youth with red hair and a prominent Adam's apple. He came into the main control room without knocking, because Captain Potter had posted standing orders that messages of urgency were to be transmitted at once and without the usual protocol that prevailed on the interstellar ships.

"Yes, what is it, Adams?" Potter snapped. The captain was tall and strongly constructed. His features were handsome and coarse, from the big knife of a nose to the heavy tufted eyebrows that gave his face a sinister character. He wore a midnight-blue uniform with gold flash marks on the sleeves, showing his years of service in the Interspace Mariners' Association. His voice was low-pitched, harsh, and resonant, the sort of voice you paid attention to the first time you heard it.

"Radio signal, sir," Adams said.

"Is it from the people on the harvester?"

"No, sir. We still haven't been able to establish contact with them. Their radio doesn't respond. I don't think it looks good, sir."

"Nobody gives a damn what you think," Potter said, his voice dropping to a sawmill rasp. "Who's the message from?"

"A man who calls himself Red Badger," Adams said. "He says he's a crewman from the *Dolomite*."

"*Dolomite?* Never heard of it. What location did they give?"

"They're descending to the surface of AR-32, sir."

Potter stared at the crewman, eyes narrowed, dark brows creased. "That's quite impossible," he said at last. "This planet is our exclusive preserve."

Adams was about to reply, but perceived just in time that Potter was talking aloud to himself.

"I'll speak to him," Potter said. "Put it through for me."

Adams went to the console and made the necessary adjustments. Badger's voice came through on the loudspeaker.

"Captain Potter? Sir, this is Crewman Badger from the ship *Dolomite*. Sir, a situation has arisen which I would like to acquaint you with."

"Go ahead," Potter said, and listened carefully as Badger told about the revolt he had led on the *Dolomite*.

"We didn't think it was fair, sir, Captain Hoban taking us into an area that was under the exclusive control of Bio-Pharm. The men asked me to speak for them. I talked with Captain Hoban, sir, in fair and reasonable terms, asking him to get a ruling from Bio-Pharm before taking us into this area. Can't say more reasonable than that, can I, sir? But Captain Hoban didn't see it that way. He ordered me and my men put into irons and held to face criminal charges back on Earth. We didn't agree, there was a fight, and me and some of the men came down to the planet."

"You're on the surface of AR-32 now?" Potter
asked.

"Yes, sir. And we're not the only ones. There's a Dr.
Myakovsky down here, too, in his own pod, sir. He's
come to this place to steal your royal jelly. He and
Hoban are criminals, and they want to put us on
charges!"

"That's very interesting," Potter said. "Do you happen to have their exact location?"

"I'm afraid not, sir, since me and my mates had to
leave ship in a hurry, so to speak. But I'll bet anything
they're heading for the hive, where they sent that robot of theirs."

"What robot are you referring to?"

"The one they call Norbert. Looks just like an alien,
sir, only it's not a real one. There's a law against that,
isn't there? The damned thing already killed some of
my shipmates."

"There's a law against it, all right," Potter muttered.
"My law, if no other!"

"Beg pardon, sir?"

"Never mind. What is this robot supposed to do?"

"Collect royal jelly, sir. And leave an electronic trail
showing Myakovsky where to go."

"Damn it!" Potter sputtered. "They could get what
they came for and be out of here before we could
stop them."

"No, sir," Badger said. "I've heard them talking to
Captain Hoban on the radio. They plan to get through
the hive by following an electronic signal that their
robot is to lay down for them. But if me and my
mates was to wipe out that electronic trail . . ."

"I like the idea of that," Potter said slowly. "Can you
do it? You would be rendering me a valuable service."

"Indeed we can, sir. We're hoping it'll be taken into
consideration when you pick us up. You are going to
rescue us, aren't you, sir?"

"You can count on it," Potter said. "There could be
a reward in this for you. Does that sound good, Mr.
Badger? Get in there and wipe out that trail. Then

come to coordinates 546Y by 23X. We'll rendezvous
with you there. You men will be rewarded for your
good work."

"Thank you, sir! You'll be hearing from us soon."

The transmission ended. Potter turned to Adams.
"Well, what are you standing around for? Get back to
the radio room! And not a word of this to the crew, or
I'll have your hide!"

"Yes, sir!" Adams saluted smartly and backed out of
the room.

Potter waited until he was gone, then looked
around the control room. The only ones present were
his chief engineering officer, Ollins, and the helmsman, Driscoll.

"Driscoll," Potter snapped.

"Sir?"

"You've heard nothing of this."

"No, sir!"

"You can take a break now, mister. Ollins and I will
finish out your watch."

"Yes, sir. Thank you, sir." Driscoll saluted and left
the control room.

Lieutenant Ollins was a grizzled old veteran of
many space flights who had served with Potter before. In fact, the two men came from the same town
in Tennessee. Ollins relaxed when Driscoll was away
from the control room. Potter afforded him great priv-
ileges when none of the men were around. When they
were, it was spit and polish and punctilio all the way,
because that was the sort of man Potter was.

"Well, Tom," Potter said. "Seems we've got a bit of
a situation on our hands."

"Seems so, sir," Ollins said. "But unless I miss my
guess ..."

"Yes? Go ahead, Tom."

"Unless I miss my guess, sir, you've thought up an
interesting way to take care of it."

Potter permitted himself a smile. "I don't know if
I'd say 'interesting,' Mr. Ollins. But 'thorough' ... Yes,
I think you'll find my way very thorough."

58

Rain hammered against the pod's hatch like shot from a battery of shotguns. The pod quivered and shook as the storm shrieked and swore to itself, its voice falling to a whisper then rising to a banshee wail. Stan and the others were suited up in all-weather outfits that would give them some protection against the elements, though not much against the aliens. It was time to go.

"Okay," Stan said. "Julie, you feel up to this?"

"I'm perfectly ready for a stroll," Julie said airily. "It's just about sunset, isn't it?"

"Yes," Gill said. "I've checked out the hive on remote sensing. The activity is reaching a peak."

"A perfect time for us to drop in," Julie said.

Stan felt a warm glow go through him when he looked at her. She was young, beautiful, and very brave. They were in about as difficult a situation as he could imagine, but she wasn't giving in a bit to it.

He turned to Gill. "What weapons do we have?"

Gill opened a locker and showed what he had brought. "Five chemical slugthrowers with fifty slug clips. These are somewhat old-fashioned weapons, but they are reliable. And their fifty-caliber slugs pack a wallop. I brought three Gauss needlers. They're recoilless, and their steel slivers ought to have a good effect against the aliens. I was only able to bring one Gyroc, and a bandolier of point seventy-five-caliber spin-stabilized rockets. Two high-impulse laser rifles, both fully charged, and that completes the arsenal, except for half a dozen concussion grenades. I would have liked a greater selection, but that was all that was available at the moment."

"You have done admirably," Stan said. "That's quite an array."

"And, of course, I also have the light tracker, a heavy-duty communicator. As well as the suppressors to get us past the aliens undetected."

"Very important, that last," Stan said. "What range do the inhibitors have?"

"They'll dampen at close to one-hundred-percent strength for approximately three meters in all directions."

"And how long will they last?"

"That's the bad part," Gill said. "They may be good for half an hour at full strength, but it could be less."

"Well, we'll just have to move quickly and hope we have some luck. Julie, have you reached Captain Hoban yet?"

"Just getting him now." Julie spoke into her wrist enunciator. "Can you hear me, Hoban?"

"Loud and clear," Hoban's voice came back to them. "I was beginning to worry. What happened to you people?"

"Nothing good," Julie said. "But we're on AR-32 and we're still alive and in one piece. Three pieces, I should say."

"What are your plans?" Hoban asked.

Julie turned to Stan. He said, "We have to get out

of the pod, Captain. The storm is shaking it to pieces.
What news do you have about your mutiny?"

"The mutineers grabbed our backup lander and
took off for AR-32. It'll be a miracle if they weren't destroyed on their way down."

"A miracle for us if they were," Stan said. "Captain,
we have our suppressors and there's only one thing we
can try that'll bring this off. We're going to go
through the hive, following Norbert's trail. That'll get
us out of the storm, which will destroy us otherwise.
We should be able to follow Norbert's trail to the far
side, where the harvester is. We'll board that and
come up to you. You, meanwhile, will take geosynchronous orbit at the harvester's coordinates. I'm
transmitting those coordinates digitally. Please ac-
knowledge."

Stan's fingers flew over the computer's keys. Soon
he heard Captain Hoban's acknowledgment. "I've got
it, Dr. Myakovsky."

"Good. What do you think of the plan, Captain?"

"It seems to me the best, given the circumstances.
Does Gill concur?"

The android nodded. "There's really nothing else to
do," he added in a quiet voice.

"It's perfect," Julie said. "What have we got to lose
but our lives?"

"Signing off, then, Captain," Stan said. "See you in
an hour or so, I hope."

He turned to Gill. "Have you any objections?"

"As I said, Doctor, given the circumstances, there's
nothing else to do."

"But you wouldn't have gotten us into this fix
in the first place. Is that it?"

"I didn't say that, sir."

"You didn't have to." Stan looked out the port at
the lurid sunset that had just begun flaming behind
the upthrust bulk of the hive. He reached into an inner pocket and brought out a small aluminum case,
like a cigar case only slightly larger. Opening it, he ex-
tracted an ampoule of royal jelly.

"Well," he said, "time for a little ride down the street of dreams, eh?" He looked at Gill and Julie, who were watching him. "I need it," he said defensively. "It's the pain. . . ." Abruptly he pulled himself together. He returned the ampoule to the case and put the case back in his pocket.

"No, I'll do it straight," Stan said. "That ought to be ever so much more amusing. Ready, then? Gill, crack the port!"

Gil undogged the hatch. It took his and Julie's combined strength to push it all the way open against the wind pressure. And then it was done, and the three of them staggered out into the raging storm.

59

There was no easy way to hold a conversation as Stan, Julie, and Gill made their painful march across the wind-whipped plain toward the great rounded mound of the hive. Behind it the sunset flared, sending streamers and columns of radiance around the basalt-blue solid-looking clouds that seemed to march across the plain like giants.

Julie looked at the sunset in awe. She did not consider herself a nature lover, yet this kindling of shapes and colors that seemed too intense to be natural almost brought tears to her eyes. The display touched off a memory.

She was a little girl in the high, carven house of Shen Hui. It was one of his holiday houses in Shan Lin Province, and there was a pool in the garden in which golden carp moved back and forth, and a wind chime in a nearby temple sent forth a sad melody that seemed to speak of ancient days and old-fashioned manners.

It was only then that Julie thought of her mother, whom she had never known, but who visited her almost nightly in dreams whose memory she lost upon awakening.

They walked for a long time, bent into the driving wind, and came at last to the base of the hive. Looking up at the great, pitted, gray-brown surfaces covered with branchlike vines, Stan saw that it resembled some exotic plant. It was pockmarked with puckered holes, many of which were large enough to admit a man. Stan wondered if the hive might not be an organism in its own right, symbiotically connected to the aliens, coexisting with its own weird life-forms.

It was an interesting fancy, but Stan thought it was more logical to assume that the aliens had constructed the hive, following instinctual instructions laid down in their DNA aeons past.

Still, it pleased his fancy to imagine that the hive and the aliens were two different types of living matter. What a startling possibility! He could see the headlines now, heralding his discovery. . . .

He smiled wryly and reminded himself that his only job now was to stay alive, to keep on going until he could find the pure and unadulterated royal jelly that might extend his life—if there was any truth to his conjectures.

He and Julie walked around the hive until they found an opening. It loomed ahead of them, a dark and ragged hole that plunged into the depths of the hive.

"Are you ready for this?" Stan asked.

Gill didn't answer. Julie said, "If that's where you want to go, I'll go with you."

There seemed no way into the hive. They found what looked like a pathway that spiraled up its side.

They climbed up the long, narrow ramp that looked to be part roadway, part vine. It went up the side of the hive in long sloping curves, and there were rough-barked vinelike things along the side that served as handholds, and other things that looked like snapped-off tree limbs and might have provided footholds for taloned feet.

Using these as handholds, they half hiked, half climbed, up the side of the hive. The storm was still buffeting them, its wind gusts swirling in from all directions. The slanted rain made the footing slick and unsafe. When Julie was able to spare a glance to the side, she saw the great plain of AR-32 spread out below, all bathed in strange red-and-violet sunset colors, cut through here and there with deep, black fissures.

She was leading the way, with Stan in the middle and Gill bringing up the rear. Stan was short of breath already, and Julie, listening to him labor as he walked, decided it didn't augur well for the future.

She was worried about Stan, but he had gotten them into this situation. She just hoped he was well enough and sane enough to get them out of it.

Then they reached an opening camouflaged against the side of the hive by a dense growth of vines. They pushed inside and found a broad roadway that curved inward and upward.

The spiraling roadway terminated in a wide opening that seemed to lead deeper into the hive. Julie was less than ten feet away from the opening when something within it, a darkness against the darkness, stirred and moved.

She whispered, "Oh, shit," and froze.

Stan noticed that she had stopped and also halted.

Gill stopped, too, peering upward, trying to make out what was the matter.

As Julie waited, barely breathing, an ugly dark head with a long backward-sloping cranium poked out of the hole above her. Its fangs were clearly visible, gleaming white, impossibly sharp and packed together, dripping with green matter.

Then the alien's muscular body came out slowly, foot by foot, and its claws grasped the spiraling track on which Julie and the others were standing. The alien began to descend, moving directly into their path.

"I think it can't see me," Julie said, praying that it was true. The indicator on her suppressor showed less than half an hour left in the batteries.

Well, she thought, half an hour is a long time. But then she wondered, What if the gauge is simply stuck at the half-hour mark?

The alien came right up to her, so close she could smell the acrid tang of its hide.

Julie moved to the far edge of the narrow pathway.

Taking a grip on one of the vines at the side, she leaned far over, giving the creature room to pass.

Its ferocious blind-looking face passed within inches of her, its hard black flank brushed her side, and then it was past, descending toward the ground.

Stan and Gill, below her, moved to give it room.

Julie slipped into the opening at the top of the hive, the others following close behind. The passageway widened out to a tube about ten feet in diameter. It curved downward and to the left, and soon there was only a ghostly memory of light for them to see their way by.

About twenty feet down, the tunnel widened into a cave. It was difficult to make out its dimensions in that shadow-infested place, perhaps fifty yards long by twenty wide, but it could have been twice that, the remaining dimensions lost in the gloom.

There were things growing between the floor of the cave and its low ceiling. Then they moved into a wider area, where they could stand upright.

Stan and his party paused here to redistribute their loads, make a final check of their weapons, take a drink of water, and have a last conference before plunging deeper into the hive.

Stan was disturbed that Norbert had been unable to lay down an electronic trail. But he was too tired to worry about it much.

He lay down on the uneven ground. He needed a moment to catch his breath. It was tough going, there was no doubt about that. His chest burned incessantly. It had been a long time since he'd had a dose of royal jelly. The case with the ampoules was still in his pocket; it felt comforting there. He wanted one now, badly. Anything to get out of this incessant pain, which seemed to radiate out from his chest and course down his arms and legs, following the pathways of his arteries and veins.

He pulled out an ampoule and hastily swallowed its contents. And then he had to scramble to his feet as he heard sounds from somewhere in the tunnel.

They had to depend on searchlights now to find their way, for the last of the natural light was cut off as they rounded another turn.

And came face-to-face with another alien.

It was moving toward them on all fours, its ugly head questing right and left, seeming to be sniffing the stale, earth-flavored air. It was clear that it had picked up a scent or cue, but apparently it couldn't tell where it was coming from. The creature slid past them like liquid black iron, and they moved on in silence.

There was a sort of grim interminability about that nightmare journey into the hive. Julie felt that time itself was standing still as they proceeded into the silence of that awesome construction. She felt she was on a dream descent into depths that corresponded in some way that she didn't understand to the depths of her own being.

Abruptly she came back to attention. Her searchlight picked out incomprehensible shapes as she moved ahead. There seemed to be huge things with tall stooped shoulders and folded wings towering above them. There were oval things scattered here and there, like ostrich eggs, only with a strange crosshatched texture of fine lines. There were plants with wide, white faces, and they turned toward the searchlight beam as if it reminded them of something they had once known a very long time ago.

Stan said, "This is some weird place, huh, Gill?"

Gill shrugged. "I suppose this hive has been in existence for a long time. Centuries, maybe. It stands to reason that a lot of different life-forms would have tried to establish themselves here. It's one of the few places on this planet that's out of the wind."

"I wish I could get a videotape of this," Stan said.

"You planning to do a TV special?" Julie asked.

"It would be a first. What's that up ahead?"

By the light of Stan's searchlight, he saw that the floor of the cave abruptly declined and became a large hole. Stan approached it cautiously and played his light along it. The sides sloped down sharply for

about five feet, revealing that the interior of the hole
was filled with a mixture of substances. Stan's flashlight picked out bones and body parts, vegetables in
advanced stages of rot or desiccation, bits of wood
and rock, and other kinds of debris he couldn't make
out.

"What is it, Stan?" Julie asked.

"It appears to be a midden. A garbage dump."

"Ugh!" Julie said.

"No, it's really very interesting," Stan said. "A midden can tell you all about the life of the hive. Look at
all that stuff! Isn't that a cow carcass down there?
And what's that over there . . . ?"

He focused the searchlight beam and looked again.

"It looks like a dog collar," he said at last.

The three of them were silent for a moment. The
memory of Mac the dog hung in the air like something
evil, something they would have preferred to forget.

"I suppose this is where they threw Mac when the
queen was through with him," Stan said. "That's certainly his collar with the suppressor attached. We can
use that for ourselves."

He leaned over the pit to pick up the collar. Suddenly the ground crumbled beneath him. Stan scrambled for footing, fell backward, his arms windmilling
wildly. Julie lunged for him and almost managed to
grab his ankle, but lost her grip as Stan pitched over
the edge with a bloodcurdling yell.

For Stan, that moment of falling into the aliens'
garbage pit was so intensely terrifying as to be almost
pleasurable. In the split second a million things
flashed in front of his eyes like high-speed movie images. Some residue of the royal jelly in his veins
kicked in, and he had a moment of pure illusion.

He dreamed in that instant that he was on a moun-
taintop, and on all sides of him were birds and beasts,
waiting to hear what he had to tell them. Mac was
there in his dream, sitting up on his hind paws beg-
ging, his tongue lolling out. Stan himself seemed to be
wearing a robe made out of a luminous golden mate-

rial, and he was not entirely surprised to find a golden halo circling his brow, casting a mellow light of its own. He was about to address all of the birds and beasts, tell them it was all right, when he struck the bottom of the pit with a resounding jar.

"Stan!" Julie cried. "Can you hear me?"

Gill came up beside her. "Is he alive?"

"I don't know yet. Stan!"

Stan stirred, then fell back.

"Stan! Call out if you can hear me," Julie cried.

Stan didn't answer, but something else did. Something that spoke in a sibilant hiss, with many overtones. It was not a single voice. It was many voices. The hissing voices were like the tumultuous waves of an acid sea. Julie tried to direct her light. Gill was beside her, his hand on her shoulder. Suddenly his grip tightened.

"What is it?" she said, and then she saw it, too.

There were passageways into the lower part of the midden. From them, heads peered; the characteristic heads of aliens. This was apparently a shortcut into a lower level of the hive. The aliens must have heard the noise Stan made while he was falling.

The aliens had come out to investigate. It was like before when they had met the alien coming into the hive. Only this time something had changed. It took Julie a moment to figure out what it was. Then she shuddered in horror.

"Gill, my God!" she said. "The suppressor must have quit. They can see him!"

61

When Stan recovered consciousness, he had one delicious moment of thinking he was ten years old and had just awakened from a particularly terrifying dream. How grateful he was to find himself in his own bed! There, just across from him, was his computer, a good one, which his parents had bought for his last birthday. His floppy-eared toy puppy was there, though of course he was too old to play with it. Still, Mr. Muggs watched while Stan did his experiments.

Now Stan stretched luxuriously and tried to think how he'd spend his day. There were some spiderwebs down near the brook that he wanted to investigate. . . .

His outstretched fingers touched something wet and sticky. He recoiled, turned his head, looked. It was Mac, dead. He had pushed his fingers into the sticky wound in Mac's throat. What he had thought was his computer was actually the skeleton of a cow. And there were aliens glaring at him, seeing him, and starting toward him. . . .

"Gill!" Julie screamed. "Start shooting! But for God's sake don't hit Stan!"

Julie was firing as she spoke. She had unslung the plasma rifle she had been carrying by its strap over her shoulder. Red-orange flame lanced out from its muzzle, painting the garbage pit in lurid colors and huge dancing shadows.

The concentrated fury of the plasma blast danced around the aliens, who had begun advancing on Stan from a passageway that led into the midden. Red, acetylenelike cutting flames poked and probed at them, lancing through their bodies, stabbing into arms and legs. Gill was firing simultaneously, caseless carbine rounds that blew the aliens off their feet, sending them halfway up the pit, to tumble back again in a welter of severed arms and heads.

The plasma fire and the caseless rounds wove a dance of death around Stan's recumbent body. The fire approached him and then, almost delicately, backed away again.

Julie ran around the circumference of the pit, firing to keep the aliens from coming up on Stan from behind. Gill held his position, blasting a way clear for Stan, who finally stumbled to his feet and made his way to the side of the pit. He tried feebly to climb back out.

"Can you hold them, Gill?" Julie asked.

"I think so," Gill muttered.

Julie slung her plasma rifle and reached out for Stan's hand. Their fingers touched and clasped. No sooner did Julie have a good grip than she heaved, putting into it every ounce of strength in her slender body. Stan seemed to fly into the air, landing on the edge of the pit.

While he tried to catch his breath, Gill finished off the last of the aliens, scattering arms and legs everywhere. Then he turned to help Stan. Stan tried to get to his feet, then slumped again to the ground. Before anyone could grab him, he slid again into the pit.

"Oh, no!" Julie said. "Hold my ankle, Gill, I'll get him."

They tried, but couldn't reach. Stan appeared to be on the edge of unconsciousness. His eyelids fluttered briefly behind his thick glasses, which miraculously had not been knocked off. His fingers clawed at the debris-strewn surface. From behind him, there was another hissing sound. An alien suddenly appeared, two others behind it.

"Kill it!" Julie cried.

"I can't!" Gill said. "Stan's in the way!"

"He's in my way, too!" Julie began to run around the side of the pit, trying to get a clear shot.

The leading alien looked somehow different to her from the others. But at first she couldn't determine how. Then Gill threw a phosphorus flare and she saw that the alien had half his shoulder chewed off. There was also damage to his midsection and head.

But what she wasn't prepared for was the look of those wounds. Instead of flesh and blood, there appeared to be cable and metal fittings in the wound, and small humming servos.

For a moment she couldn't process this information. Then she understood.

"Norbert!"

62

Since they pulled him out of the midden, Stan had drifted into a different place. He seemed to be in a spaceless space and a timeless time. It was a world filled with little blue-and-pink clouds. There were stars in the background, and pools of water. He was not surprised to see Norbert standing in front of him. Nothing could be strange to Stan any longer. He had passed beyond weirdness, into a place where all effects were the same, all part of the great symphony of death, whose opening notes he could hear as though coming to him from a great distance, but getting louder, louder.

This couldn't have been an illusion because it answered him.

Norbert said, "Yes, I am here, Dr. Myakovsky. I am functioning at only twenty-seven percent of capacity."

Stan blinked and his vision cleared. He was in the

alien garbage midden, lying on his back on mounds of refuge. In front of him, bending over, was Norbert.

"It must have been quite a fight," Stan said, surveying the robot.

"I would say so, Doctor. I killed three of them in a running battle through the hive. Unfortunately, they did damage to me that I fear will prove terminal."

"Are you afraid?" Stan asked.

"Not in the personal sense, Doctor. By fear, I meant regret that I will no longer be able to serve you as you designed me."

"Can't you turn on your self-repair circuits?" Stan asked.

"I tried that, Doctor. They are down. And you did not equip me with self-repair units for the self-repair units."

"In the future we'll have infinite backups for all systems," Stan said. "Including human ones, I hope. Including mine."

"Are you all right, Doctor?"

"I've definitely had better days," Stan said. "My self-repair circuits aren't working right, either." He felt something in his hand and held it up. "Look here! Mac's collar! I've got it!"

"That's fine, Doctor," Norbert said. "I have something, too."

"What is it?" Stan asked.

"This." Norbert reached into the gaping wound in his shoulder and drew out a gooey mass the color of honey.

"What is it?" Stan asked.

"Royal jelly from the queen's birthing chamber," Norbert said. "I was unable to provide a proper container. I'm afraid it's gotten some oil on it, and some blood."

"Doesn't matter," Stan said. He reached out and took the mass. It had a waxy consistency. He put it in his mouth, made himself chew and swallow it. He experienced no immediate effect.

"Great work!" Stan said.

Behind him he heard big objects move and slide around as something came from the interior of the hive.

"Better get going, Doctor," Norbert said. "They're coming. I'll cover your retreat as well as I can."

"I don't see how," Stan grumbled.

"I improvised a weapon. I hope it will suffice."

Stan pulled himself onto his hands and knees and worked his way toward the edge of the pit. Behind him he could hear sizzling energy beams as Norbert and the others fought off the aliens. Norbert was buying him time.

Stan tried to pull himself up the side of the pit, but the crumbling structure gave way under him and he fell to the bottom again. Pain washed over him in great uncontrollable waves, and in each one he thought he might drown, only to come back again and again, each time more feebly, to the surface of consciousness.

He felt Julie's hand in his, and then Gill's hand. He was lifted into the air. Below him he heard Norbert's battle still raging, and the shrill screaming sounds that the aliens made as they died in the violet-edged bolts that Norbert's impromptu weapon cast. But the aliens kept on coming, and as Julie and Gill pulled Stan out of the pit and beat a hasty retreat down a tunnel, they heard the sounds of Norbert being pulled down and torn apart.

63

Glint asked, "Is this the place?"

Badger checked the crude map he had drawn following Potter's instructions. Yes, there were the two fan-shaped rocks, and over there was the fissure cut like a curly S.

"We're at the spot all right."

"Okay," Glint said. "But where is he? Where's the rescue pod?"

They were standing on a wide flat rock shelf. It stood practically under the shadow of the hive. The wind had died down for a moment. They could look out over the nearly featureless landscape. Toward the west there was a line of lime-green haze, possibly sent up by some natural circumstance. So much about a place like AR-32 was simply incomprehensible.

Yet, even on Earth, despite his thousands of years of occupation, despite his long acquaintance with

bird, fish, and fowl, things could still surprise man as
well. Strange animals turned up every year. Mysteries
abounded. Even the status of ghosts was still uncertain. No one had ascertained for sure whether or not
the Yeti or the Jersey Devil really existed. Were there
such things as werewolves and vampires?

But on AR-32, the anomalous and the unexpected
happened all the time.

You tended to think of such things on a planet like
AR-32. Mankind had known of the place for less than
ten years. No genuinely scientific expedition had ever
visited it. Only commercial vessels called, and for the
sole purpose of stealing (though they called it collect-
ing) the aliens' jelly. The men who went on such ex-
peditions were as hard-bitten a lot as conquistadores
of old Spain. Like them, they cared little for what lay
below them or what it might mean in the scheme of
things.

It was not unusual that Badger and his men, who
were as much of the conquistador type as the crewmen on the *Lancet*, were surprised but not absolutely
astonished when a creature raised its head from behind a rock and looked at them.

"What in hell is that?" Meg asked.

Badger and the others turned. The creature was
sitting there looking at them. It had a large head
somewhat the size and shape of a hogshead. Eight little skinny legs came down from its sides, terminating
in blunt claws. Something about the creature was
reminiscent of a pig, right down to the way it snuffled
and oinked at the crewmen. It had a small curly tail.
It was colored pink, and it had a black saddle marking
in the middle of its back.

"What do you suppose that thing is?" Glint asked.

Badger said, "It's some critter indigenous to this
planet, I think. Boys, I'll bet we're the first ones ever
to look at this thing."

"G'wan!" Meg said. "One of the *Lancet* people
might have seen it first."

"No way to prove that," Badger said. "But this thing

could be rare, and never take to hanging around the places where humans live and work. Like the bobcat and the wolverine on Earth. If there's animals like that on Earth, why not here?"

"Here, fella," Meg called. "Why'ncha come over here?"

The piglike thing lifted its little triangular ears and stared at them with bulbous blue eyes. It lifted a forepaw and pawed the ground. Then it trotted over to Meg.

"Hey, ain't that nice?" said Meg. She reached over and scratched the creature above its ears. It made a high-pitched grunting sound that had about it a tone of approval. No mistaking that sound for a cry of pain.

The others crowded around. "Cute, ain't it?" said Glint, who had raised hogs in Arkansas.

Meg said, "I wonder why it came to us?"

"Can't tell about alien life-forms," Badger said. "I wonder if we should take this fellow along with us. Back on Earth sell him to a circus, make a lot of money off'n him. I wonder what he eats?"

"I'm sure he'd tell us if he could," Meg said, scratching the creature's back. "Where do you come from, fellow?"

The creature cocked its head at them as if it were trying to understand. It seemed to be listening to something. Or for something. It was hard to tell which.

Badger listened, too. And after a few moments he heard a high-pitched buzzing sound, like locusts, only heavier somehow, meaner. As he listened the sound changed. It turned into a heavy thumping, as if a thousand bass drums were advancing up the ridge. Then Badger realized that the two noises were going on simultaneously. He wondered what it could be, and suddenly he didn't want to know.

"Lock and load!" he shouted to the men. "I don't like the sound of this!"

The creatures came over the top of the little hill, a

couple dozen of them, though of course that was only the first wave. They were different from the creatures they had seen before. They were the size of large dogs, and their heads were big and shaped like raptor birds. They had no feathers, however, just two tails apiece, and those tails appeared to be barbed. Their mouths were filled with long sharp teeth—that seemed to be a rule here on this planet—and they were making a buzzing sound as they came.

Behind them came another group of creatures, a little smaller than the others, about the size and general shape of woodchucks, and colored a lime green with bluish features. They all had mustaches, like walruses. They made a booming sound as they walked, but Badger couldn't see how they produced it.

They came on, all of them, and they didn't look friendly.

"Hit 'em with it!" Red shouted, and he and his three buddies began to pour in fire. They had the caseless carbines going so fast that the firing mechanisms began to grow hot, but they ignored the pain and kept on firing.

One thing was plain from the first: these creatures were hard to hit. They weren't coming on fast, but their dodging and swerving made them difficult targets. Nevertheless, Red scored a hit, and had the satisfaction of seeing one of the woodchuck blow up like an overinflated beach ball.

Meg scored, and then Glint, who shouted in triumph.

Then one of the raptor-headed creatures got under the line of his fire and grabbed his foot. It bit, twisted.

Glint's foot came off at the ankle. He stared at the stump, too surprised to feel pain yet, and tried to take a step away. But he toppled over and they were on him, a dozen of them, biting and tearing. One long-necked creature buried his head in Glint's belly. Glint screamed and tried to tear it away, but the bird-thing was stronger. It got its head deep inside Glint's belly, and then pulled the rest of itself in. Lying on the ground, Glint went into convulsions.

Badger dropped his empty carbine and picked up a plasma rifle. He turned it to full fire and sprayed the area. He caught Meg, out on the periphery, with his blast and saw her wither and collapse before he could turn it off her.

"Damn it, sorry, Meg!" he shouted. It was just the sort of unfortunate thing that happens sometimes in combat.

Meanwhile, Min Dwin, firing from the hip, was seized from behind by an alien. It caught her by her long hair, and she turned, still firing, and put four rounds into the creature's head, had the satisfaction of seeing it blow apart. But it still held her hair in its dying claw, and from its ruined head a gout of acid sprayed, catching her full in the face.

"My eyes!" she screamed, and fell to the ground, clawing at her face. She writhed for a moment, then lay still. The acid had penetrated to her brain.

Andy Groggins tried to turn his carbine to face an alien that had just come up on his side. His feet were yanked from under him. An alien had him by the ankles, another seized his arms. They tugged in opposite directions, and Andy triggered off his entire magazine, spraying the area and nearly catching Badger, who had to dive to escape the blasts. Then Andy roared as his left leg was ripped off at the hip.

The alien who had been pulling his feet fell backward. The other caught its balance and came at him. Badger triggered off a burst and blew the creature away. Groggins was dead before the carbine's reverberations died away.

Looking around, Badger saw that he was alone. The others were dead. The original beast, the barrel-shaped thing, was nearby, sitting on its haunches and watching expectantly.

"Damn you, you Judas goat!" Badger said, and blew it away with a short burst.

The area was a shambles of blood and gore. All

Badger's people were dead, and he expected to go next, but the attack had ended. There were no aliens in sight now except dead ones, and no other creatures, either.

Badger stood there, sobbing with fatigue and anguish, and saw a shadow appear as if from nowhere. He looked up.

There it was, Potter's ship, the *Lancet*, and he had a chance to get out of this. "Drop a line! Pick me up!"

They were down level with him, and he saw four of the crew watching him from one of the big glassite windows. He screamed at them, and finally they opened a hatch and threw out a rope ladder. Badger scrambled up with his remaining strength and collapsed inside the ship.

"Did you get all that on tape?" Potter asked.

"Yes, sir," the second-in-command said.

"The scientists will be interested in these creatures," Potter commented.

"Yes, sir," the second-in-command said. "But the killing of all those men was a little gruesome, wasn't it?"

"Oh, edit that part out," Potter scoffed. "And mark it in the log that we didn't reach the surface in time to save the rest of the mutineers." He turned to go, then stroked his chin. "Not that one ever really wants to rescue mutineers. They set a bad example for the rest of the crew. But don't put that in."

"Yes, sir." The second-in-command saluted and began to walk off. "We did pull one of them out."

"Take him to the medics," Potter said. "We'll get his story later."

"Yes, sir." The second saluted and left the control room.

"And now, Dr. Myakovsky," Potter said to himself, "it is time to deal with you."

64

Stan and his group went through a maze of pathways. They found no sign of Norbert's electronic trail. No sign of Norbert, either. He had dropped behind, after making a gallant stand against the aliens. Stan had last seen him submerged under a writhing mound of black alien bodies.

Stan's breathing was laboring, he could hardly drag himself along. When was the royal jelly going to kick in? Julie and Gill helped him all they could, but they needed to keep their hands free to use their weapons. Because now more and more aliens were appearing, coming out of different turnings in the tunnels. They came in ones and twos, no mass attack yet, but it was probably only a matter of time.

It was clear that the suppressors were no longer doing their job. Stan, Julie, and Gill had to be constantly on the alert, because the creatures were attacking silently, suddenly springing out of the shadows.

Julie was leading the way. Her searchlight beam probed ahead into the profound darkness. She thought she had never seen such darkness before. Even the darkness she saw when she closed her eyes was not as deep as this. This was the darkness of evil, the darkness that cloaked a place where unspeakable creatures performed horrifying rituals. This was the darkness of childhood terrors. This was the darkness out of which monsters swarmed, the place where they tortured little children, and ate them, and then spit them up to make them live again so they could kill them anew.

Glancing back, Julie saw Gill falling back to help Stan, fighting half turned around to keep the aliens from running up their backs. He showed no expression when the searchlight beams occasionally illuminated his long, serious face. The android did his work methodically, but then he wasn't really human, it was all the same to him, he had no feelings, not really. He'd act just the same if he were on an assembly line screwing down machine parts. He's lucky, Julie thought, because it's not all the same to me, no matter how hard I try to make it so.

And Stan? In a way he was lucky, too. Too exhausted to care any longer, and in too much pain, to judge from his twisted features and the sweat that dripped from his face. She felt so sorry for him, and yet, in a way, she envied him. He was too far gone to feel the terror that engulfed her mind and turned her legs to jelly.

Gill plodded along, an efficient machine doing what it was supposed to do. His peripheral vision was enormously extended, and when he caught movement at the outer edges, he wheeled and fired in a single economical movement. When a group of three or more aliens came at him, he switched to the small thermite bombs he carried in a pouch on his left side, setting the proximity fuse with his thumb just before he let them go.

It was like a dance—turn, swing, fire—the only dance he had ever done. Turn, wheel, extend the arm. *Boom! Blam!* Turn again, gracefully duck, turn, fire, fire again, then go forward. . . .

He heard Stan gasp and slip. Gill scooped him up and put him back on his feet. "Can you go on?"

"Yes. Thanks . . ." Stan was saving his breath.

Gill was worried about the doctor. That dose of pure royal jelly hadn't seemed to help any. He knew how much Stan had been expecting to find some sort of divine elixir that would cure his cancer. Gill had no particular hope that this would happen. It was illogical. The royal jelly was not a cure; it served merely to diminish the pain. Why should a pure strain do more than the other, adulterated strains?

He knew that humans liked to entertain farfetched notions. All of the humans, in a way, were like those Spanish conquistadores he had learned about during his hypnopaedic learning sessions, those men in armor who had painfully trekked across the American plains, searching for the Seven Cities of Cibola, imaginary places that had never existed outside the dreams of mythographers.

Stan's belief in a cure for his disease was like that. It was forlorn, even silly. No android would be capable of such folly. Yet Gill didn't think that made him better than Stan. Quite the contrary, it made him subhuman, because he could not participate in the delusions, both the pathetic and the sublime, that made the human race what it was.

The aliens were massing behind them. Gill had to slow down more and more to flight rearguard actions.

Julie pressed on ahead, hoping that the turns she took were leading them toward the outside of the hive rather than deeper into it.

Gill switched the plasma rifle to automatic fire and laid down a sheet of flame as half a dozen aliens came crawling out of a pit and, rearing to their feet, loped toward him.

Stan stumbled and fell, and lay still. Gill scooped him up and draped him over one shoulder, leaving one arm free to aim and fire the heavy plasma rifle.

By now the aliens were coming from side turnings as well as from behind. The little party wasn't surrounded yet, but it looked imminent. Gill threw his last thermite grenade, shifted Stan higher onto his shoulder, and noted that the charge in the plasma rifle was almost depleted. He turned, ready to fight to the end.

Then Julie cried, "There's light ahead! We're almost out of it!"

Gill turned and saw the faintest glimmer of grayness penetrating the profound gloom of the hive. He let go of the depleted plasma rifle and pulled a chemical slugthrower out of a side pouch. Four quick shots blasted a close-packed group of aliens with high explosives. Then Gill turned and ran, with Stan on his shoulder, toward the light.

His feet slid on the hard-packed clay of the tunnel's floor, and then suddenly he was out of the hive and into the sepulchral gray light of AR-32.

Behind him he heard Julie say, "Get out of the way, Gill."

He managed to stagger a few steps farther. This gave Julie a chance to reset her plasma gun to full heat. She held it steadily, hosing the entrance to the hive through which they had come.

It took Gill a moment to understand what she was doing. Then he put Stan down, rummaged in his pouch, and found a plasma-rifle refill. He reloaded and swept the spot where Julie was beaming.

The beams glittered and coruscated on the hive face. The aliens were forced back, deeper into the cave, to wait until the noise and heat died down.

But Julie had something else in mind. She kept on firing until, with a sudden thunderous roar, the cave mouth collapsed. A cloud of dust and smoke arose, and then it was quiet.

Julie turned off her weapon, as did Gill.

"That'll do it for a little while," she said.

"Until they find another exit from the hive," Stan said.

"Well, it's better than nothing. Now, where in hell are we?"

Stan pointed. "You've done a great job, Julie. Look down there."

Julie looked, and saw, less than a hundred yards away, the squat hull of the harvester.

"Now we're getting somewhere!" she said. "We just have to get aboard."

"Yes," said Gill. "But there's a difficulty." He pointed again.

It took Julie a moment to see it. But then she saw the small black dots moving at the base of the hive. She could finally make them out: aliens! They had found another exit from the hive sooner than she expected. And they were blocking the way to the harvester.

She asked, "What now, Stan?" But Stan was unconscious again.

Julie and Gill looked at each other, then glanced up as a shadow crossed them.

It was a ship. For one moment Julie's hopes flared. But then she took in the ship's markings and design, and a great despondency came over her. That was not the *Dolomite*. That was the *Lancet*, commanded by Potter, the Bio-Pharm man. It hovered in the air, and nothing about it stirred. It seemed obvious to Julie that Potter was going to let them die here, watching and maybe videotaping their final agonies.

Stan revived and sat up. "The harvester, did you say?"

"It's right down there." Julie pointed.

Stan looked and nodded. He struggled to his feet. "We've got to get there. From there, something may be possible."

"There are quite a few aliens in the way," Gill pointed out.

"So I see," Stan said. "Have you ever heard of the old American Indian stunt of running the gauntlet?"

"I don't believe so," Gill said.

"You're about to learn history in a very practical way," Stan announced. "Load what's left of the ammo and we'll be on our way."

Despite the mortal danger of their position, Julie could have kissed him at that moment.

65

Stan gave the signal and they were off, trotting down the rocky path that led from the edge of the hive to the plain. Fifty yards away, more or less, was the harvester. In the sky above them, the *Lancet* hovered, silent, watching.

And then the aliens came.

They came singly and in pairs, and then in threes. They seemed to crawl out from under rocks and to appear out of holes. They came in silent ferocity, fangs bared, talons extended, forming a rough line between the hive and the harvester. Stan and the others ran through the line, blasting as they went. They had all shifted now to rapid-fire weapons. Never did Julie display better hand-eye coordination. She managed to move at full stride, at the same time keeping a look on all sides of her and releasing sizzling bolts of energy at anything that moved. The rocks turned white-hot under the glancing energy beams. The aliens surged forward, and died. Julie and Gill were doing fine. . . .

And then Stan collapsed.

He had been doing very well, for a man in his condition. But his illness and general debilitation were not to be denied forever. Pain coursed through his chest like a sea of fire. He gritted his teeth and tried to continue, but now everything was turning dark before his eyes. He couldn't see where he was going. His feet stumbled on the rocky surface, a pebble turned under his foot. He felt himself falling, and a black pit seemed to yawn in front of him. He threw his arms wide as he fell, but before he hit, Gill scooped him up.

"Don't stop for me!" Stan said.

"Order denied," Gill said, setting him on his shoulder and running again.

They cut their way through the ranks of the aliens. Flesh, blood, and bile spilled in all directions. It was like a free-for-all in a slaughterhouse. Julie hadn't imagined there was that much gore in the whole world. Scattered parts of aliens lay everywhere, arms and legs, long ugly tails, heads with the teeth still snapping. And still they came on. Julie thought that every alien on the planet must be here, or on its way.

She was firing two weapons now, cutting a path for herself through a growing mound of living matter— the locked bodies of aliens, still trying to get at them. Gill, running along hard on Julie's heels, with Stan bouncing up and down on his shoulder, was cutting wide swaths in the clustered aliens. Julie saw her left-hand weapon flare and die. Firing right-handed, she snatched a vibraknife from her waist pouch to set it on high. The blade had to make physical contact to do any harm, but it had come to that now with the aliens pressing ever closer. It seemed to her that this was the end; aliens pressed in and she had no idea where she was. And then Gill was shouting, "The harvester, Julie!"

They were there. Gill raced up the landing platform and dumped Stan inside through the entry port. Then he turned, feet braced, firing a bazooka-style weapon that gave out great gouts of green flame. Julie ducked into the harvester under his arm.

She saw Stan, lying on the floor, unconscious again. Something big and black and many-toothed was bending over him. It was an alien, damn it! The harvester was filled with the creatures—two, no three of them. She cut them down. "Gill!" she screamed. "Get inside so we can close the door!"

Gill cut and slashed and backed through the door. Julie cut down an alien and now there was one left. It stood in the doorway, towering over her, and just at that instant her gun began to fail.

She must have screamed, because Gill slung a handgun across the harvester to her. She caught it, aimed, and triggered it in one rapid moment. The alien was in her face, but she had no choice: at extreme close range she blasted him.

The alien's throat exploded. One wildly waving claw came completely off. His forelimb, severed at the wrist, waved wildly in the air. The milky white acidic substance that was the blood of the alien spewed forth in a stream.

Some of the acid hit Julie. She screamed and went down, and it seemed to her that she could hear Gill yelling something, too, and then she didn't know anything anymore.

Stan returned to consciousness angry that the dose of pure royal jelly hadn't done anything for him. Luckily he still had some of the older product left. He'd take some of that soon.

He was not really surprised that the pure royal jelly hadn't helped him. He had always suspected that it was too good to be true, the idea that some other form of the jelly would cure him in some miraculous way. It just doesn't work like that, he told himself.

His mind raced back to earlier days. He thought of all the work he had done, all his accomplishments. He'd had a lot of chances in the poker game that was his life. Could he have played his cards some other way? He didn't really think so. And it was strange, but he knew that for some strange reason there was no place he'd rather be than here, right here, at the end of a glorious venture, with Julie and Gill, his friends.

Gill was at the other side of the harvester, looking after Julie. There really wasn't much he could do for her. Just see that she was comfortable. Most of the acid had missed her, but some drops had fallen along the side of her neck and penetrated deep under the skin. Her face was ashen, her breathing labored. Her vital signs were diminishing.

Gill found himself struggling with new emotions, things he had never felt before. He realized that there was a comfort in being a synthetic man. The trouble with android status was that nothing ever felt very good. There was no joy, no exultation. But the advantage was that nothing ever felt very bad, either.

Strange, though. Now he was filled with unaccustomed emotions: pity for Julie, and something else, some tender feeling that he couldn't quite identify, couldn't quite find a name for. He touched the vein on the side of her neck. It pulsed, but not strongly. He reached over to make Julie more comfortable and only became aware then that his left arm was missing a hand and half its forearm. He had been too busy to notice when the hand went off-line. It was that advantage, again, of being a synthetic: you felt no pain. Now, looking back, he could reconstruct how it happened. The harvester's hatch had been closing, and he had just managed to get inside. But not quite all of him had made it. One hand had still been outside as the alien's big claw closed over his wrist. Stan had pulled, and the alien had pulled back.

There had been a deadly tug-of-war, with the alien pulling one way and Gill the other, sawing his arm back and forth along the door frame. None of the others had been in a position or condition to help. Stan had been out cold, and Julie, staggered by her acid bath, was out of action, too.

Gill and the alien had fought their deadly game. Gill hadn't been exactly sure what happened next. Presumably the door edge had severed some of the cables that controlled his arm movements. Or the combined pulls of Stan and the alien had pulled the skin welds on his arm apart. Suddenly, and with an audible pop, his arm had let go several inches below the elbow. Cracks had appeared in the tough synthetic skin, and had immediately widened. Fine-control cables had come under tension, pulled taut until they sang, and then snapped.

Cables and wires had coiled around Gill's wrist, then pulled free when Gill pulled what was left of his arm the rest of the way inside the ship and the hatch slammed shut. It had been a good sound, that sound of the hatch closing. After that, Gill had been too busy looking after Julie and ascertaining Stan's condition to pay much attention to his own condition. He looked to himself now.

He could see that there was no way of fixing himself. He could have tried a jury-rig if he'd had spare cables with him. But in the close confines of the pod he hadn't brought along the repair and spare parts kit that every synthetic tried to keep with him at all times. And even if he'd had the cables, he was still lacking several transistors and capacitors. Reluctantly he took the arm off-line. He had no motion in it at all. From the shoulder down, it was as dead as a hundred-year-old Ford.

"Gave you a little trouble, did they?" Stan's voice came from over his shoulder.

Stan had revived, calling on reserves he never knew he had. He had even gotten to his feet. He was filled with a strange knowledge; that he was both a dead man and a living one. The two sides of himself were warring now, each trying to establish dominance. Stan thought he knew who was going to win.

Somewhat unsteadily he crossed the harvester and gazed at Gill's wound.

"Pulled it right off, did they?"

"Yes, sir. Or perhaps I did."

"Comes to the same thing," Stan said. "Doesn't give you any pain, does it?"

"No, Doctor, none at all. I register the loss of my

arm solely as an analogue of loss, not as the real thing."

"It's abstract for you, is that it?"

"I suppose you could say that, sir." And yet, Gill knew it wasn't quite true. No human could really imagine what it was like to be a synthetic. And to be a synthetic suffering loss—that was really beyond their scope. Except, he thought, maybe Julie could understand it.

67

"Well, Gill," Stan said, "I think it'll be best if you look after Julie for the time being. I have some work to do on the radio."

"I don't think much can be done for her, sir. Not without regular medical facilities."

"No, I suppose not," Stan said. "Maybe there's not much that can be done for any of us. Still, we must avail ourselves of every twist and turn. That's what it's like being a human, Gill. You avail yourself of every little opportunity. You assume you're not dead until you can no longer move. I hope you're taking note of all this."

"Indeed I am, Doctor," Gill said. "Is there anything I can do for you?"

"I'm afraid not," Stan said. "Unless you happened to bring along a replacement body. No? I didn't think so. But the royal jelly is finally starting to take effect. I'm all washed up, Gill, but I'm feeling a lot better."

"Glad to hear it, sir."

"Thanks. We'll talk more later, Gill."

Stan turned to the radio. Gill watched him, and he was disturbed. It seemed to him that Dr. Myakovsky was in some sort of shock. He was hardly registering his grief at Julie's condition. Was it a callousness about him that Gill had missed? Gill thought it was something else. He had noticed that humans from time to time went into a condition they called shock. It was when something terrible happened, either to them or to someone close to them. It was how humans shut down when they experienced overload. But synthetics could never shut down.

68

As Stan turned to the radio it suddenly burst into life. An unfamiliar voice said, "Hello? Is there someone aboard the harvester?"

Stan sat down at the instrument panel. "Yes, there is someone here."

"I thought as much. This is Potter, captain of the Bio-Pharm ship *Lancet*. You are trespassing on Neo-Pharm territory. Identify yourself at once!"

"I am Dr. Stanley Myakovsky," Stan said. "There are only three of us here—myself, a woman, and an android. We are all that is left of a survey expedition sent to inspect the hive on AR-32."

"I knew you were here, Doctor," Potter said. "That says it all, I think."

"Maybe you don't know everything, Captain," Stan said. "Our ship was damaged during the recent storm. We require help badly."

"I understand," Potter said. "I am sending men to

pick you up. Be prepared to leave the harvester. That is all for now."

Stan put down the microphone and turned to Gill. "He says he's sending help. I suppose you can guess what kind of help Potter is going to offer."

Gill didn't answer. He was watching through one of the view panels as the *Lancet*'s primaries flared briefly and the great ship dropped slowly and majestically down through the sky in a shining glitter of landing jets. The big ship settled effortlessly on AR-32's plain. Soon after the landing, there was a sparkle of bright lines along the ground, and then something almost transparent that looked like the ghost of a wall erected itself around the *Lancet*.

"I see you have your force field up," Stan said. "A wise precaution, I can assure you."

"We're able to throw some protection around your ship, too," Potter said. "My men are coming now."

A bay door in the *Lancet*'s side cracked open, then let down to the ground, forming a landing ramp. Stan watched a dozen men come running down the ramp. Carrying bulky weapons, they were masked and shielded, and wearing full space armor.

"You waste no time, do you, Captain?" Stan said.

"You're damned right," Potter said. "The sooner I get you people out of the harvester the better."

"One way or another," Stan said mildly.

"What was that?"

"Oh, nothing," Stan muttered. "But it looks to me like your men are running into a little difficulty."

69

The armed men were moving across the corridors between the force fields that lay between Potter's ship and the harvester. The force fields shimmered faintly in the pelting rain. Low, flat lighting, grim and without shadows, illuminated the scene, and this was aided by the search beam from the *Lancet,* which flooded different areas with its sulfurous, yellow light. The men moved at a brisk trot, helmet shields up so they could communicate better.

Their troubles began slowly and built fast. The first man to scream was hardly noticed, so rapidly were the others moving. But then the squad leader became aware that something was amiss.

His name was Blake and he was from Los Angeles. He was used to skulking around smoking ruins and walking down ruined streets. So he wasn't entirely surprised when he saw one of the men throw his arms in the air as something long and black snaked out from seemingly nowhere and grabbed him around the neck. But what had it been? Blake wasn't sure. He stared, gaped. Another man screamed, and was dragged away shrieking. Then Blake realized that somehow the aliens had gotten into the uninterdicted corridors between the force fields, and were grabbing soldiers as they crossed from one field to another.

Seeing this, Blake shouted some orders. His little squadron was already cut in half. He ordered the remaining soldiers to fight back-to-back. They were closer to the harvester than to the *Lancet*, so he ordered them to continue.

You could see that the men didn't want to go. What had begun as a nice little bug fight had turned into a slaughter of humans. It wasn't fair! But there was no one to complain to.

They fought, their weapons flashing and flaming, and they caught a group of aliens as they were preparing to charge, caught them dead on and blew them to hell and back. The air rained black body parts. The acid from the aliens' wounds sprayed far and wide, and the ground sizzled beneath them. Luckily the soldiers were in acid-proof armor, or the acid would have made short work of them.

The sun came out as the slaughter continued, and the men seemed to be holding their own. Then the aliens got around the other side of the force field, and the soldiers were caught between two attacking alien groups.

They continued fighting, falling one after another. The lucky ones were dead when they hit the ground. Some of the others, wounded but not yet dead, weren't so lucky. Aliens draped them over their shoulders and retreated to the hive. These soldiers would make fine hosts, just what the queen needed.

Seeing this, Blake fought hard to keep his composure. It was unnerving, seeing friend after friend pulled apart, torn to bits, or dragged away unconscious to be glued to the wall of the hive with something small and deadly growing inside him, after the facehugger had done its work.

Blake turned back. It was all happening too fast. When he looked around, he saw the last of his men collapse, scream, and get dragged off. Blake saw his chance and sprinted to the harvester. He got there before the aliens, but just barely. He pounded at the door. "Let me in! Please, please, let me in!"

Stan's mild-mannered face peered back at him through the viewport. His lips moved. Blake couldn't hear the words, but Stan was saying, "Sorry, I can't open the door. I don't have the strength to close it again."

Blake pounded again, and then the aliens were on him. A claw came around his shoulder and grabbed his face at the forehead. It pulled, tearing the skin right off. Blake felt his nose pull away, felt his lips leave his mouth, felt all this, and then another claw had seized him by the neck, it was pulling out the tendons of his neck! And then Blake felt no more.

70

Potter was shouting, his voice grating on the speaker. "Damn you! What have you done to my men?"

"Not a thing, Captain," Myakovsky said. "They brought it on themselves. Nothing I could do for them. Can you get us out of here, Captain?"

"It seems scarcely worth my time," Potter grumbled. "I ought to nuke all of you."

"But then you'd lose the contents of the harvester," Stan said.

"True enough. But I could always come back for it after things have cooled down."

"I have a better plan," Stan said. "Something that will be of use to us all."

"Hurry up and tell me what it is," Potter said. "I don't like leaving my ship down here."

"It's too complicated to explain over radio," Stan said. "But I think you will like it. Listen, I have an android here who has been damaged in recent fighting. I could send him over to you. He'd explain the whole thing."

"I don't know if I should even bother." Potter was obviously thinking aloud.

"I think you'll be interested in my scheme," Stan continued. "And after all, it won't take very long."

"All right," Potter said. "Send him over. This better be good."

"It'll be very good," Stan affirmed.

"How are you going to get him through the aliens? If my own men couldn't make it, how do you expect your android to get here?"

"Modern technology is a wonderful thing," Stan said evasively. "He'll be right over, Captain. Signing off."

"Julie," Gill said. "Can you hear me?"

Julie's eyelids fluttered. Pain contorted her face. She gave a long shudder and then looked around. "Oh my God, is this where I am? I was having such a nice dream, Gill. There's this lake I know of. I went there just once when I was a little girl. I remember fields of spring flowers, a little lake. There was a rowboat. I was drifting in the rowboat, and there were willows hanging down over the boat. Oh, Gill, it was so pretty!"

"I'm sure it was," Gill said.

"Have you ever had a dream like that?" Julie asked.

"No, I have not," Gill replied. "I do not dream."

"Well, you can have half of mine," Julie said sleepily. "It wasn't really a little lake, I don't need it all. . . . Where's Stan?"

"He's right over there," Gill said. "He's trying to save you."

Julie grimaced. "I'm afraid he's cut it a little too fine this time. Poor Stan. He has such great ideas. But I'm glad I came, anyhow. He's not long for this world, you know."

"I know," Gill said.

"It's too bad. He's such a brilliant man. But they've done nothing but crowd him. He hasn't had a chance. Except this one. And I think this wasn't much of a chance."

"I suppose not," Gill said.

She looked at him. "Your arm! What happened?"

"Ran into a little trouble," Gill said.

"You're using understatement, just like a human."

"I suppose it rubs off," Gill said. "A lot of things do. I feel . . ."

"Yes?"

"I feel like I understand a lot more about humans now," Gill said. "It's . . . interesting, isn't it?"

"I suppose it is," Julie said. "Are you all right, Gill? You've got a very strange expression on your face."

"I'm fine," Gill muttered. "It's just that . . . well, even an android can run out of time."

Suddenly Stan's voice came from across the cabin. "Gill? What are you doing?"

"Just looking after Julie, sir."

"That's good. But she needs to rest now. Come over here. I have some instructions for you."

"Yes, Dr. Myakovsky." He turned to Julie. "Julie . . ."

"What is it, Gill?"

"Try not to forget me." Gill stood up and crossed the room.

Stan Myakovsky was huddled up in the control chair. He appeared to be experiencing no pain for the moment. But he had changed. Gill noticed that the doctor seemed to have shrunk inside his own skin, to be falling in on himself.

"Now pay attention," Stan said. "Forget about Julie for a moment. I have work for you to do."

"Yes, sir."

"You are going over to the *Lancet* to parlay with Captain Potter."

"To what end, sir?"

"Ah, yes," Stan said. "Negotiations usually have a point, don't they? Ours will be different. There's no point at all."

"But what do you want me to accomplish, sir?"

"Oh, that I can easily tell you," Stan said. "I want Potter to take his ship away from here. I will retain the harvester. I will find some way to make rendezvous with Captain Hoban, and we will go back home with our ill-gotten gains. How does that sound to you?"

"Wonderful, sir. But I'm afraid—"

"Yes, I am, too," Stan said. "The captain is not going to like it at all. That's why I have something else in mind. Come over here to the workbench, Gill. I have a modification I must make in you."

Gill hesitated. "A modification, sir?"

"You heard me. What is the matter with you?"

"I wouldn't want to change my thinking on certain issues."

Stan looked at Gill then glanced over at Julie, who was resting with eyes closed. "I think I understand. You've undergone quite a little course in humanization, have you not?"

"I don't know what to call it. But I've never experienced anything like it."

"I won't change any of those qualities you call emotional, Gill. They are rare and special, I agree with you on that, and sometimes they are a long time coming to men—and to androids, never. Or just about never. No, it's your command structure I need to modify. And something I need to wire into you. It will make it easier for you to do what you will have to do, unless things go a lot better than I imagine they will."

"I wish you'd explain a little more," Gill said, letting

Stan take him by his remaining hand and lead him over to the workbench.

Stan checked out his instruments. "Better not to explain too much," he said, fitting magnifying lenses over his glasses. I'll know what to do when the time comes. And so will you."

72

There were heavy ground mists when Gill left the harvester and started his trek to the *Lancet.* The ship loomed eerily in the mounting mists. Gill walked between the force fields. There were aliens out there, and he walked past them. The aliens were searching, but they didn't seem to know what they were looking for.

Gill knew that he had a certain amount of natural immunity, since androids did not smell like men. But to be on the safe side he had taken the last suppressor. Gill touched it on his wrist for luck. He wasn't superstitious, but he knew that men were, and of late he had been seeking to emulate them in every way.

The suppressor was working. It had been Mac's, but that was quite a while ago and now Mac was a bundle of wet fur on a garbage heap in an alien hive.

Gill knew he had to keep his mind on business. Usually, this was no problem for an android. Artificial men weren't bothered by random thoughts, stray insights, weasel realizations that came to them like thieves in the night. Not usually. But this time was different.

Gill found that his attention was divided. Part of him was observing the terrain he passed over, noting the presence and position of the aliens, watching as he drew nearer to the *Lancet*. But with another part of his mind he was thinking of Julie, seeing her as she had been just a day ago, vibrant and laughing, filled with life. He had felt something special for her then.

What was it? Was it what the humans called love? How could he find out? No human had been able to explain love to him. Even Stan grew embarrassed and turned away when Gill had asked him to explain the concept and give it a quantifiable value.

Humans were so strange, so filled with odd compunctions that covertly ruled their behavior. And now he had the most understanding of them he would ever have. It all came from stray thoughts, he told himself, and he worked hard to banish Julie's image from his mind as he approached the entry port of the *Lancet*.

73

Two of Potter's crew, heavily armed, were waiting for him in the entryway.

"I don't know how the hell you got through," one of them said.

"I've got a pass," Gill told them. They just stared at him. Gill decided that his first attempt at that key human quality, humor, hadn't been a success. But he reminded himself that he was new at it. Perhaps he would get better as he went along.

The two guards looked through the port visor. They could see the aliens, slowly drifting toward the ship, forming up against the almost invisible walls of the force field. They didn't do anything. Just stood there, their heads facing the ship, and it was as though some great power of attraction held them there. They were surrounding the force field that protected the harvester, too, more and more of them, and the sight of them was singularly uncanny and disquieting.

"We better tell the captain about this," one of the guards said. To Gill he said, "Come on, you. Raise your arms. We're going to search you."

Gill did as he was told. "I carry no weapons," he told them.

"Sure. But we'll just check you anyhow. What happened to your arm?"

"I lost it at the movies," Gill said. Again, the guards did not laugh. They just stared at him like he was crazy. Gill wondered what he was doing wrong. This humor thing was going to take some studying.

74

"Julie, can you hear me?"

Julie had been lying on the deck of the harvester near one of the heaters. Stan had found a blanket in one of the back bays and wrapped it around her. She looked better than she had since the accident.

"Stan?" she said. "I'm very cold."

"Let me see if I can find another blanket," Stan said. "I already have these heaters going full blast."

He stood up to go, but Julie reached out and grabbed his arm. "No, don't leave me, Stan. We're in a lot of trouble, aren't we?"

"To one way of thinking, yes, we are. But to another, we're in no trouble at all. We're together, and we're going to stay that way. Here, Julie, I have something for you. For us both, actually."

He reached into his jacket pocket and brought out the little case containing the Xeno-Zip ampoules.

There were six of them. He uncapped one and lifted Julie's head so she could drink. When she took down the first ampoule, he matched her with one, then uncorked another.

"We aren't supposed to take more than one, are we?"

"I've got a special dispensation," Stan said. "Don't worry, it'll do us no harm."

Julie swallowed the contents of a second ampoule. She shuddered, then laughed. "You were right, Stan. I feel a lot better."

"Me, too," Stan said, sitting down on the deck beside her and holding her close to share the warmth. "This is nice, isn't it?"

"It's very nice, Stan," Julie said. "We never found much time for this before, did we?"

"Unfortunately not. Sometimes it takes a long time to realize what a good thing is."

"As long as it happens sometime," Julie said.

"Don't worry, Julie. We're going to get out of this."

"I'm sure we are," Julie told him. "One way or the other." She could feel the pain leaving her body. How miraculous the Xeno-Zip was! What a pleasure it was to be free of pain.

She knew it had to be the same way for Stan. For the moment they were both young and strong and were going to live forever. This could only last a little while. But perhaps, she thought, it'll be long enough.

The radio kicked into life. "Dr. Myakovsky! Are you there?" It was Captain Hoban from the *Dolomite*.

"I have to issue a few last-minute instructions," Stan said to Julie. "Excuse me, my dear, I'll be back as soon as I can."

75

On the *Dolomite*, Hoban had been working hard to keep the location of his ship a secret. He had no doubt what Potter would do if he knew there was another ship in the area, and where it was situated. He had no intention of sharing the fate of the *Valparaiso Queen*, the wreck that silently circled the planet. He hadn't known quite what to do. But then Stan's message had come to him, and he had no choice but to make contact.

"Sir," Hoban said, "I need to tell you, by radioing me, you have compromised this ship's position. You shouldn't have done that, sir."

"Now, now," Stan said. "I have a plan whereby Potter and his crew will be neutralized. There will be nothing to prevent you from making rendezvous with us at these coordinates as soon as possible."

"I understand, sir," Hoban said. "But there is a

problem. From your present location, it is going to take me at least twenty minutes to get to you."

"As long as that?" Stan exclaimed. From where he sat, he could see through one of the viewports as the aliens massed in front of the force field, not trying to get through it—that would have been impossible—but coming together in ever-growing numbers, those behind pushing away those in front. They were crowded as close to each other as they could get, and some of them were mounting on the back of others, and others were climbing on top of those.

Stan saw at once what was going to happen. They were going to keep on piling themselves up until they were able to topple over the rim of the force field, which was only about twelve feet high. Then they'd come for him and Julie.

He didn't want to think about it, so he took refuge in analysis.

This swarming behavior was probably some sort of instinctual mechanism for getting them over barriers that were otherwise impassable. It was really very interesting. Ari had to see this.

Stan took out the cybernetic ant, poised him on a fingertip, and lifted his hand so Ari could see through the viewport.

"See what's happening, Ari? Are you taking it all in? Future generations are going to be very interested in what we have done today."

The little creature gave no sign that he was listening, yet he showed a certain alertness.

Stan continued, "You've been a good companion, Ari. Silent and uncomplaining. Who could ask for anything more? I only wish Norbert were here, too. You'll have to tell them how it was with us, Ari. If you get out of this, that is."

Ari, as usual, was silent.

"Stan!" Julie called.

"I'll be right over," Stan answered. He broke the connection with Hoban and changed frequencies. In a moment the sullen face of Captain Potter appeared on the viewscreen.

"About time you called, Myakovsky. I don't have much patience."

"Not much more is required," said Stan.

"I will listen now to your offer."

"Yes, Captain. What I suggest is that you forget all about this matter and take your ship some distance from here. While you are gone I will take this harvester ship and get away. You needn't worry about losing the royal jelly aboard. There's plenty of it down here for you. You can easily milk yourself another harvester load."

"That's great," Potter said. "And just why should I do that?"

"Because I have a legal claim to this stuff which is every bit as good as Bio-Pharm's claim. And because I want you to."

"I think you've flipped out."

"You're not going to do it? No harm in asking, was there?"

"You're wasting my time," Potter spat. "There's no deal, Myakovsky. I don't need to negotiate with you. I'm taking what I want."

"Right," Stan said. "Gill?"

Gill's face appeared in the viewscreen. "Yes, Doctor?"

"Activate Subroutine Diogenes," Stan said. "Signing off, Captain Potter."

"That doctor of yours is really crazy," Potter said to Gill. "He must think he still swings some weight. You can just forget any order he gave you. Things are going to be a little different now."

"Yes, they are," said Gill. The time was finally at hand.

He put his remaining hand to his mouth and popped in one finger. With a single wrench, he tore the finger off.

"What are you doing?" Potter said. "Stop that!"

"Subroutine Diogenes is beginning," Gill said, tearing off a second finger. "You know the old story about the rich man's house?"

"What are you talking about?"

Off came another finger. "In the rich man's house," Gill said, "a guest has a problem if he wants to spit." Off came the fourth finger.

"You're crazy," Potter said. "Stop or I'll shoot."

"In the rich man's house," Gill said, "there's no place to spit but in his face." The fifth and last finger came off. There was a frozen moment in the control room of the *Lancet*. Then Gill blew up. Literally.

The explosion of the artificial man enclosed the *Lancet* in a rosy glow shot through with yellow diamonds.

76

"What was that?" Julie asked.

"Just somebody knocking at the door," Stan said.

It came again: a heavy booming sound. Stan noted that the aliens had gotten over the top of the force field, scrambling up on each other's shoulders and toppling over. Now they were pounding and tearing at the entry port to the harvester. Stan could hear the metal start to buckle under their blows.

"It's very loud," Julie said dreamily.

"I think our friends are becoming agitated," Stan said. "It won't be long now."

"Is there any more of that royal jelly left?" Julie asked.

"Let me just see. . . . Yes, my dear, we have another two ampoules. Here, let me uncork that and hold it for you. . . . That's better, eh?"

"Much better," Julie smiled as Stan swallowed his ampoule.

The radio squawked into life. "Doctor! What in hell is going on! Potter's ship . . ."

It was Hoban. Stan said, his voice very low, "It was nice, eh, Captain?"

"What did you say, Doctor?"

"Gill made a satisfactory explosion, didn't he?" Stan said. "Gill did his part very well. How close are you, Captain?"

"Another five minutes."

"I'm afraid I don't have that long," Stan said. "I hope I won't be alive to see the last act. Hoban, it's been a pleasure knowing you. I hope you have no trouble clearing your name on Earth and going on with your brilliant career. Tell them on Earth . . ."

"Yes, Doctor?"

"Oh, tell them anything," Stan said, suddenly testy. "Over and out." He shut off the radio, then turned to Julie. "Good-bye, sweetheart."

"See you again soon," Julie said.

They kissed. And they were still kissing when the entry port shattered and the aliens came into the harvester.

77

Stan thought that was all. But it wasn't, not quite. There was a long blank stretch. He was vaguely aware that Julie was dead. All the others were dead, too, of course. Ari? He didn't know what had happened to Ari. And as for himself, he was surprised to find he was looking down on a corridor floor. He realized that the aliens had suspended him to the wall. He was in no pain. The royal jelly was still working. But something was growing inside him. He could feel it.

He was about to give birth. And die.

Now Stan summoned up all his courage and all his remaining strength. He opened his mouth and yelled. It was a long, hard, satisfactory yell. He could feel his body vibrating as he yelled. And a poem came to his mind. . . .

> I would have mourned the loss of my life
> If I had not been already dead.

And then he felt the chestburster come crashing through his chest, its expressionless face already questing for food. And then there was only darkness, and it was warm, like Julie's kiss.

When Captain Hoban finally brought the *Dolomite* down to AR-32's surface, he found the remnants of Potter's crew. Julie was still alive, and Badger was missing, but everyone else was dead. Along with Julie, only Ari, the cybernetic ant, was left.

Once he was back in the ship, Hoban wasted no time trying to read the ant's memory files. But they were locked with an unbreakable molecular combination. Only Stan knew the combination, and Stan had forgotten to unlock the files to permit the final details of his story to be known.

Hoban's Afterword

That was the end of it, all except for cleaning up what was left. When Gill blew himself up, he disabled the *Lancet*'s control system. It took several days for Potter and his remaining men— those who hadn't been killed in the blast—to repair it. It gave me the time to bring the *Dolomite* down to the harvester, where Stan and Julie had made their last stand.

We had a brisk firefight with the two aliens we found inside. But we managed to put them down without further loss of human life. They were carrying containers of royal jelly. All the rest of the aliens were gone.

We didn't know at first where they had disappeared to, or why.

It took us a while to figure it out. First we had to get Julie in the ship and into emergency medical. We did that, and she finally came through it all right. She was nearly well when we got back to Earth. I don't know what she's doing now; we lost touch.

I did see Badger again. He came to visit me one day shortly after I bought my new house on the Pacific Palisades. I had been reinstated, and I was doing well again as a spaceship captain. I owe it all to Stan. It wouldn't have happened if he hadn't stolen that ship, which brought the whole thing to the attention of the authorities and resulted in the reopening of my old case. This time a jury found for me, and against Bio-Pharm.

Badger arrived when I was between flights. He just wanted to say hello. We talked a while. Potter had brought him back to Earth in the *Lancet*, after he'd fixed the damage Gill caused.

"He didn't like me," Badger said cheerfully, "but he couldn't very well kick me out. I was the one who'd tipped him off to you and the doctor."

"And got Stan killed," I pointed out.

"He did his best to get me killed," Badger said.

"That was not intentional."

"No? Well, neither was my blowing the whistle on you to Potter. I was just trying to save my own life."

I didn't know what to say to that.

Badger was curious about one thing. When we'd gone back to get Stan and Julie, why had we only found two aliens, instead of the hordes that had been swarming over the harvester? And why hadn't they gotten to Julie?

"That bothers me, too," I said. "No one will ever really know. But I've got a theory."

"I'd like to hear it," Badger said.

"I figure there'd be communication of some sort between the aliens and their queen. I think she sent them an order that overrode everything else they were doing."

"Why do you think that?"

"You know all that royal jelly that Potter's men had

packed into the harvester? It was gone, all of it. I
think the queen told them the first thing to do was to
recover all the stolen royal jelly and bring it back to
the hive. Then they could go back and finish off whatever humans were left. But we had come and gone by
then. I can never prove it, but that's what I think happened."

Badger stared at me, taking it in.

I began to laugh. Badger said, "What's so funny?"

"It's not really funny," I said. "But it is ironic. That
the royal jelly that was ultimately responsible for
Stan's death should also be responsible for saving Julie's life."

ABOUT THE AUTHOR

ROBERT SHECKLEY is the author of over fifty books in science fiction, fantasy, and mystery. His novel *Immorality, Inc.* was recently made into the movie *Freejack*. The cult classic *The Tenth Victim* was made from his original short story. Mr. Sheckley is a New Yorker currently residing in Portland, Oregon, with his wife and children.

They are the pinnacle of evolution, the universe's perfect killers . . .

ALIENS™

BASED ON THE SPECTACULAR HIT MOVIE from Twentieth Century Fox and the bestselling Dark Horse graphic novels, the *Aliens* series chronicles a whole new adventure in terror for the last remnants of humanity.

ALIENS, BOOK 1: EARTH HIVE   ____56120-0
by Steve Perry $4.99/$5.99 in Canada

ALIENS, BOOK 2: NIGHTMARE ASYLUM   ____56158-8
by Steve Perry $4.99/$5.99 in Canada

ALIENS, BOOK 3: THE FEMALE WAR   ____56159-6
by Steve Perry and Stephani Perry $4.99/$5.99 in Canada

And now:

ALIENS: GENOCIDE by David Bischoff
____56371-8 $4.99/$5.99 in Canada

Buy all the *Aliens* novels on sale now wherever
Bantam Spectra Books are sold, or use this page for ordering.

Please send me the books I have checked above. I am enclosing $____ (add $2.50 to cover postage and handling). Send check or money order, no cash or C.O.D.'s, please.

Name _____

Address _____

City/State/Zip _____

Send order to: Bantam Books, Dept. SF 8, 2451 S. Wolf Rd., Des Plaines, IL 60018
Allow four to six weeks for delivery.

Prices and availability subject to change without notice.   SF 8 9/95

Aliens™ © 1986, 1995 Twentieth Century Fox Film Corporation. All rights reserved.
™ indicates a trademark of the Twentieth Century Fox Film Corporation.